.

It's a Kink Thing

SWEET AND KINKY

M.C. ROTH

Sweet and Kinky
ISBN # 978-1-80250-589-4
©Copyright M.C. Roth 2024
Cover Art by Kelly Martin ©Copyright January 2024
Interior text design by Claire Siemaszkiewicz
Pride Publishing

Published in 2024 by Pride Publishing, United Kingdom.

Pride Publishing is an imprint of Totally Entwined Group Limited.

SWEET AND KINKY

Dedication

For Q

Chapter One

Rowes

It must've been dizzying to be tossed about on the gentle breeze, floating on wings that were so much larger than your body, an updraft from the small pond like a hurricane that could suddenly twist and plunge you into the sea. Rowes watched the butterflies flicker around him, their powdered wings glistening in the filtered light as the humidity condensed on the glass inside the conservatory.

An echo of the floating butterfly lay on the cobbled path, its wings broken and mottled. Blue surrounded it like a halo, a shoeprint laced across its middle. He'd almost sent one just like it to its doom before Izzy had caught him, tugging him off balance to save the little insect. He'd landed against Izzy's chest, basking in the private moment for the few seconds that he could.

They'd come here on a whim, spotting an advertisement on a passing bus that had piqued Izzy's interest. One call to their manager and they'd had exclusive tickets where they could stay as long as they liked without the hassle of a crowd.

Perhaps 'manager' wasn't enough of a word for Lorena. She took care of everything for them, including screening their contracts, arranging flights and lawyers and even having a juice box and a snack within easy reach.

"Do you like it?" asked Rowes, tilting his head back to peer through the branches of the tropical trees. There were butterflies lining the glass above them, pulsing their wings as they presumably looked for an escape. Come winter, this would be the safest place for them. He wasn't sure if they would even live that long, trampled by another tourist just like them.

"It's hot." Izzy grinned, rolling up his sleeves. He must've expected it to be air conditioned, because he was overdressed, especially for the summer warmth outside the giant greenhouse.

The material of Izzy's shirt looked thin, but it had to be stifling in the air that was close to one hundred percent humidity. The little pond with two turtles and a handful of koi did little to cool anything, only making the air thicker. Even the stray drops of a nearby waterfall didn't take the edge off for Rowes, and he was in a T-shirt.

"But it's pretty," said Rowes, spinning around in a circle. Another of the delicate creatures floated past his face, close enough that he could feel the beat of its wings. "I never expected to find a bit of jungle here. It's like the last time we were on a world tour." He closed his eyes at the memory before settling back against Izzy's side. Izzy's arm was around him in a moment, steadying him in the dizzy spell that followed.

They'd hit so many countries in so few days that the memory of their trip had turned into a blur. Their ratings had gone through the roof, though, and the show had finally hit it big after the first season with a mediocre fan base.

"Only I'm not puking as we pass over the equator," said Izzy, rubbing the back of Rowes' neck where most of his sweat had gathered. "Come on. Let's get out of here before I melt." His brown hair was looking a tad darker than normal, almost black and clumped with sweat. That, and his shirt was sticking to him and showing off every dip and curve of his torso.

Rowes loved the heat of the place, almost warmer than the man next to him. It was so much better than the closeness of the set some days.

But the best thing about the butterfly conservatory was the quiet. There wasn't another person in sight, except for the nervous-looking staff member who was hovering on the path close by and probably hoping for an autograph or for them to leave so she could go home. Both options had equal appeal.

"Just five more minutes," said Rowes, stepping closer to the waterfall. There was a thin cobbled pathway that led under the narrow outcropping where a stream splashed into the pond below. The railing was speckled with water, the drops tapping a pattern against his exposed arms.

Izzy sidled up behind him, pressing against his back. He was tall enough that he could easily see over Rowe's head to the koi swimming in the pond below them. The pounding of the water flushed everything out, and for a split second, it was just the two of them.

"*Now*, Rowes," said Izzy, trailing his fingers down Rowes' arm to his hand before tracing the bumps of his knuckles. The gentle move was the opposite of the strain in his voice. "Frosty the Snowman wouldn't last two seconds in this place, and right now, I'm melting, too."

"So dramatic." Rowes let out a sigh, tilting his head to lean onto Izzy's shoulder. "Just one more minute." With his eyes closed and the white noise around them, he could almost imagine he was somewhere else. Izzy traced his knuckles again before settling his hand completely over his.

This is the life.

The peace lasted until the moment they stepped outside. Every relaxed muscle snapped tight, his skin prickling when a crowd appeared out of nowhere from the parking lot. One of the conservatory staff stood to the side, looking intrigued and a touch sheepish.

Fuck.

A camera flashed in his face, temporarily blinding him as summer air coated his heated skin. A shiver ran along his spine as he stumbled, trying to blink away the tears. A few minutes to themselves, and this was how he paid for it.

Rowes tucked his head against Izzy's shoulder, inhaling sweat and cologne, as the cameras continued their assault. It was Dior, and the same one that Rowes had bought him for his birthday, with a touch of flowers from the artificial habitat. Each breath was like being back in the jungle with only the trees and the air between them.

How do they always seem to know where we are? Even with a tip from the employee, they hadn't been here that long. At the same time, there were some pretty devoted fans out there, which meant that their private moments had turned into anything but. It wasn't quite what he'd expected when he'd auditioned for season one.

"Rowes! Mr. Laurie!"

Rowes flinched at the shout before forcing a smile onto his face and straightening. Professionalism was key, despite what names people called him. He was only twenty-eight, but the way they shouted his last name sounded like he should have been forty with a house of his own and two cats that he fed pieces of his dinner. *The American dream.*

Izzy chuckled, wrapping his arm around Rowes' shoulders and pulling him close. Rowes sank into the touch before grinning at the crowd of gathered reporters. He recognized a few who had stuck with them for a long time, but there was always a fresh face or two.

The crowd blocked the walkway, leaving them nowhere to go, let alone run. Getting to their ride would be next to impossible, and retreating into the conservatory would probably do no good. The most patient hunter was one with a camera.

Izzy went tense at his side, probably coming to the same conclusion. If only he could melt into Izzy, letting the other grab him in a ruthless hug so they could plow through the crowd together.

But that would probably land them in the wrong part of the news. Reporters loved labeling actors as assholes if they were pushed too far and finally snapped.

It was much preferred to meet reporters at a press conference. That way it was on Rowes' terms, and their manager Lorena would be there to kick some ass and shut certain conversations down.

"Isthmus!"

Izzy nodded at the sound of his own name as he reached for his phone, and Rowes could almost feel the mask slipping into place over his best friend's features. He hated the false façade that Izzy wore in public. Acting was one thing, but this was something else — something cold where nothing could reach Izzy.

"Good evening, folks," said Izzy, the grin on his lips looking so genuine that even Rowes almost believed it. The crowd went quiet, probably ready to write down the next uttered quote.

"I want to go home," Rowes whispered through his teeth, hoping only Izzy could hear him. It had been a long day and an even longer week. He'd hoped for a few hours of reprieve with their trip to the conservatory, but that didn't look like it was happening.

Biting his tongue, Rowes tried to draw back from Izzy, clasping his hands as he fought his frown. The water bottle in his grip crackled. He'd gotten it at the last-minute from the vending machine, his mouth dry despite the humidity of the jungle.

Izzy didn't seem to care that he was trying to escape, his grip going tight on Rowes' shoulder as he refused to let him go. The cameras were there to catch it all.

Are we too close? If I move now, is it obvious? Either way, there were sure to be new rumors in the morning. With social media, every clip went viral, distorting the truth before anyone even learned it.

With every eye looking his way, Rowes let out a breath, risking a glance at Izzy. He was staring back, his blue eyes pinched with concern and one eyebrow raised, probably wanting the answer to the only question that Rowes couldn't give a response to.

Are you okay? The answer was decidedly no. He'd wanted to spend the day with his best friend and not be harassed about it or asked if he was gay. He wanted one moment when horny housewives weren't imagining them kissing behind the scenes.

He gave Izzy a smile that hopefully reached his eyes. Izzy seemed convinced, moving to grab his hand and squeezing once. Looking out into the crowd, Izzy slipped back into his professional mode in the blink of an eye.

Gone was the fluffy sweetheart that pulled Rowes' chair out for him or sent him a picture of a cat to cheer him up. No, the man he saw before him was the one who half the planet had fallen in love with, a sensual smirk on his face that always made him an instant favorite.

He glanced to the side where the sun was trapped behind layers of dark clouds. There was a garden beyond the grass where a butterfly fluttered. Maybe it was one that had escaped the conservatory, only to find that the jungle was the only place it would survive. It was one of the lucky ones.

The life of a television star was less glamorous than Rowes had predicted. When he'd gotten the part, he hadn't expected much to come of his role — and neither had anyone else. The series had promised to be like so many that were canceled on a yearly basis, and the first episode had aired with little fanfare. It was only much later that the network realized what a gem they had put their investment in.

"What's your bet?" asked Izzy, a smile on his face as he ducked to Rowes' ear. "I'm thinking five this time — Wait — make that six." He glanced at one member of the crowd who had a Bristol board sign with Izzy's and

Rowes' names on it surrounded by a giant red heart. *Is that really necessary?*

Rowes rolled his eyes, squeezing Izzy's hand once before he remembered himself and dropped his arm to his side. His fingers tingled — cold and empty as the last of the heat fizzled away. His skin prickled, longing for touch just as much as he did. It wasn't the touch itself, but the support it gave him — the calm.

After all this time, he still couldn't understand why people were so obsessed with them and what their *status* was. Four seasons in and the speculations had only gotten fiercer. Sometimes he read the online articles, just for a chuckle. They popped up on his feed often enough that they were hard to ignore.

Five reasons why Rowes and Isthmus are perfect for each other…

Isthmus getting possessive…

Jealous Rowes moments…

Are they already married? Five true facts that prove they are…

People couldn't comprehend that he and Izzy were friends, and that was all. Maybe they were closer than most traditional friends, but Izzy certainly didn't star in any of his sexy dreams. Rowes liked to cuddle and hold hands with pretty much anything that moved, Izzy included. Izzy just happened to indulge him more than most.

Their fellow actor Connley could hardly stand to be touched and frequently shrugged Rowes off him. Even with that, there were still a few rumors that the two of them were dating, or that Rowes was cheating on Izzy with Connley.

With Ainslie, an actress on their crew, he could cuddle and snuggle with her all day and not a single rumor erupted. It was as if people thought they were siblings — or that he was gay.

And as for getting possessive? It was hard not to get a little pissy when he seemed to be the brunt of a lot of jokes. He didn't have Izzy's allure, Connley's skill or even Ainslie's wicked sense of humor, but he was still a great actor... *Okay, a decent one.*

Sometimes he wondered how he had landed the part. Up against the others, most days he struggled not to fall back on his high-school drama days when his voice still cracked, and he sweat every time he spoke in front of two or more people. Izzy's encouragement was the only thing that kept him from quitting.

"I'll say four," said Rowes with a shrug. Izzy had moved his hand to Rowes' lower back, the warmth of his palm spreading across the space in a way that was almost distracting. The shouts had resumed so Rowes leaned close. *Fuck they're loud.* He was going to have to take some medication later.

"I already texted Lorena, so hopefully she gets us out of here before the fifth," said Izzy, dangling his phone in front of Rowes' face. Lorena's contact info glowed in front of him. *Thank God.* Izzy was always the thinker. He'd probably texted Lorena while Rowes had been stuck in his own personal pity party.

Izzy chuckled, slipping his phone into his own back pocket before reaching for the water bottle in Rowes' hand. "Can I have some? I think I lost ten pounds of sweat in there."

Rowes nodded, rubbing his hands together. After twisting off the cap, Izzy took a deep drag, emptying all but a swallow from the bottle in no time flat. Sweat dripped down his neck and into the collar of his shirt as the sun shifted in the sky. It was probably a great picture. There was no breeze to speak of and the summer heat was just as unforgiving as the conservatory's.

Before he could finish it, Izzy polished the rim of the bottle with the edge of his shirt, handing it back to Rowes. "You should drink some. It's only going to get hotter once the questions start."

"Don't I know it." Rowes took a small sip, ducking his gaze when he noticed the reporter with the sign watching them with a look of glee on her face. She was probably going into overload. *I drank Izzy's water. Oh gosh! It must be an indirect kiss!* The flash of the cameras certainly seemed to think so as they sped up. If it had been dark out, he would have been completely blinded.

People needed day jobs — preferably ones that involved sitting on the couch to watch their show and not stalking them to the middle of nowhere at a goddamn butterfly conservatory. *Is nothing sacred anymore?*

"Oh, thank Christ," said Izzy.

Rowes shot his head up, every muscle in his body relaxing as he spotted Lorena. She was always dressed to impress, and this evening was no different. She was the only woman he'd ever met that could pull off any shade of red. Anything from pink to maroon complimented her perfectly, and her shoes were out of this world.

They must've interrupted her from a dinner date, though. Rowes tried to squash his guilt. It had been her day off. Her skin-tight blood-red dress swooped down to nearly her navel and her black shoes had straps that went halfway to her knees and glistened with some kind of sparkling jewels.

She gave them a little wave, a muscle twitching in her cheek the only thing that gave her away. A few of the smarter reporters parted for her, but one was too slow. An elbow to the back of the head took care of him.

"Oh, I'm so sorry, dear. These shoes... I swear, I've been tripping on them all night," she said as the last reporter parted. She raised one eyebrow as she reached them, and Rowes nodded, his throat clicking as he tried to swallow. *Yeah, she's pissed.*

He'd take the real reason as to why to his grave. It wasn't the first time that he and Izzy had been caught on something that could be considered a date, and each time it pissed Lorena off a bit more. She detested the rumors about them, almost as much as she hated gluten.

"Thank you everyone for meeting us here," said Lorena, tossing her hair over her shoulder as she addressed the crowd. She was the type of woman to do that—throw everyone off guard as they questioned whose idea it had been. With every eye locking onto her cleavage, she rarely had to raise her voice.

"We have the stars of our show with us today, including everyone's favorite, Isthmus Linton." She winked as the crowd gave a little cheer, the one with the sign whistling and shouting.

Rowes could see the change almost instantly. She had them exactly where she wanted them and could probably convince them they were on her payroll at this point. "We picked this special place to bring awareness to conservation. I know Rowes is a big supporter of establishments like this, and Izzy has already made a generous donation."

I missed that memo. Rowes blinked, glancing at the door. He knew Izzy wouldn't miss the cash at all, but it would have been nice to know. Maybe that was what Lorena had meant when she said she could buy out the place for a few hours.

Izzy raised his hand in a little wave, his beaming smile winning over every person in the crowd. Rowes snickered, shooting his elbow into Izzy's ribs. It was like meeting a brick wall that didn't have the ability to flinch.

"So humble," said Rowes as he rubbed his elbow. Izzy snorted under his breath, lowering his hand. There was a moment of reprieve when the cameras paused, waiting for their next move.

"But so true." Izzy's smile never dimmed, and the shouts of the crowd only grew as he threw his arm back over Rowes. Rowes felt his face flush as Lorena sent him a look over her shoulder. He wasn't wearing a spot of makeup, so everyone would see it.

He could only imagine the articles later.

"What can we expect from season five?" shouted one of the reporters. The hush fell again. The months of waiting had taken their toll on people's patience.

"Without giving too much away," said Lorena, clasping her hands together as she took control again, "if you thought season four was hot, you've got another thing coming. Season five is faster, hotter with more firepower."

That pretty much summed it up. Rowes chewed his lip. He'd never thought he'd know so much about guns from being an actor, but he was basically an expert at this point. His character *loved* guns, which went hand in hand for a show about mobsters.

"Will Kemble be taking over the family business?" asked another reporter, using Izzy's screen name. His character's father had been shot to death in season three and Kemble had spent almost all of season four trying to get out of taking over as the head of the family. It didn't help that he looked even better with a gun in his hand than he did without.

Rowes bit his tongue before he could shout out the answer. He'd only gotten snippets of the script so far, but it wasn't hard to put the pieces together. He *hated* direct questions because he could never seem to find a way out of them. Asking something vague and he could dance all day, but he was a walking spoiler alert. It was probably one of the reasons Lorena always tried to answer before them.

"I *can* tell you one thing," said Lorena, her hair shining in the sunlight. The wind picked up, and Rowes caught the scent of perfume that tickled his nose. He much preferred the smell of sweat coming from Izzy. "You will *not* be disappointed."

The fan cheered, even as the reporter narrowed her eyes, obviously miffed about not getting a straight answer. "Will Kemble and Salem finally be getting together?"

Letting out a groan, Rowes thumped his face into Izzy's shoulder at the mention of his own character's name. Lorena was going to kill him. What was he supposed to do, though? Probably not shift closer to Izzy, tucking as tightly as he could.

"That's one," Izzy whispered into his ear.

"Fucking hell." In the show, his character and Izzy's were best friends but nothing beyond, just like in real life. People still didn't get it in either case, though.

"It would be a great move for the LGBTQ community," said Izzy, shouting over any reply Lorena may have had.

Oh fuck. Rowes shook with laughter at his friend's gall. It was the same thing that Izzy had said to the directors during the previous season, but the crowd had a much different reaction. That had been a set meeting that Rowes hoped he forgot sometime soon.

The cheer from the one fan was almost deafening, but when he peeked out from his spot against Izzy's shoulder, Lorena had turned, the look on her face sucking away every bit of humor.

Leaning away, he stared off into the crowd and toward the fan who was completely flushed, their sign slightly ripped from the way she was waving it so frantically. The red heart surrounding their names wobbled.

There were so many signs and supporters at every event and forum. It was too bad they would be disappointed. The directors had made it very clear that there would be a gay secondary character this season but that Izzy's character would still be vying for the attention of his extremely female co-star.

Some of the scenes had blurred the lines in past seasons. There were times that they were too close, a whisper in an ear or laughter about a joke that had more than one meaning. It was fun to tease, and the fans greedily soaked it all up.

Rowes still shivered when he thought of the season finale. Izzy had been so close, with the sounds of gunshots and shouts echoing behind them, and the bulk of his body blocking the cameras and the CGI bullet from Rowes' prone form.

That, and Izzy's character hadn't gotten the girl. The producers still hadn't seemed to realize that that particular ship had sailed. Rowes and Izzy had a connection on set that was beyond fantastic—much to the fan's delight.

It was another story with his female co-star. They bickered like siblings and had the chemistry of old baking soda in watered-down vinegar—one bubble and it was done and ruined.

"We do have some exciting developments with Ainslie's character," said Lorena, reining the crowd back in and sweeping them away. Ainslie played the female lead and had a following of her very own. She was a kick-ass woman who could take down a guy with a gun any day.

"You okay?" Izzy glanced his way, squeezing his wrist with his fingers wrapped around Rowes' pulse. Shifting, Rowes slowly pulled free. It was a battle not to lean into the touch, but he knew Lorena could look at them at any moment.

"Fine." *If only I hadn't signed that fucking contract.* It was the stupidest thing he'd ever heard of—a piece of paper banning him from having a relationship with any of the cast members. *But I signed it anyway.*

Rowes slumped, crossing his arms before he could stop himself. He'd thought the fine print on the contract had been for his own protection, at first. Izzy was the star, and everyone was in love with him. Lorena and the producers wanted to make sure that nothing affected the fan's love for the show. She'd thought that if Izzy became attached to someone in his personal life, the fans would somehow stop loving him on screen.

So Rowes had signed above the dotted line on a contract stating that he couldn't enter an intimate relationship with any of his co-stars. He hadn't found out until after that apparently hand holding and snuggling were a part of that list, according to some.

"Did you need another water?" asked Izzy, his eyes seeing straight through Rowes. "Lorena should be able to shake these guys soon, then I'll get you back to the room and get you something to eat."

That sounded like perfection. Closing his eyes, Rowes gave in to the need to lean on Izzy's shoulder. The lack of breeze was starting to wear on him. It wasn't that much cooler outside than it had been in the conservatory, and he was in desperate need of a snack and a cool drink.

But if he were hot, then Izzy must've been roasting. Even the heat of his skin through his shirt was blazing.

"Roll up your sleeves," said Rowes, tugging at the collar of Izzy's long-sleeved shirt with sudden concern and dipping one finger underneath. They must've slipped down since they'd stepped out of the building. "Oh my God, you're roasting in there." He tugged harder, even as Izzy sent him one raised eyebrow.

"Who says you can tell me what to do?" asked Izzy, tugging his shirt back into place. "I'm a badass mafia bitch, and I've got to look the part." He smoothed his hand down his chest, one fan shouting hysterically at the display. "See?"

Yep. Just because he wasn't gay didn't mean that Rowes couldn't see the appeal. Izzy was perfectly proportioned and toned, and he'd be envious of the guy if he wasn't his best friend. Izzy was the biggest sweetheart out there, too, so it wasn't even in the cards to get mad at him about his good looks.

Shaking his head, Rowes crinkled his water bottle before shaking it threateningly. There were only a few drops left, but he'd dump them straight onto Izzy's head. "You're super sweaty, and it's starting to ruin your hair."

"Oh." Izzy ran his hand through his sweaty locks, his fingers tangling in his hair gel. He always insisted on putting the stuff in, even if they weren't planning on doing a public event. It was probably why he looked so much more presentable than Rowes. "Is it really? I guess you're right then." He rolled up his sleeves, exposing his forearms. "Much better."

Lorena was still speaking and slamming through questions one after the other, but the crowd seemed to pause at the sight of Izzy's forearms, the toned skin tanned to perfection.

"Good." Rowes poked him in the pec, wrinkling his nose at the amount of sweat there. "Have you been working out more?" They usually worked out together, but he didn't remember Izzy being quite so ripped. His shirt looked three sizes too small now that it was clinging to all that sweat. Either that, or Izzy was puffing out his chest.

"Nah, Lorena gave me this shirt for Christmas last year, but I think she got the sizing all wrong. I wasn't going to wear it, but all my laundry is out. Is it bad?" Izzy flexed, showing off the way the fabric strained to contain him. Rowes was pretty sure he saw someone in the crowd faint.

"Nope. You still look like a badass mafia bitch, just maybe undercover," said Rowes, waving his hand at one reporter as Lorena drawled on about a few of the spoilers that had already been released.

"Shouldn't it be 'bastard'?" asked Izzy, scratching at his chin. He must've missed a few hairs when he'd shaved that morning. He always complained about how they would itch if he didn't keep clean-shaven. "I thought 'bitch' was more of a lady term and 'bastard' was a guy thing."

"Bitch, please," said Rowes, waggling one finger in the exact way his character usually did when taunting someone.

"You love me," said Izzy, grabbing Rowes around his waist and pulling him in tight enough that he stumbled. Did he not see the cameras? The skin prickled on the back of his neck. Lorena was going to kill him.

Love wasn't the problem. He loved Izzy, but as a *friend.* Lorena shot him a look, her lips pressed in a thin line. "That's all for today, folks. I've got to get these boys back to their rooms so they can get rested up for their next shoot."

If only everyone else could figure out that they were friends. *That's all we'll ever be. I promise.*

Chapter Two

Isthmus

"I'll grab ice if you order dinner," said Izzy, tapping his key card against the sensor for the door. He always missed the scent of chlorine that lingered in hotel rooms, along with the fresh faces in the halls.

Outside of press conferences, he was rarely recognized—not like Rowes. Rowes was the hottest thing in the show, which meant he was the one on the cover of magazines more and in the eyes and hearts of every fan.

"Sure." Rowes shrugged, slipping out from under Izzy's arm and pushing his way into their hotel room without a backward glance. It was the third time Rowes had pulled away from him in the last three hours. Ever since prep for the latest season had started, it was as if a switch had flipped.

Izzy narrowed his eyes, pausing at the door and holding it for a moment longer. Rowes looked and moved the same, slipping his shoes off and padding around the room like he always did. *Maybe it's nothing?*

"Hey." Izzy slipped through the door, letting it shut behind him before he reached for Rowes' hand, halting him in his place. "Ro, what's going on? Talk to me. Do you want to go out for dinner instead?"

He looked around the room from the cheap lamps to the two hideous queen-sized beds. They could afford better—way better—but Izzy liked the rustic side of things. He was content with air conditioning and fresh sheets, but maybe it was a little too rustic for Rowes.

"Is it the room? I can call down to the desk and get us a better one. They had the penthouse available, but this one looked like more fun. And the view is pretty sweet." Glancing toward the window, he caught the sight of the sparkling city lights. There really was nothing like the view of the city at night—always awake, even if almost everyone was sleeping.

"No." Rowes took a breath, sagging his shoulders before he slowly turned back to Izzy and closed the space between them. He looked so young, and vulnerable like that, and more like a kid who had never been in the television business. "I think I just need a hug."

That can't be all. If Rowes had his way, he'd be locked in a permanent hug with at least three people, and Izzy was more than happy to be the one who indulged him. It was what best friends were for, after all.

"Anytime, buddy." Wrapping his arms as tight as he could, he brought Rowes as close as possible, until there was no space between them at all. Warmth and the scent of Rowes sank into him, washing away the strangeness of the hotel room. "I don't mind in public

either, if that's what you're worried about. The fans
love it."

Izzy wasn't quite sure why, but every time he even
looked at Rowes, the crowd seemed to go wild. He was
more than happy to indulge them. Rowes was the most
beautiful person he knew, and he literally loved giving
him hugs. His life wasn't full without them.

He would never describe Rowes as handsome,
exactly. There was something delicate about Rowes
that made him pretty, his fine features and sweet smile
anything but rugged.

It was another story when he slipped into the
persona of his character and became something fierce
and *dangerous*. That was why Rowes was the fan pick —
even if he denied it.

Rowes went stiff, tugging away from Izzy's arms as
he sniffed. His eyes were wet, the flush on his cheeks
something that threatened to break Izzy's heart. "Not
everyone likes it."

Am I missing something? He fought the urge to crack
his knuckles as he immediately tensed. Sometimes
people didn't understand how truly sensitive Rowes
was and how much a small comment could affect him.

"Did somebody say something to you, Ro? One of
the bodyguards? I swear, if one of them — "

"No." Rowes threw out his hand, his face nearly
frantic and his voice cracking. "Nobody said anything.
Just…I don't know if we should hug and stuff
anymore." His face flushed as he dropped his gaze to
the worn pink carpet. "There are already so many
rumors, and I don't want someone to think that
you're…you're…" He trailed off, clasping his hands
behind him.

Snorting, Izzy reached for the empty bucket for ice, pulling out the little plastic bag and flicking it open. Rowes flinched at the sound, worrying his lip between his teeth. *Unreal. Un-fucking-real.*

Isthmus Linton was one hundred percent gay and proud of it—a real live homosexual who loved cock more than ice cream. That didn't mean that he was fucking his best friend.

Playing with the edge of the bag, he shoved it into the bucket. He didn't mind explaining that to the few thousand people who felt it was their right to ask him, but he'd thought it was pretty clear between the two of them.

Rowes was just different. Nothing had an expectation to it or that longing that he got when he needed to get laid. Their simple touches didn't give him the shivers, and seeing Rowes naked was as natural as breathing. They just *were.*

Hopefully it was just a misunderstanding.

"Can you get me a steak, Ro? And maybe peppers or something on the side?" He ruffled his friend's hair, grinning at the shy smile he got in return. "And a chicken Caesar wrap for you…extra croutons."

Rowes' face lit up, all shyness dropping away at the promise of croutons. "You think I could get extras?"

It was crazy how much Rowes watched his carb intake. He was literally perfection, inside and out, but he still counted the things. Bread was his enemy, for some reason. Personally, Izzy loved watching Rowes stuff his face with a sandwich. It was something only he got to see.

"You've been really good," said Izzy, shooting him a grin. "And I looked into the menu before we got here. They make their croutons in-house with sourdough."

Rowes let out a groan. "Where's the menu?"

Izzy paused as a knock sounded on the door. Turning to the sound, he furrowed his forehead. He didn't think they'd been recognized on the way up to their room, but there was always a chance. Or it could just be their co-worker Connley, hoping to steal their basket of tea and coffee samples.

Glancing through the peephole first, Izzy grinned before throwing the door open to reveal Lorena. Of all the agents he'd ever had, she was by far the best. She didn't have the slave driver attitude of some, and she took care of them like family, even bringing them cookies every once and a while.

"Lorena, baby!" Izzy opened the door wide, welcoming her inside. "Thank you so much for rescuing us! Sorry about the slip-up, but I'm doing my best to convince the directors to include some LGBTQ characters. Do you think they're pissed?"

He wasn't actually sorry at all. On their way back from the conservatory, he'd checked his social media. The clip of his shouting about the LGBTQ community was already going viral.

Lorena surveyed the room quickly, pursing her lips as she caught sight of Rowes, who was still frozen like some kid who had gotten caught with his hand in a bag of sugar. She usually stuck to the luxury suites instead of the ones that were a bit more basic.

"I'm here to talk to Rowes about something. Do you mind if we borrow the room for a minute?" asked Lorena, tossing her hair over her shoulder as she strolled to the coffee maker before slipping one of the pods inside and starting it up. "There are some changes to the script for next season that I wanted to run by him."

"Okay." He looked to Rowes, hesitating at the door. Was it just his imagination or had he paled a few shades? Maybe he was coming down with something. He'd been off all day. "I'll be back in five."

Grabbing the ice bucket, Izzy took one last look over his shoulder. Rowes wasn't even looking at him, busying himself with the menu instead. Narrowing his eyes, he shot a look at Lorena. "Make it quick, okay? Rowes isn't feeling well."

She raised her hands, giving him a soft smile. "It will only take two minutes, then I'll be out of his hair. Did you guys want me to order some food for you? Or maybe some soup, Rowes?"

Shaking his head, Rowes didn't even look up. Izzy huffed out a laugh. Sometimes his best friend was so painfully shy that he got second-hand embarrassment — only Rowes wasn't even smiling.

"Or maybe I'll stay," said Izzy, tossing the bucket back on the counter and bypassing Lorena. Taking a seat next to Rowes on the bed, he threw an arm over his shoulder, leaning in close.

Rowes was trembling, the tiny shiver in his frame barely perceptible. Izzy could feel it like a blaring alarm, though, and he wasn't leaving until it stopped. Whatever was going on, it would have to go through him first.

"You were saying?" asked Izzy, directing his question to Lorena while keeping his gaze locked on Rowes. His face was too pale, the menu in his hands starting to shake. Izzy grabbed it before setting it on the bed. "I'll order room service while you guys chat. Don't mind me."

With one last glance at Rowes, he twined their fingers together, moving just far enough away to grab the phone and dial room service. He tried not to listen as Lorena spoke, he really did, but he failed utterly when he heard the word 'gay', dropping the receiver just as he finished ordering.

"The directors made the choice that Salem's love interest would be a rival gang member — probably one of the background men from this season," said Lorena.

Rowes tightened his grip, nearly crushing Izzy's fingers.

"They want to have that inclusive culture going forward, and I think it's about time," Lorena continued, tucking a strand of hair behind her ear.

What the hell is she talking about? She'd never supported any of Izzy's ideas for a gay character. In private she was accepting of him, but in public she was strictly professional, supporting what she felt was best for the show in the public's eyes.

Izzy made a face. His shaking had worsened, and he looked even paler than he'd already been. *This conversation better be over.*

He knew what it was like for someone to judge you on your character alone, and Rowes' character was top-notch. There was no way he would get with a nobody, especially not a rival. Izzy's character, on the other hand, was a bit of an unpredictable maniac.

"Why not Kemble?" asked Izzy, grabbing the phone and hanging it up with a click. He'd apologize to reception later. "I am the only out gay man on the main cast list, and Kemble is a hot shot who does what he wants."

Lorena pursed her lips. "From what I understand, the relationship won't get much screen time. It's not going to be one of the main plot points —"

"Well, maybe it should be," said Izzy. Rowes looked like he was about to pass out, and Izzy could sympathize. Whenever he had to kiss a woman on screen, it felt like an inner betrayal. He couldn't eat the whole day before just knowing what was coming. It didn't matter how beautiful they were. It took a lot out of him to create the desire he needed from nothing. It was *exhausting*.

"Isthmus." Lorena let out a sigh, tugging at her hair in the way she always did when she was starting to reach her limit. The last time she'd done it, she'd fired her assistant. "It's going to be a few shots, maybe three minutes of screen time and one kiss. That's it. Your character is going to have another female love interest this season. We have to appeal to the majority of the fans, and the fans are saying that they want Kemble with a woman."

Snorting, Izzy rolled his eyes. What part of the internet were they getting *that* from? Maybe some of the conservative sites. But they didn't like the show to begin with. *Gunlover* idealized the gangster lifestyle, which didn't sit well with a lot of people. It was still hot as fuck, though.

"It's fine," said Rowes, speaking up for the first time. His grip on Izzy's hand was fierce and matched his own. They were going to accidentally hurt each other if they kept it up. "Izzy, it's fine. One kiss won't be that bad."

"Excellent!" Lorena perked up, already turning for the door. "I'll let the producers know that you're on board. I'm sure you'll bring the same passion to this season as you have in every other."

The door snapped shut, and Izzy turned a hesitant smile on his friend. His color was starting to come back, and his shaking had eased. Maybe he'd just been nervous about the role. *Well, I can help with that.* "My own little baby gay. Can I coach you?"

Rowes shrugged him off before throwing a punch into his shoulder. It barely stung.

"You know I'm straight, right?" asked Rowes, raising one brow as he lay back on the bed. Every ounce of tension had evaporated the instant the door had closed. If Izzy squinted, he could almost see a pure image of his best friend. *Everything is all right.*

"Uh, I think I missed that memo," said Izzy, rolling his eyes. "Just kidding. I am very aware of how painfully straight you are. No corners or nothin'." He squeezed Rowe's knee, tickling the flat surface until Rowes kicked out with a giggle.

"Quit it."

Of course he knew. They spent most of their time together on and off set. Between sharing hotel rooms and living in a studio apartment back home, they were rarely apart. It was damn inconvenient when Rowes brought a woman home, even if he tried to be discreet. Izzy always kept his lovers away, making sure that their place stayed distinctly theirs.

"I think she thinks I'm gay — or at least bi, though," said Rowes, his voice going quiet as he stared up at the ceiling. "Everybody thinks that. Lorena probably told the directors that one to push that decision through." He gave Izzy a pleading look.

"It's just a kiss?" Izzy asked, scratching at his chin as he shifted along the bed so he could lean against the pile of pillows. Tugging Rowes' arm, he urged him closer. "You know as well as I do that a kiss isn't just a kiss."

One shot could turn into a dozen, with those same lips against yours as you tried to dredge up a passion that you didn't feel. But that was acting. He kissed women all the time for the show, but somehow this felt different.

A knock on the door cut him off, and Izzy let out a sigh as Rowes leapt off the bed and pulled the door wide without looking. "Oh, food!"

He must've been fucking starving or something.

Izzy took care of the tip as Rowes set the food out on the bed before taking a seat on the ground. It was the same way they always ate in a hotel—with Izzy sprawling over the bed and Rowes below him, spilling shit everywhere. The only difference at home was that they usually chilled on the couch, Rowes sitting on a cushion on the floor.

It had always been like that for them, even in high school when they'd first become friends. Rowes just seemed to have some sort of issue with sitting on a bed or couch to eat—something about them being too squishy threw off his balancing act with his plate.

Grabbing the remote, Izzy flicked on an old action movie, tucking into his steak. Rowes' mouth was already full of his wrap, crunching away on what sounded like more croutons than anything else.

"So what's up with you and Lorena?" asked Izzy, flicking a bit of carrot to the side of his plate and shoving a pepper into his mouth instead. "It's awkward as hell between the two of you lately, and don't think I haven't caught all those looks. You guys hooking up?"

Rowes spluttered, lettuce and chicken going absolutely everywhere. Izzy passed him a napkin with a roll of his eyes. The constant spills were one reason he never argued with Rowes chilling at his feet, even if it made him feel like some kind of owner.

"I said I was straight, not suicidal," said Rowes, grabbing for his phone and propping it against his knee. Izzy watched him scroll through a few apps as if aimlessly searching for something. *How many games do you have on that thing?*

Without fail, it was something Rowes did when he was nervous — avoiding the situation by burying himself in his phone. Izzy wasn't buying it this time.

"She's very pretty — gorgeous, even." He had eyes, even if his spectacles were tuned for men. It was like having 3D goggles that picked up on gay dick instead of layered images on a theater screen — and he could get a good taste of the image instead of a mouthful of popcorn.

"And married," said Rowes, tapping through his phone at record speed. He paused at one screen, his shoulders going tense. His wrap lay forgotten, a few croutons spilling out onto the plate, along with some shredded lettuce on the floor.

Izzy peered over his shoulder, recognizing one of the platforms for social media shorts. He did his best to stay away from them, but occasionally they dragged him in for a few hours. The headline on this one caught his eye, though.

Are Kemble and Salem actually Dom and sub?

Well, that was a new one. He glanced at the television, muting the commercial for toothpaste as Rowes hesitated, staring at his phone as if it were a bomb. The thumbnail didn't give much information other than the words and a blurry picture of them. It could have been their stunt doubles from the picture quality.

"You should play that one. It looks interesting," said Izzy, wiping a bit of sauce from his lips with a nearby napkin. The steak wasn't half bad for getting to them so quick. The staff must've recognized who they were when they checked in.

Rowes jumped, his phone hitting the floor as he looked over his shoulder. His eyes were wide, his face nearly red as he flushed. A small piece of lettuce clung to his lip. Izzy wiped it away with his napkin before tossing the tissue toward the trash. "I...I—"

"Come on. Just play it. I don't usually watch those things, but it looks neat." It was interesting that someone who didn't know them thought they were in a BDSM relationship.

People calling them too cuddly was one thing, and Izzy would agree with them if he gave a fuck. The truth was, he was not Dom material.

Rowes would make a good sub, though. Not that he was thinking about it.

His romantic feelings had lasted all of twenty minutes for Rowes. One laugh together and he knew that he never wanted to risk losing their friendship. The occasional stray thoughts were only natural for someone as handsome as Rowes, especially when they spent so much time together.

Rowes bit his lip, bringing his phone back up and shuffling so he was leaning against the bed frame more. Izzy set his plate to the side and scooted forward a bit so he didn't have to strain to see the picture at all. It wasn't so blurry now that he was a bit closer.

"You can see okay?" asked Rowes softly, his finger hovering over the play button. One of his nails was chipped like he'd been chewing at it again.

I have to figure out what's bothering him.

Putting Rowes out of his misery, Izzy reached for the phone, hitting the play button before settling on his elbows. Rowes was stiff, his hands trembling so the screen shook, making it nearly impossible for Izzy to see.

"Just relax," said Izzy, reaching for Rowes' hair and tugging the strands. His hair was so soft, and even after their trip to the conservatory and battling the crowd with Lorena, he looked completely put together. He didn't need the hair products and gel Izzy relied on.

Rowes let out a sigh, lolling his head to rest against the side of the mattress and raising the phone so they could both see clearer.

The music in the background of the video was dark and throbbing as words started to scroll across the screen against a black background. Izzy shifted, trying to get comfortable as his stomach twisted. He was sure why, but something about that music just called to him. It was something he would hear in a club while grinding a hot guy and picturing himself eight inches deep.

It wasn't something he'd ever think to listen to with Rowes.

A fresh batch of words scrolled across the screen and he blinked back to attention, hoping his stray thoughts would stay far away.

"I wasn't convinced that Kemble and Salem were in a D/s relationship until I saw today's footage. Now they can't deny it."

Izzy rolled his eyes. He could deny a lot of things, especially something as ludicrous as that. People thought a single light spank was hard-core kink nowadays. It was crazy.

"What's D/s?" asked Rowes, tilting his head to lean into Izzy's hand. "Just a second, I'll look it up." He moved to pause the video, but Izzy stopped him.

"It's Dominance and submission—the 'DS' in 'BDSM'," said Izzy, reaching to turn the volume up. A male singer had started in the song as the screen faded to red before the first shot of them appeared on the screen.

"How do you know that?" asked Rowes, his eyes wide.

"Shh." Izzy held a finger to his lips, the music and the picture momentarily taking his breath away.

It was a shot of them on their way back from the conservatory, Rowes looking more tired than Izzy had realized. It was right outside the glass doors of the hotel, the sparkling lights from the entrance almost as bright as the sun that was low on the horizon. Izzy had one hand on Rowes' neck, his fingers on his pulse point with Rowes' eyes closed in what looked like bliss and his face tilted to the sky.

Holy fuck. His gut throbbed, his words swept away as his mouth went dry. For the life of him, he couldn't remember that moment, but there it was before him. They looked like lovers who were caught up in an intimate moment. And the way his hand was wrapped around Rowes' neck, his finger tangling in the bit of his hair that had started to grow out as the back, made him question everything he knew about them.

Rowes seemed to be lost in the picture, the trembling in his hands finally still. What did he see? Could he remember the bliss in a moment that Izzy had somehow forgotten?

The picture changed, starting to snap through clips so quickly that he could barely keep up. Some were grainy shots in the darkness that he could shrug off, but others were crystal clear and undeniable.

One was of them at a conference, with Izzy's arm around Rowes' shoulder. Izzy was leaning in, whispering into Rowes' ear with a grin. As he watched, Rowes flushed bright, his eyes tracking the crowd as a smile flicked over his lips. It was probably something dirty that Izzy had been joking about—not that he could remember now.

The camera dragged slightly to the side as the person must've been bumped, catching Lorena, who looked anything but impressed as she stared their way.

Rowes seemed to change in an instant before the camera as soon as he glanced toward Lorena. His lips went tight, his face shuttering as he pulled away from Izzy in a way that made Izzy's heart ache to see it. The video faded, fresh text appearing on the screen.

"I'm convinced that their manager is trying to keep their relationship under wraps, even more so because of the way some people view kink. As soon as she is out of the room, though, all bets are off."

It flashed to another video of them, this time inside the hotel. It had felt so private behind the layers of glass in hindsight, but apparently, someone had been filming them the whole time.

His gut clenched tight as he gritted his teeth. Fan videos had never felt off before—as soon as their show had started to do well, he'd known that his private life was over. But this…? It was violating.

Izzy touched Rowes' chin on screen, tilting his head up with a fond smile on his face. Rowes had looked so gloomy that day, and Izzy remembered doing everything he could to cheer him up. Rowes happened to be crazy ticklish under his chin, not that it looked like that was his intent...*at all.*

The video showed Izzy sliding his hand down Rowes' neck to his back and Rowes immediately standing straighter, rolling his shoulders once before seeming to settle.

"Fixing his submissive's posture is one thing that a Dominant would do. Salem responds right away and doesn't let his shoulders droop again."

Okay...things were getting a bit far-fetched. Rowes had been complaining that his back was aching after the press conference, and Izzy had offered a back massage later, giving him one pat as a taste.

"You could try to fight that, but what about this one?"

Groaning, Izzy fought not to look away. Could it get any more incriminating? *Not fucking possible.* He knew himself and Rowes. They were friends and nothing more. Rowes certainly wasn't into kink.

But looking at all this, maybe he was so, *so* wrong.

When they'd initially checked into the hotel, there had been some confusion about their room, and they'd had to wait about ten minutes. Looking back, the staff had probably been confused as hell as to why famous television stars were staying in such a crappy room when the penthouse was free.

As they'd waited, they'd settled on the couch in the lobby in their usual fashion.

The video showed them walking over to the couches in the small waiting area of the hotel, setting their bags on the carpet as they went. On screen, Izzy pointed next to the couch and, like magic, Rowes dropped to his knees in that spot before settling against the side of the couch and getting comfortable between Izzy's legs.

Izzy's hand was in Rowes' hair a moment later, the look on both of their faces pure contentment and bliss.

Izzy couldn't look away, his heart pounding.

Rowes' eyes closed on screen, his throat bobbing as he swallowed and tilted into the touch. Izzy had grabbed for the paper, skimming through the pages as he explored Rowes' hair with his hand never pausing. The camera zoomed in, the shot going blurry as it tracked Izzy's hand.

"I'm so happy for them. Until next time, peeps."

The music cut off as the video ended, the replay button appearing in the center as a new one started to load. His heart had never beat so fast, his gut so tight that he wasn't sure if he could eat another bite of his steak.

"You see why I don't like to watch them?" asked Rowes, his voice surprisingly calm as he broke the silence between them. "They blow everything out of proportion." He shrugged. "You're looking at a mosquito bite on my neck, and they think you are choking me. Not to mention, when we sit in the lobby like normal people and I'm what? Your slave or something?"

More like my boy.

"Uh, yeah," said Izzy, clearing his throat as he wiped his sweaty palms on the bed sheets. Had it always been like this, and he'd just been blind? Even now, Rowes was below him eating a meal with extra croutons that Izzy had told him to get because he was *good.*

I'm not a Dom. He pulled his hand out of Rowes' hair, looking at his fingers with fascination. There was rarely a time that they were in the same room and weren't touching in some way. Even if their touches weren't

41

sexual in the least, it apparently didn't look innocent to anyone else.

"How did you know about that Dominance and submission thing?" asked Rowes, shooting him a curious glance as he tossed his phone and picked up what was left of his wrap. "Are you keeping secrets from me?" He winked, his laughter faltering when Izzy just stared.

"One of my first boyfriends was kinky," said Izzy, rolling off the bed before grabbing his plate. There was still one perfectly good piece of steak left, but there was no way he could stomach it. "You want this last piece?"

He plucked it from the plate without waiting for an answer, pressing it to Rowes' lips. Rowes took it without comment, scraping his teeth over Izzy's skin and probably trying to make sure he got it all.

Clearing his throat, Izzy turned away, heading to the bathroom to wash the plate. *I'm still doing it.* He hadn't even thought about feeding Rowes the bite before he did it. They shared food all the time. *I didn't... Ah fuck.*

Izzy turned on the sink, rinsing the plate as he gritted his teeth. With the hum of the bathroom fan overhead, he could almost tune out the rest of the world...but only for a minute.

"My wrap is better," called Rowes, cutting through the sound of the fan easily as Izzy scrambled to try to remember the last time Rowes had fed *him*. He could recall countless occasions where he'd fed Rowes or offered him something out of his glass or off his plate, but Rowes never did the same thing to him. *Maybe he doesn't like to share?*

That didn't fit either.

Turning the taps on full cold, Izzy splashed water on his face, scrubbing hard before he returned to the bed.

Rowes hadn't budged, little bits of croutons and lettuce spilled all around his place on the floor.

"Make sure you clean up your mess," said Izzy, biting his lip and covering his mouth with his hand when his brain caught up to what he'd just said. *Stop it!* Telling their sub to clean up was something a Dom would do. Friends didn't do that, did they?

"I will." Rowes was staring at the television, his phone long since forgotten. He'd upped the volume again to a level that would keep their neighbors happy. It was the same kind of rerun that was always playing in hotel rooms.

Izzy half expected a *Sir* at the end of it, letting out a sigh of relief when it didn't come.

"This kinky boyfriend," said Rowes, tossing a look over his shoulder as Izzy settled on the bed again, "did he like to get spanked and stuff or did he just call you Daddy?"

Izzy choked, patting his chest as he wheezed. He hadn't thought about those days in a long-ass time. They were still fresh in his mind, though, the humiliation and thrill of it crystal clear.

"I—uh—called him Daddy, yeah," said Izzy, crossing his arms as he looked away. He had been a different person then, and innocent enough that he'd thought he was a submissive. It hadn't been hard to believe that with an older man.

Rowes spluttered, abandoning the rest of his dinner before crawling onto the bed. He paused a few inches away from Izzy, his eyes practically glowing with mirth. A stray piece of parmesan clung to his lip and Izzy wiped it away without a thought, bringing his finger to his own mouth and sucking it clean.

"*You* called him Daddy? Oh my God, you're a bottom!" Rowes snorted, rolling onto his back as he let out a laugh. "Here I had to listen to all these stories about you pounding some guy's ass, and it's been the other way around the whole time. You're so cute."

"Hey." Izzy poked him with his toe, resting his foot on top of Rowes' belly to get him to stay still. "I was young, and he was twenty years older than I was. I had no idea what Daddy kink was or who I was at that time in my life. I didn't even know I was going to be an actor at that point."

Rowes sobered in a heartbeat. "Wait. He didn't take advantage of you, did he?" His eyes were laser focused as they swept along Izzy's body, as if he could remove the hands of his past simply by looking hard enough.

No. Thank God. Izzy shook his head. "He was a nice guy, but our kinks didn't line up, so we didn't last long together."

The 'Daddy' ship had sailed almost as soon as he'd gotten on board, and he'd never managed to find his sea legs after that. There were times that he wondered if he should have been the one who was called 'Daddy', though. He wouldn't have minded if Rowes called him that.

Where is this coming from? Half an hour before, they'd been nothing but best friends, but now he was picturing Rowes calling him Daddy? He was never watching a fan video again.

Chapter Three

Rowes

He must've swallowed swamp water or something because his breath was terrible. Groaning, Rowes rolled onto his side, thudding against something warm and sweaty. With all the time zones they'd been going through for the past few weeks, his body was so ragged that he had to blink his eyes open before he remembered who was with him.

Izzy, obviously. Rowes grinned to himself, wrapping his arms around Izzy's chest and nuzzling in close. He wasn't daisy fresh, but so distinctly Izzy that Rowes couldn't care less. He'd seen Izzy drunk and covered in puke and it hadn't bothered him — a little sleep sweat didn't bug him, either.

After another full day, they'd fallen asleep in their hotel room during a movie marathon. The television was still humming in the background, the sound so muted that it was nothing more than a distant muffling of voices. With the remote nowhere to be found within reach, Rowes ignored it, along with everything else.

At some point Izzy had taken his shirt and pants off, leaving himself in nothing but a pair of boxers. Rowes almost felt overdressed in his actual pajamas. He would have been in the same state if Izzy hadn't told him to put pajamas on before bed, but he'd put off brushing his teeth, chomping down on wine and chocolate instead as he'd tried to stay awake.

"Your morning wood is stabbing me to death over here," said Rowes, as he shifted away a touch. He giggled as Izzy let out a groan and pushed at him with one arm.

"And your morning breath is like daisies on a spring morning," said Izzy, scrunching up his nose without opening his eyes. "And stop squishing it or it will get attached to you."

Rolling off the bed, Rowes stretched, wincing at the sheer number of cracking noises. Once their promotional tour was done, he was getting back to the gym ASAP.

"And I'll make my fresh breath scent into the next perfume," said Rowes, letting out a yawn as he reached for the remote, which was in the middle of the floor. He was a kicker when he slept, so he'd probably nailed it straight off the bed and across the floor.

Izzy chuckled, rolling and faceplanting into his pillow. "I'm going back to sleep."

His nonchalance was so relieving that Rowes let out a breath. It had been two weeks since they'd watched the fan video together, and he'd started to worry that things had changed between them.

He'd watched enough of the stupid things to know when to shrug it off and when to take constructive criticism, but this one had seemed to linger. He could still hear the beat of the music in his dreams...and the way Izzy had looked at him.

He closed his eyes, letting out a sigh as goosebumps inexplicably prickled over his skin. He'd have to turn the heat up if he was wearing these pajamas again.

The video *was* causing issues for them. All their touches suddenly seemed purposeful, and it was driving him insane. He just wanted to chill with his best friend, but now he had to wonder if there was someone watching them and where the hell he was going to sit. He *liked* sitting on the floor...mostly because he loved it when Izzy played with his hair. Sometimes it was the only way he could relax after a long day.

And trying to look up BDSM on his phone was completely out of the question. He rarely had any time alone, and Izzy would probably quiz the fuck out of him if he saw him searching for something like that.

"Have you ever thought about being a Daddy?" asked Rowes, opening his suitcase and grabbing the closest pair of boxes before doing a sniff test to make sure they were clean. He was going to need some laundry services at the next place or he would be freeballing soon.

Izzy jerked on the bed before throwing the covers back and sitting up. His morning wood was straining at his boxers, and Rowes averted his eyes as he lowered his own pants. They were alone, but he wasn't sure if it was okay for him to look or not. He didn't know the boundaries of their new relationship since they'd watched that video.

"Like...kids?" Izzy asked, his voice pitching. Rowes glanced at him, snickering at the shock he found there.

"You hate kids." Rowes grinned to himself. Perhaps hate was too strong of a word, but Izzy couldn't stand being around the little rascals. Rowes didn't mind them, but he didn't want a dozen to call his own someday, either.

"You aren't talking about kids." Izzy flushed, scratching the back of his head before flopping on the bed.

"Uh...no." Rowes glared at his suitcase, his bravery starting to fail. He was usually the follower, but he couldn't stand the tension between them. In their room, it wasn't so bad, but as soon as they left, it was as if Lorena was watching over his shoulder all the time. It would only get worse when they started shooting again in the next few weeks.

"I just thought maybe that was what has been bothering you the last little bit. Maybe you missed the kink aspect you had with your boyfriend and hadn't thought about it much since that fan video shoved it in your face." Rowes risked a glance at Izzy, wilting at his thinly pressed lips and furrowed forehead. "Shit. I never should have let you watch that," said Rowes, cursing himself for the hundredth time.

Maybe Lorena was right. Maybe he *was* too close with Izzy and was stomping all over his game. He could have a hundred guys waiting for him, but Rowes was simply in the way.

"That's not it exactly," said Izzy, doing his own stretching routine, which managed to be much more athletic than Rowes'. "But I have been thinking if maybe I've crossed a few lines with you that I shouldn't have. I don't want you to be labeled a submissive if that's not who you are. Being told you're something that you aren't can be really hurtful."

Ugh. Sometimes Izzy was too thoughtful for his own good. "You didn't cross any lines. I mean, there are literally hundreds of those videos. Not D/s ones, but ones about us hooking up and all that. They started back in season one and are still going strong."

From what little he'd been able to figure out about submission from the few searches he had risked, he was a textbook sub. He tried not to think too hard on the fact that Izzy seemed one hundred percent a Daddy.

"Well, show me some more then. Maybe it will help me figure some stuff out once and for all."

Wait…what? Rowes bit his lip, clutching his jeans to his chest. He had not been prepared for that. He'd hoped that Izzy would take his word for it like he always did. On one hand, maybe the videos would clear things up, or maybe they would make it so much worse.

What if Izzy started to doubt their entire relationship? *No.* There was nothing between them except friendship, and that was the only thing there would ever be—but not according to the rest of the world.

"Are you sure?" *Why did I open my mouth?* He tugged on his pants, grabbing the shirt from the top of the case and pulling it on. He was pretty sure it was the same one he'd worn the day before, but it would have to do.

"Yeah, what's the harm? They are all over the internet, right?"

Izzy may have been Daddy material, but he was also apparently naïve. It was like someone going online looking for all five-star reviews on their show and having a mental breakdown at anything less. Rowes had spent years trolling himself on the internet and was used to the haters. Izzy, though?

"Fine, but you have to promise me something," said Rowes, searching for his phone and finding it tucked under the pillow on the bed. Izzy had barely moved other than to cover his lap with the duvet from the bed.

"Anything."

He said it so easily, as if Rowes could ask him for the world and Izzy would somehow deliver. He probably would. He'd been craving fried chicken one day, and Izzy had taken a cab all the way across town to get it for him.

"Don't take anything personally. I mean it." He gave Izzy a steady look. "People are assholes, especially people on the internet. Seriously, just let it slide off."

Izzy shrugged, leaning against the headboard and patting the spot next to him. Rowes was more than happy to snuggle in close, the coolness of the room sinking in. He must've cranked the air conditioning before bed because it was frigid. Izzy tucked him right under his arm like he belonged, morning body odor and all. Rowes couldn't complain because he still hadn't brushed his teeth.

Bringing up the video app, he scrolled through his feed until he found one that caught his eye. It was an older one, but it had a lot of views and a mind-boggling number of comments.

"Last chance to back out," he hovered his finger over the play button, waiting for Izzy's nod before he pushed it.

Unlike the D/s video, this one was much more upbeat, with a sparkly pop song and no text comments throughout. It was just shot after shot of them together in places that Rowes barely remembered.

The first one was a short of them at Niagara Falls. Rowes was terrified of heights but had wanted to look down into the swirling mass of water right at the base of the falls. His hands had been shaking as he grasped the metal fence that had been slick with the never-ending mist.

He wasn't sure how Izzy had known, but he'd been there in an instant, pressing his chest to Rowes' back and wrapping an arm around his waist to hold him firm. He'd braced his other hand on the fence, leaning them as far as he dared while clutching Rowes tight.

He'd felt so safe, the plunge and danger fading to the periphery of his thoughts as he'd gotten his first good look at the whirlpools below. His smile of thanks had been caught on camera, along with the way he'd tilted his head to Izzy, their lips so close to touching.

He curled his toes into the bedsheets as Izzy shifted against him, the warmth of the blankets almost too much. He'd seen it all before, but he remembered the first time and how off guard it had taken him.

"Did you want me to stop it?" he asked softly, reaching for the screen.

"No," Izzy answered, his voice even quieter. He sounded almost resigned.

Rowes swallowed, wincing at the next shot of them. It had been at a photoshoot and Rowes had just tripped over absolutely nothing, splaying on the ground and scraping the hell out of his knee through his way-too-expensive pants. Izzy had helped him to the nearest chair before kneeling and rolling up his pant leg to check on the scrape. Izzy had been the one to grab a bandage from the first-aid kit, touching the wound that had barely been bleeding.

The rest were no less incriminating. Shots of them holding hands, leaning close or smiling at each other, their gazes appearing to hold a thousand secrets.

Rowes was sweating by the time Izzy asked for another video, and by the third, he had to kick the blanket off them, wishing that he'd turned the air conditioning even higher. He didn't dare look at Izzy, whose breath was steady against the side of his neck, his heart thudding a steady beat, unlike Rowes' racing one.

He wasn't sure how long they sat together, going through video after video, some of them with the same shots and others completely unrelated. They probably would have sat there forever if Rowes' stomach hadn't growled, demanding breakfast and effectively calling an end to their screen show.

Shutting off his phone, Rowes tossed it across the bed, slowly leaning away from Izzy and standing. The air was so tight he could scarcely breathe, his gut twisting in a way that made him wonder how the hell he was going to eat.

"You okay?" asked Izzy, the sound of shuffling following him as he presumably stood. He patted Rowes' shoulder, the warmth of his hand sinking in. There was no hesitance, only friendship and support.

"Yeah." Rowes let out a sigh of relief. Leaning into the touch before shooting Izzy a smile. "I'll order breakfast for us."

"Get me the waffles, Ro, and you should try the pancakes. The menu promised real maple syrup and fresh fruit toppings. You could get the blueberry."

With the way Izzy said it, how could he resist?

Chapter Four

Isthmus

There was a warmth on his cock that could only mean one thing. Izzy let out a low groan, easing his hips forward to slide a little deeper. He knew a mouth when he felt one — and the tight pressure of someone taking him down their throat. The buzz of their hum only added to his pleasure, slamming him closer to the edge.

"Shit." He let out a sigh, reaching for their head. He loved being in control and choosing exactly how fast and how far they went, even if they choked a little. Most guys liked that.

His arms moved so slow as he strained for them, and when he touched their hair, it was nothing like he'd expected. His eyes were pinned shut, but he knew exactly who it was, their head bobbing as they swallowed around him.

"Fuck, Rowes."

Izzy started, blinking awake in the dark hotel room. His cock was throbbing, painful and urgent as his gut thrummed with how close he was to the edge. A steady, warm pressure was against his cock, the friction dry and hot.

Only it was Izzy that was moving, and the person in his arms was Rowes, not some one-time hookup that would spend the night asking for a selfie that 'of course, they would never share with anyone'.

He froze, forcing his body to go still as his heart hammered. Rowes was in his arms, his face plastered to Izzy's chest with a bit of drool on his pec. When they'd settled down to watch a movie, Izzy had been too tired to move to his own bed. It wasn't like they hadn't slept together before, although they usually didn't end up quite so close.

And Izzy wasn't usually this hard, either. He had an active enough sex life that his desires were usually kept to a minimum, and he was the lucky kind of person who forgot his dreams when he woke.

But he wasn't going to forget that one anytime soon. It had been Rowes – *Rowes* – on his knees somewhere in the world. There had been the sound of a director shouting in the background, and the hum of conversation from his co-workers.

What the hell?

"You okay?"

Izzy bit his tongue, nearly choking at Rowes' words. Rowes shifted, moving his leg where it was jammed between Izzy's thighs. He had to stifle his gasp, his cock throbbing as snippets of his dream came rushing back.

It had started as an innocent kiss during a scene, with Rowes leaning in and his eyes closed. Seconds later it had turned into a battle of teeth and tongue until Rowes had dropped to his knees.

It wasn't real.

M.C. Roth

"Did you have a nightmare?" asked Rowes, rubbing his cheek against Izzy's pec. "Your heart is pounding, and you're sweating like crazy. It's okay. It was just a dream." His voice was sleepy, and so utterly adorable that the guilt grabbed Izzy tighter. His friend was just looking out for him, and he was a few solid strokes away from coming.

"Can you move?" asked Izzy, his voice strained as fresh sweat broke over his skin. He could smell the saltiness that reeked of panic and uncertainty. "I have to get up." He started sitting up when Rowes didn't move right away.

"Comfy," Rowes protested, wrapping his arms around Izzy's neck and clinging tight as he tried to sit up. Rowes shuffled his legs, freezing as Izzy let out a pained moan and the firm pressure of Rowes' leg turned into something excruciatingly good.

"Are you...hard?" Rowes pulled away as if he'd been snapped with static, his feet tangling in the sheets and sending him sprawling back on the bed.

Fuck. Izzy tried to look away—he really did—but he failed miserably. Rowes was splayed out on the bed, his hair dark against the white hotel sheets. His shirt had rucked up, displaying the lower edge of his abs and the dusting of hair there. It drew Izzy's gaze like a beacon, his dream sinking his claws in.

It didn't help that Rowes had an impressive semi. It was something Izzy had seen so many times before, but he'd never reacted to it. He was gay, but Rowes just...wasn't his type.

"Nice dream?" asked Rowes, letting out a laugh. "It wouldn't be the first time." He shrugged.

Izzy couldn't laugh with him. Something was lodged in his chest, and he could barely breathe through the urgency of it.

"Those fucking videos," mumbled Izzy, drawing a hand through his hair. Without them, he wouldn't be in this situation with his cock throbbing while his best friend was giggling away like one of them had had a wet dream at a sleepover.

"What?" Rowes paused, his hand hovering in the air where he'd been reaching out. "The videos?" He swallowed, the click of his throat audible.

"That's not what I meant," said Izzy, throwing back the rest of the covers before scrambling off the bed. It looked even worse with his cock jabbing straight out, the thin material of his boxers doing very little to hide him from view. He was the kind of guy who couldn't exactly hide what he was packing. "I just can't seem to get them out of my mind," said Izzy, letting out a sigh as he very pointedly avoided Rowes' gaze and searched for his pants instead. Why the hell had he taken them off in the first place?

His heart throbbed until he could feel the beat in his throat. "How many people have watched them and seen the same things? Every time I look at you, they think that all I can focus on is the thought of kissing you." He tugged his hair, pulling a few strands up by the roots.

"Are you?"

Izzy finally looked at Rowes, swallowing when he met pale skin and wide eyes. Rowes looked fucking terrified of the idea. *Would it really be so bad?* Izzy shook his head. Of course, it would be. His relationships never ended well, and he was not dragging Rowes through that trash fire.

But why am I even considering it?

"I'm going to go," said Rowes, pulling the hem of his shirt down to cover his exposed belly. Izzy followed the move with his gaze, focusing on the peek of skin just beneath his shirt. He didn't need to wonder what Rowes looked like underneath because he knew every inch. He was without flaw and probably one of the most beautiful people Izzy had ever met. But that was nothing to the *person* he was.

"Rowes, don't." Izzy reached for him, but Rowes shrugged him off before starting for the door and grabbing his shoes along the way. "Rowes, please, it's not like that. I shouldn't have said anything."

"I'm going to crash with Ainslie for tonight," said Rowes, letting out a yawn as he reached the door. They'd stayed up too late watching movies again, and he looked so fucking tired. "I just don't think I can stay here right now."

"Rowes." He let out a sigh of defeat.

"Not tonight, Izzy. I can't. With Lorena, and now this... I just can't." He reached for the door, slipping out before Izzy could say another word.

"Fuck!" Izzy grabbed his hair, tugging tight as he went to his knees. What the fuck was happening with them? He was still hard, but now he was alone, their friendship starting to shatter like dropped glass on pavement. "Rowes...wait."

He scrambled to his feet, grabbing the door handle and twisting it open. It didn't matter that his key was still in the room somewhere, or that it was deathly quiet with early morning stillness. "Rowes!"

The hall was empty, with no sign of Rowes on the patterned carpeting. There was a distant sound of a humming ice machine, and a whisper of someone's television, but otherwise nothing.

What is Ainslie's room number? They'd talked about it when they'd arrived at the hotel, and Ainslie had been going on and on about the view she had been hoping for. They were near a river and the water sparkled in the daylight and all that crap.

Sixty-five. That had to be it. It was two floors above, and the nicer rooms were higher up in his experience. Rowes had probably taken the elevator, so he darted for the stairs, pounding up them and throwing his way through the door to the sixth floor.

Passing a very startled-looking teenager, Rowes pushed his way through, stumbling to Ainslie's room and knocking as loud as he could. Someone down the hall poked out of their room, shaking their head and slamming their own door when Izzy didn't quit knocking.

"Ainslie, open the door. I know he's in there," Izzy growled, trying the doorknob, even though it was still locked. He heard a click on the other side, then a scraping noise as the deadbolt was presumably slid back.

Izzy took a step back, blinking when Connley was the one who opened the door. *Do I have the wrong room?* Connley had talked about being close to the gym, which was the opposite to the room with a view.

"Yeah, you caught me," said Connley grimly, his lips pressed into a thin line. "What's your problem?" Connley slipped into the hall, pulling the door shut behind him.

"Is Rowes in there?" asked Izzy, trying to see inside before the door slid shut.

M.C. Roth

"Nope," said Connley, flicking a bit of dust from his shoulder that Izzy couldn't see. "Haven't seen him since the bus."

He must've had the wrong room. Maybe he mixed up what Ainslie had said...but he could remember it so clearly.

"Where's Ainslie?" asked Izzy, looking up and down the hall. He lowered his voice when he saw the person looking out from their room again.

Connley shrugged. "Sleeping, I guess." He looked a bit relieved, which didn't make any sense. Izzy didn't care because there was only one person on his mind.

"We can check the gym for Rowes if you want. I was going to head there in the morning anyway, so why not three a.m.?" Connley rubbed his eyes with the back of his hands before cracking a yawn. "Let's go."

"No. He said he was going to stay with Ainslie. He won't be in the gym," said Izzy, shaking his head.

"Did you guys fight or something?"

Izzy swallowed, his throat clicking with how dry his mouth was. This was so much worse than a fight. The base of his nose ached as he held back his tears.

Connley must've taken his silence for a yes because he hummed under his breath before patting Izzy on the shoulder. "Then he probably went to the gym to cool off. There is nothing better than punching something when you're upset."

That made way too much sense for so early in the morning, especially when it came to Rowes. He was the unfortunate type who liked to go for a run to blow off steam while Izzy usually stuck to the free weights.

Connley turned, shuffling his socked feet down the hall before gesturing Izzy onward. "Come on. The halls should be empty, so we won't run into any fans of yours."

Izzy padded after him, his heart starting to slow. Connley always had that effect on people. Izzy had never seen him riled once, not even after numerous retakes when he still managed to make everyone believe in the role. Someone could come into a shoot pissed off, but once Connley got a hold of them, they couldn't even remember why they were angry.

"So, what's this fight about?" asked Connley, heading for the stairs. Their socks were going to be ruined after the trek. Even in the midst of summer, there were still stray bits of sand and dirt that made its way onto the carpet of every floor.

"A misunderstanding," said Izzy, dragging a hand through his hair as he let out a sigh. "I just want to explain myself, is all."

Connley nodded, holding the stairwell door open for him. "You guys will figure it out. You always do." He let out a small smile. "I remember the first time you two worked together on set. You were still bickering as if you were in high school and fixing each other's hair. The makeup artist absolutely *hated* you."

Izzy shook his head. Those had been the times. There had been no pressure back then, only hope and effort. The effort was still there, but now that they'd made it big, he'd lost that little part that had made his career so special. Rowes was probably the only one who kept him going.

"Then there was the season two rewrite," said Connley, barely out of breath as they reached the bottom floor. The guy was like a machine, plodding on in a steady rhythm. You'd never know from his wiry frame. "I thought you were going to walk out when they tried to kill off Rowes' character. It's a good thing you made that threat. My life wouldn't be the same without you two."

As they reached the gym, Connley held the door open for him, padding over to the elliptical as Izzy straddled the nearest weight bench. There wasn't much to lift in the gym, which always seemed to be a fallback of some hotels. Maybe they didn't expect their patrons to want to work up as much of a sweat as they did at a twenty-four-hour place, or they were worried about a lawsuit if someone dropped a weight on their neck.

"You didn't tell me what you guys were really fighting about," said Connley as he started up the machine, somehow making the flailing look elegant. Izzy was terrified of that particular piece of equipment. He could always picture slipping, his leg ending up between the pedals and snapping in two.

"Have you ever watched a fan video?" asked Izzy, casting his gaze around the too-clean gym. It was a stupid idea to look for Rowes here, but maybe it was a good thing to give him some space so he didn't feel like he was being pressured.

"I presume you mean the ones where you and Rowes are lost in each other's eyes." Connley snorted before upping his speed. "It's hard to miss them. All my apps are plastered with you guys, no matter how many times I snooze you. What about them?"

"Did you ever believe them?" asked Izzy, his gut going tight. Black weights from five to twenty kilograms called to him, but he made no move to reach for them. They would probably slip right through his fingertips if he made the attempt.

"I do my best not to picture you two naked. I see enough of that on set."

"They've made me question a few things," said Izzy, putting his hand flat on the bench. His palm sank into the cushion, the material sticking to his sweaty palm. He was out of shape if he was sweating just from the stairs.

"Like..." Connley trailed off, raising one brow. Somehow he kept his voice steady, even as he upped his speed.

"Just...things." *Real fucking mature.* But he did not want to explain a wet dream to his co-worker—not when he'd already humiliated himself enough for one day.

Connley rolled his eyes. "Okay then. You two will figure it out. As for the fan videos, they are just like the set. They show things in a different light, with makeup and innuendos, but it's only a play. The only people who know the truth are the two of you."

Chapter Five

Isthmus

"It's good to be home," said Izzy, sucking in a lungful of air as he stepped off the bus. Connley tapped his foot impatiently, still trapped behind Izzy. He was too busy taking in the view to rush.

Connley hadn't stopped complaining during the last two hours of the journey, and it had almost been enough to push Izzy to his breaking point, all things aside. Connley was one hell of an actor — probably the best he knew — but sometimes he was a spoiled brat.

He was sure his ass wasn't the only one that was numb. They'd all been sitting in the same type of seats. And they were all hungry. The last few days had been a whirlwind of travel, and it was always hard to keep on top of mealtimes during stints like that.

He ducked to the side, letting Connley past him and out into the crisp summer air. For once, it wasn't humid, and the sun's rays weren't nearly as unbearable as some parts of the world this time of year.

Connley screwed up his face as he stretched his arms over his head. "You grew up here? Weird." He turned to Izzy, letting out a chuckle at the glare sent his way. "I'm only kidding. It seems...nice."

Sometimes Izzy had no idea when Connley was joking or not. The guy was just that good. That, and he had the sense of humor of a potato.

"It's not weird. I know this whole city," said Izzy, leaning against the side of the bus as the rest of the crew started to file off. He wasn't going to admit that he was waiting for Rowes, but he'd thought Rowes was right behind him.

The hotel where they were staying was in the heart of downtown where skyscrapers roamed among the old brick buildings that give the city life. He remembered grabbing ice cream on the street corner as a kid and skateboarding along the rails at city hall. His childhood had been a fantastic blur of movement and people.

"Down that way is the park," said Izzy, leaning up on his toes to try to get a peek at the trees. They were too far away for him to see a thing from the ground, but maybe he'd luck out with the hotel. "And on the other side of town there's an industrial area that always smells like fresh-baked bread or burnt tires."

That bread factory had been there since Izzy had been young, and he could still remember guessing what batch they were making when he'd driven by with his parents. When they messed up a batch, the whole block knew.

"And that way..." Izzy faltered as Rowes stepped off the bus, dropping his hand to his side. He hadn't been to *that* side of town in a long time, and from what he'd heard, it wouldn't be the same anymore.

"What?" asked Connley, apparently oblivious to Izzy's struggle.

Pointedly keeping his eyes off Rowes, Izzy looked to where he'd been pointing. "Nothing. Just a club. I just remembered it's not there anymore."

Connley kicked his heel against the pavement. "Too bad. I could use one hell of a drink after that ride. It's a good thing that this is the last stop, and we can get back to filming. I'm starting to dissociate."

It would have been funny if Connley had been joking. He had the strange habit of slipping in and out of character amid conversation. The first time it had happened and Connley had taken on an English accent, Izzy had been worried for his mental health. Now it was second nature.

"Yeah, me, too…" Izzy trailed off before glancing to Rowes. He was standing next to the bus and looking at the hotel with his hands in the back pockets of his jeans. To an outsider he probably looked relaxed, but Izzy knew better.

'Cause I fucked up. Shaking his head, Izzy grabbed for his bag and slung Rowes' over his opposite side when he spotted it. They settled heavily against him, the straps digging into his shoulders. He didn't care how tense things were between them at the moment, he was determined to fix everything.

The first part of that was rooming together again.

If I wouldn't have watched those fucking videos… Every time he looked at Rowes now, all he could do was analyze him. Was he feeling more than Izzy was? Was that the light catching his eyes, or did he detect a hint of longing? His lips looked soft, glistening with the balm he always used. It smelled like honey, but did it taste like that?

Fuck. He'd never dealt with something like this before. When he wanted someone, he went out and got them — as long as they were consenting, of course. He'd never come up against a brick wall with someone he was not allowed to have.

They'd stopped sleeping in each other's beds the first night after the incident. Rowes had suddenly sat up before crossing the room to his own bed. Izzy had laid awake all night, listening to the sound of soft breathing and fighting back tears as he longed for his best friend. Rowes wasn't the only one who needed touch.

At the next stop, Rowes had insisted on his own room, claiming that he didn't want to keep Izzy up with his snoring. Lorena had been all too happy to book the extra one, even going so far as to offer Rowes a pat on the back.

The thing was, Izzy couldn't sleep a wink. He needed that noise and the sound of Rowes' rasping breaths to get him through. And he fucking missed his friend. He'd never been so stressed or lonely before.

After sitting apart on the bus, Izzy was desperate to get his best friend back by any means necessary. His crazy-ass plan was probably the worst idea he'd ever had, but he'd had too many sleepless nights flipping through his phone and wondering.

"Rowes, you're with me. I booked us the presidential suite," said Izzy, supporting the straps of the bags with his hands so he wouldn't be tempted to reach out. He wasn't exactly sure *why* he was afraid to touch Rowes, but Rowes seemed almost grateful about it.

"Thank Christ," mumbled Connley. "I thought you were going to be in the doghouse forever. The angst was starting to turn me gray." Connley pushed past them, grabbing his own pinstripe bag and lugging it into the hotel. Even if he did go gray, his light blond hair would never show it.

"What's that supposed to mean?" asked Izzy, shouting after Connley. He turned to Rowes when he didn't get an answer. "Do you know?"

Rowes only shrugged, because apparently they weren't on speaking terms, either.

Fucking hell. If he was going to go through with his plan, he was doing it tonight. It was only about two in the afternoon, so he had a solid few hours of power napping before he had to do anything. That would hopefully put things into perspective.

Lorena checked in for them, getting their keys in record time. The smell of chlorine was powerful as they waited in the lobby, but for Izzy, it wasn't as comforting as usual. Hotels were supposed to be fun, but he was just so tired that it barely mattered.

"You okay with the suite?" asked Izzy, desperate for Rowes to say anything. The shrug of a reply only made him bite his tongue, more frustrated than he could put into words. "Well, come on, then."

Doubling the bags up on one shoulder, he reached for Rowes, throwing his arm around him and pulling him close. His shoulder ached from the strain of too much weight on one side as it pulled him off balance. Another curse of being on the road too long meant he had little time for keeping fit. He was turning into a car potato.

Breath going out in a whoosh, Rowes glanced at him in confusion before immediately looking around as if he expected Lorena or someone with a camera to be standing right next to them. There were a few actually, speckled on the exterior of the hotel behind a small black rope. They could see straight into the hotel's glass windows if they cared to look.

Look all you want. They weren't doing anything wrong.

Gunlover was getting a lot of hype in the media, and the fans had been flocking alongside them for their entire press tour. A few fan meets had been absolutely insane.

"Worried we'll get caught?" Izzy asked softly, lowering his head to speak into Rowes' ear. Rowes shot him a glare, his lips pressed into a thin line. There were dark shadows under his eyes, so he'd probably slept even worse than Izzy. It was strange to sleep in silence when you were so used to someone breathing beside you, even if that someone was in a different bed.

"Caught with what?" asked Rowes as he scowled. "With my hands on your ass? Or are you worried someone might find the little bag of weed in your suitcase that you think I don't know about?"

Even as he said it, Rowes moved his hand around Izzy's hip, settling low on the waistband of his sagging jeans. His palms were warm enough that Izzy could feel them through the fabric, Rowes' grip unsteady. He wasn't speaking loud enough for everyone to hear, but Ainslie snickered next to them, shooting them a smile.

"That weed is for you," said Izzy softly, forcing a smile on his lips as he blinked toward the muted flash of a camera. He could already imagine the headlines, and he couldn't care less. Rowes was touching him. *Finally.* "There's a hell of a thunderstorm coming, and I know those always give you migraines."

"Oh." Rowes dropped his gaze, something flitting over his face before it was gone. "Sorry." He shifted his feet, feeling so close to pulling away. Izzy squeezed him tighter, ignoring his bag as it slid from his shoulder to the nook of his elbow.

"Don't be," said Izzy. *Fuck, I'm doing this all wrong.* All he wanted was a straight-up conversation with his best friend, but he could barely focus. "Let's talk in the room. I hate what's happened these last few weeks, and I want to put it behind us." A camera flashed to the side and Izzy made sure to turn his head, shooting the fan a little peace sign before shrugging as the second bag tried to slip down his shoulder. "Also, what do you have in this bag? It weighs a ton."

Biting his lip, Rowes looked away, flinching as Ainslie let out a little laugh at something Connley said. The two had their heads together, giggling over something Connley had said. "I bought you kombucha."

Izzy's chest gave a pang. Maybe things weren't so hopeless after all. He loved kombucha, but Rowes absolutely detested the stuff and went so far as to turn his nose up at even trying the new varieties Izzy would buy. He must've been feeling the tension between them too if he had gone out of his way to buy it.

"Your room key, boys," said Lorena, passing them each a small paper packet with a white card within. "It's 4604. I'm surprised you guys are going splits on the room again. I thought that Rowes was enjoying having his downtime alone."

Izzy stiffened. It was hard to get a good read on Rowes, but he looked almost guilty? *Shit.* Maybe he'd been wrong all along.

Rowes dropped his arm from around Izzy's waist, clutching his key with both hands. "Come on, Izzy. I'm tired."

As soon as they were through the room door, Rowes grabbed his bag from Izzy's shoulder and stepped away, peering through the room as if he actually fucking cared what it looked like. *Jacuzzi, fireplace, same old, same old.* Once he'd started staying in hotels frequently, Izzy had stopped caring about the way the fancy ones looked, with posh decorations and outrageous armchairs. Honestly, the menu was usually the highlight for him.

"Oh, a minibar," said Rowes, his voice flat as he opened the little cupboard below the television that had looked like a dresser drawer.

Now that was just sad. There had been a minibar in literally every other room they'd stayed in during the tour. It didn't matter that this one seemed to have some pretty top-shelf stuff. Any other time they could have indulged, but not today.

"Too bad we won't be drinking from it," said Izzy, tossing his bag on the ground and falling back on the nearest queen bed. He sank into the duvet, the scent of clean laundry enveloping him. Hotels always seemed to have the same citrus scent to their sheets, no matter where they were in the world.

"No?" asked Rowes as he ducked down, grasping one of the liquor bottles and twirling it around to read the label.

You've got to be kidding me.

"Come here, Rowes," said Izzy, patting the bed and sitting up. Rowes looked to him, biting his lip before he slowly complied, the liquor bottle still clutched in his hand like a lifeline. His lips were so pink, like he'd been biting them during the whole bus ride. They still looked soft…soft enough to kiss.

Forget about it. If only he could. But he wasn't going to let his friendship burn because of what a few people had to say on the internet.

"I'm sorry," said Izzy, taking a breath of Rowes' scent as he neared. Rowes was still tense, but he let out a little sigh, leaning his head against Izzy's chest. "I should have listened to you before, but I took other's opinions too seriously and started second-guessing what's between us."

Rowes went tighter against him, his spine rigid. The trembling that racked his frame set Izzy on edge. He needed to do something—anything—to make it better.

"I just kept wondering if I was getting in the way of something for you," said Izzy, squeezing him even tighter. "Or maybe I wondered if I should feel differently. But I know you're my best friend, and I want you with me for the rest of my life, show or no show. I feel like watching those videos ruined what we had, making me deny everything I believed about us."

Letting out a shaky breath, Izzy fought not to pull away. He wanted to run, hide and bury his head under the sand to avoid anyone who looked at them like that again. At the same time, he never wanted Rowes away from his side, and he would fight to make sure that happened.

"You're still my best friend," said Rowes, his voice just as shaky as Izzy's. "But you're right. Things are different, and I don't know how to fix them."

Enter the infallible plan…

"I think I might," said Izzy, gritting his teeth. It was such a terrible idea that he'd thought of hours into a sleepless night. But once it had come to mind, there was no denying it.

Rowes pulled away, twisting in Izzy's arms with wide eyes. "You aren't going to kiss me, are you?"

Was it terrible that Rowes' mind had gone there first? Izzy couldn't help but flicker his gaze to Rowes' lips and wonder how soft they were.

"That wasn't the plan, but I can if that's what you need." That had been the first plan that he'd rejected after two moments of rational thought. He'd been thinking that they could try a kiss, then when they felt nothing, they could go back to normal.

Only, there was a one percent chance — or less — that Izzy might actually like kissing Rowes. Then everything would be fucked. Rowes was beautiful, sweet and charismatic, so a good kisser would probably go right along with that.

The second plan was so much better…and worse.

"I want to take you to a club," said Izzy, running his hand through his hair. "A kink club."

He could hear Rowes swallow in the sudden quiet, his heart racing. It had sounded so much better in his head.

"It was that first video — the D/s one — that really started whatever it is between us, and I thought that if you saw what really went on in a kink club and how Doms and subs acted with each other, it would put your mind at rest. It's really nothing like what we have — like this."

He squeezed Rowes tighter before lacing their fingers together. They fit perfectly — they always had. It was just so fucking infuriating that he was questioning anything about them.

Izzy needed to see the club again, too, just to make sure. He was starting to wonder about a few things. Maybe there was a reason he'd stuck mostly to one-night stands, and maybe it had nothing to do with his crazy schedule and dollop of fame.

"Besides, kink isn't about sex," said Izzy. Of everything, that was one thing he was completely certain of. He'd seen completely non-sexual couples go through intense scenes without any arousal whatsoever.

Rowes spluttered, snorting with laughter as he tugged free of Izzy's arms and stood. He rounded on Izzy, his face bright red and his eyes shiny. "You have got to be joking me. You think a kink club is going to fix our friendship?"

Well, it sounds silly if you put it that way.

"Yes?" Izzy scratched his chin, trying to figure out where he'd gotten the idea from in the first place. He had been a little low on sleep lately, and the stress of constant traveling had been taking its toll. That, and not having someone to bounce ideas off of was messing with his head.

"It will be confidential, with waivers and everything, and no pictures allowed, so we don't have to worry about the press." Izzy listed off the few things that had come to mind right away. It had been a long time since he'd been anywhere near the community, but he remembered them being a trustworthy group...for the most part.

Rowes shook his head, covering his mouth with his hand, and he started to laugh in what looked like disbelief. "We barely talk for days, and instead of counseling, you want to dive into BDSM. We are so fucking doomed."

He's probably right.

Chapter Six

Rowes

When Izzy had said a club, he'd expected something downtown, with music busting his eardrums and strobe lights that made his eyes ache. He'd also expected a lot of leather and high boots with maybe some latex. He wasn't a complete prude, after all.

A castle of a house outside of town after a long gravel lane had not been his first guess. It didn't even look intimidating...or sexy—just modern with a nice flow to it and little birds fluttering through the trees while chirping alarms. There wasn't even any music, loud or otherwise.

The cars in the lot outside ranged from a beat-up Ford to a BMW with every model in between. Rowes peered toward the door where a man was leaning against the frame. He would have looked intimidating if his eyes hadn't lit up, a smile stretching over his face when he spotted them.

"Are you sure this is the right place?" Rowes whispered as he stepped out of the car door when Izzy held it open for him. Izzy chuckled as he nodded before sending the stranger a polite smile. Izzy's eyes were slightly pinched, but he let out a breath as Rowes touched his arm.

The man waiting at the door was attractive as hell, but so far away from Izzy's type that Rowes had to question Izzy's judgment. With graying hair and a suit that reeked of money, he was the opposite of the men Izzy usually had flings with.

Not that Rowes was keeping track. They had a simple code between them to steer clear of the room if either of them received the '*Busy. Give me an hour*' text. Rowes always tried to be generous and give Izzy at least three, but he'd still managed to run into a few guys on their way out.

Thin, twinky with dark hair and big blue eyes fit almost all Izzy's hookups. This guy was pure Sugar Daddy material. *Just like Izzy.* Rowes shook his head, warding off those thoughts before they could develop into more. They were here to prove they weren't kinky, not that they were.

And Izzy would know. He'd been a part of the scene, if only for a short time. He'd kept pretty tight-lipped about it, not that Rowes blamed him. They weren't ones to get into stories of former conquests, no matter how good the lay was. They did swap embarrassing stories sometimes, but even those were few and far between.

"Hi, Malone," said Izzy as they approached the door. "Thanks so much for meeting us here. It's been a long time."

Malone smiled, showing off every perfect and white tooth in his beautiful mouth. His jawline was nuts, too, with just a hint of scruff that would probably feel fantastic during a make-out session. *Stop it!*

Rowes' gut churned. He didn't want to imagine the two of them together, with Izzy's fingers carding through that silver hair or going to his knees. He clenched his jaw, looking off to the side as a chipmunk scrambled across the gravel.

"Isthmus," said Malone, offering his hand. Izzy clasped it, but it looked the same way it did when he shook the producer's hand, not the way he would touch an old hookup. Rowes took a step closer to Izzy, unconsciously trying to tuck himself under his arm. Izzy didn't even look at him before throwing an arm over his shoulders and drawing him in. Just being there again drained some of his tension. Izzy was the only thing that always made sense.

"I couldn't believe it when you called me, Isthmus, but it's great to see you," said Malone, dropping his hand to his side. His gaze was steady on Izzy, only sparing Rowes a soft glance. "You've gone places since I saw you last… You've grown."

Izzy seemed to stand an inch taller at the words, his chest puffing out like the director had just told him he was the best actor he'd ever worked with. Rowes fought not to snicker, shooting an elbow into Izzy's side instead.

"Is this your submissive?" asked Malone, a bucket of ice falling directly on Rowes' shoulders. It sounded so dirty coming from Malone's lips with his deep voice that twisted his insides. "I didn't realize you two were together."

"Uh…I'm—" Rowes started, cutting himself off as Malone looked his way. Those eyes spoke of things that Rowes couldn't imagine. This was someone who knew exactly who he was and what he wanted. Next to him, Rowes couldn't help but feel like a stumbling idiot.

"Ro is my best friend," said Izzy, squeezing Rowes tight. "Something came up recently, and we thought we would look into Dominance and submission." He was such a good bull-shitter, but Rowes could imagine him preparing that speech the whole way over. "I couldn't remember enough to be helpful, but there were a lot of good people the last time I was at Unkinked."

Nodding slowly, Malone gave them a soft smile, looking at Rowes with something sweet in his gaze. "There are still good people. Clint runs the place, but his husband passed some time ago. This build is new, but the people are still the same." He motioned to the doors.

Rowes' gut clenched as something clicked in his mind. Malone was something *different*. There were very few in the world that treated actors like real people. To most, they were stars or someone to fantasize about, which was exhausting.

"Things are a little different out here, too," said Malone, reaching for his phone. "No pictures, videos or anything that can be downloaded, uploaded or posted online. Anything you see or hear, you keep between you and your play partner. If you don't like the look of something or it's not your thing, don't make a scene, just leave quietly. If you see anything that concerns you or if you suspect something isn't right with a scene, then report it to me or the Dungeon Master."

Rowes needed a pen and a pad of paper to start taking notes. They'd signed some online forms that Malone had sent them before they'd gotten there, but he hadn't read them very carefully, too excited and nervous about the place.

"Sounds familiar," said Izzy, nodding. "I gave Ro a bit of a rundown on the way, and we got those forms signed before we left. Thanks for getting that to us on such short notice."

Malone only shrugged. He must've owned his own business or something to have such a flexible schedule. Izzy had called him shortly after two, and it was still daylight now—barely.

"You remember about consent, right?" asked Malone, settling his gaze on Rowes when he didn't respond along with Izzy. "Nothing happens without consent—not a touch, not a scene or anything close to it. No second chances."

"Got it. Keep my hands to myself. No second chances," said Rowes, tucking his hands under his armpits. There were a lot of rules… Was he allowed to look? If he caught someone's eye, was he going to be banned for life?

"And that tongue, too," said Malone with a wink. "Unless you're here looking for a Daddy, try not to flirt too much. I have a lovely boy of my own, but I always have a friend who is looking."

If his face got any hotter, he was going to pass out. The air was suddenly twice as humid, the sound of crickets and a few birds way too loud. Izzy was unyielding next to him, his hand going tight where he'd moved it to Rowes' waist.

"He's not looking," said Izzy, his voice surprisingly sharp.

Thank you. At least Izzy hadn't lost his power of speech. Rowes wasn't much of a flirt usually, but he didn't want someone to take him too seriously when he was already feeling way over his head.

"Thought not," said Malone, shooting Izzy a wink as if he knew something they didn't. Hopefully, this guy didn't have the same track mind as everyone else in the world.

"We aren't sleeping together — Izzy and me, I mean. If you saw it online, it's not true. We're friends. That's all." Rowes swallowed when two heavy gazes settled on him.

Letting out a soft sigh, Malone nodded, folding his hands behind his back as he regarded them. "I meant no offense. Kink isn't about sex, and for some partners, it's a limit."

Luckily, that was another term Izzy had explained to him. If something was off the table, all he had to do was call it a limit, and they were good. If Malone asked him, he was going to tell him *everything* was a limit for now.

"Kink is about power exchange, trust and intimacy. Sometimes the greatest intimacy is between friends," said Malone.

Okay, so maybe the guy was actually a sweetheart. Rowes probably had stars in his eyes, because he couldn't remember the last time he'd heard someone speak like that to anyone. And for the first time in weeks, he felt *good*.

No one had ever told him it was okay to be exactly who he was and nothing more or less, but Malone seemed to get it, and they'd just met.

Malone held the door open for them and Rowes followed Izzy's sure steps, letting himself be ushered inside a place that would probably change his life forever. He could already feel it prickling along his skin as if looking for somewhere to sink deeper, until he was nothing like the man he'd been this morning.

Last chance. He looked back as the door fell shut, air conditioning wrapping around them like a temple. *Too late.* There was no going back now. Whatever happened, they wouldn't be the same people when they left.

"I'll give you a quick tour of the place before I show you to the open play area. There is no demo tonight, so if you need somewhere quiet, you're welcome to use the stage area."

So many rooms. Rowes was overwhelmed in moments. There was so much more than just latex and leather, and as for the people they came across, most of them he could have passed on the street and not known that they were kinky. Hollywood had gotten it so wrong.

He'd thought they wouldn't see anything scandalous, until they came across a mostly naked man with a G-string, dog collar and suspicious tail. He wasn't acting like a dog, but he was sitting at another man's feet, his head tilted to the side with his throat exposed. He barely blinked when they approached, his eyes half-lidded and appearing more satisfied than Rowes had ever been.

"These are the private rooms, and if you two ever apply to become members, access to them will be included with your membership fees after a waiting period," said Malone, motioning to a hallway with a hell of a lot of doors. "Not sure if you remember, Isthmus, but each of them has themes." He tapped on the nearest door, and the engraved name. "This one is called 'impact' so everything inside is based off impact play."

Tilting his head, Rowes leaned into Izzy before whispering softly. "What's impact play? Sounds terrible."

He really needed some time alone with his safe search off. His time in television had obviously kept him naïve to a lot of things in the world, even as a sex symbol.

"Don't be afraid to ask questions," said Malone, obviously catching Rowes' whisper. "Impact play can be anything from spanking, paddling or even a whipping. If you were interested in exploring that, I would set you up with an experienced Dom to show you the ropes."

Rowes couldn't shake his head fast enough. A little spank during sex was fine, but they weren't here to talk about sex. In fact, Rowes was doing his best to think of anything but, even with the pulsing beat coming from a nearby hallway. It sounded so similar to the song in one of the fan videos that it caught him off guard.

"I think we were in a room before," said Izzy, rubbing his forehead as he presumably tried to remember. "I think it was called 'Spoil'?"

Nodding, Malone turned from the hall. "My favorite room."

Rowes frowned, looping his own arm around Izzy's waist. Izzy deserved to be spoiled at every opportunity. He didn't need a special room for that to happen.

More rooms flickered by, one leading to a basement that Malone said would be off limits to them. They didn't get to see anything past the engraved names, but the names themselves were pretty self-explanatory. Rowes didn't have to think very hard to figure out what went on in the 'wet' room. He doubted it was swimming lessons.

"That's pretty much it except for the open play area," said Malone, moving easily past a couple who were speaking in hushed voices. "There are a few people there now, so you'll get a peek at play partners. Are you both feeling up to that?"

Well, there was no way in hell he was leaving now. Rowes had had a semi since he'd seen the man in the G-string, and he'd spotted a woman in a corset who was smoking hot. He'd worn tight pants for a reason, and after a simple adjustment, none of the others would notice his situation.

There is no way kink has nothing to do with sex.

"We're good," said Izzy, threading his hand through Rowes' hair as he nodded. Rowes leaned into the touch, his heart slowing as he took a deep breath. Without Izzy at his side, he wouldn't have made it more than a few steps inside the door. But he didn't have to be worried, not when Izzy was cuddling with him in the same way he had before the videos had ruined everything between them.

I can do this.

They stepped into the open play area, and Rowes' lungs flattened like popped balloons. He couldn't breathe. Izzy's hand in his hair could do nothing to protect him as he was completely overwhelmed, every sense flaring to life until he was drowning in pure need.

I can't do this.

The things around the room were like something out of a horror movie mixed with a gothic torture chamber, with a few couches strewn into the mix. There seemed to be stations set all around, a few of them occupied while others gleamed as if they were trying to draw him in. And the people...? He forced himself to blink. He'd never seen anything like it.

I need to get out more.

Izzy moved easily beside him, as if he'd expected the skin and the sex all along. Maybe it was easier because he'd seen the club before, or at least, the community. Either way, his gaze didn't linger, even as Rowes couldn't drag his eyes away.

I am woefully unprepared.

"Hey, Clint," said Izzy, raising his hand as someone approached them from his spot on one of the couches. Clint was handsome, even though he looked exhausted, with black under his eyes and bedhead to match. His shirt had at least three holes that Rowes could see, but it suited him in the same way that an alley suited a scruffy cat.

How could Izzy remember all these people? Rowes clenched his jaw so he didn't start to grumble. *It's in his past.* Still...he couldn't help but wonder how many of them Izzy had slept with and how many had seen him naked.

"Isthmus. I never thought I'd see you back in my neck of the woods," said Clint, tugging at his shirt collar before offering his hand to Izzy. "I'd ask where you've been, but I'm a huge fan." Shaking his hand a few seconds too long, he turned his gaze on Rowes, his eyes going wide.

"I..." Clint trailed off, his mouth hanging open as he stared slack-jawed at Rowes.

The speechlessness of fans was something that Rowes could easily deal with. Ducking out from under Izzy's arm, he grabbed Clint's hand that was still outstretched from his greeting with Izzy, plastering a dazzling smile on his face.

"Nice to meet you, Clint," said Rowes, ignoring Izzy's snort. Izzy thought the face he put on for his fans was hilarious. Well, Izzy's wasn't much better, but was maybe a touch more believable. "Thank you for allowing us in your—uh—establishment."

What the hell was he supposed to call it? He glanced sideways at a funky-looking cross that had someone strapped to it who was getting swatted with something that looked like a riding crop. It was closer to a pipe dream than what Rowes usually expected from reality.

Maybe Clint should have called the space 'a chamber of pleasure' or something. The guy getting whipped looked like he was blissed out, with the man dealing out the blows in a similar state.

"Holy shit. Rowes Keppel is in my place." Clint flushed, before going pale. "*Holy shit.*" He tugged at his shirt again, choking as his eyes only went wider. Clint was starting to wobble, his legs looking unsteady.

Please don't pass out. That had happened a time or two before. Rowes' face ached with the effort of keeping the smile on his face.

"Easy, Clint," said Malone, reaching out to steady his friend with a hand on his shoulder. Clint blinked before shaking his head and wiping a bit of drool from the corner of his mouth.

"Welcome!"

Rowes winced at the volume of Clint's yell that drew every unoccupied eye their way. From the whispers, he could tell they'd been recognized. He made a mental note to get a lawyer, just in case someone did try to post their pictures online.

"This is fantastic," said Izzy, covering his mouth with his hand. Rowes shot him a mild glare, toning down his smile for Clint as he turned back. Maybe he was just overwhelming the poor guy.

"Holy, hell," said Clint, rubbing his chest as he drew his hand back. "Hi—um—hi. Did you find the place okay? Did Malone show you around? Can I get you anything to drink?"

Rowes' eye twitched, and he almost lost his composure as Izzy started to break down into laughter behind him. Clint seemed like a sweet guy, just a little starstruck was all. It was strange because he didn't seem that way with Izzy. Most of the fans flocked to Izzy's corner, and Rowes had become used to being second best.

"Aren't you a fan of Izzy?" asked Rowes, probably a little rudely with the way Clint bit his lip and looked between them.

"Yeah, but you're *Rowes Keppel*," said Clint. "*The* Rowes Keppel. You're like the hottest guy out there—and don't get me started on your abs. Was that really you in season four, episode ten, or did they use a double?"

Shooting an elbow back as Izzy started to get a little too loud in his laughter, Rowes bit the inside of his cheek. Izzy was always the one to crack up on set and in real life, but now was not the time. He'd rather do a hundred retakes than humiliate himself in this place.

"That was all me," said Rowes, putting his hands on his hips. He was mighty proud of his abs, especially with the amount of time he'd put into the gym. It almost seemed like a waste to have months of working out summed up in a few seconds of screen time.

Clint's brain seemed to go offline as he dropped his gaze to the level of Rowes' belly. Rowes always felt bad for pregnant women and the way people wanted to touch their bellies because fans treated him the same way, even if they just ended up looking.

"Clint." Malone's voice was so much sharper this time, stealing the mirth from their bubble. Even Izzy quieted down while Rowes reached for him, clutching his hand tight.

"We're going to watch a scene together from one of the couches. You're welcome to join us, Clint," said Malone, smoothing over the situation as if it were nothing. The guy would make a great manager, not that it looked like he needed the money.

Couch. Good. Rowes glanced in the direction that Malone was leading them. *Or very, very bad.* The view before him was breathtaking. *So much for just a semi.*

Chapter Seven

Isthmus

It was almost exactly as he remembered the old club in town, and strangely enough, it was like coming home. Something had eased off his shoulders as soon as he'd spotted Malone, not only because it was good to see an old friend, but because Malone looked at him as another Dom, not like an ex-sub.

Malone adored his subs, but he treated them like boys—which was exactly how they wanted to be treated, for the most part. The way he spoke with another Dom or even acted was completely different. It was the breath of fresh air that Izzy hadn't known he was seeking.

He'd dreaded the moment of seeing Malone again—hoping against hope that he hadn't been wrong all that time ago when he'd realized that he never wanted to go to his knees again.

Glancing at Clint, who was still frozen, Izzy let out a chuckle, easing onto the couch next to Malone and pointing to a spot on the floor for Rowes.

He stared at his hand in shock. The move had been so automatic that he hadn't even realized he'd done it.

Something twisted in his gut, and he opened his mouth to protest, but Rowes was already dropping smoothly between Izzy's spread thighs and crossing his legs. The way he tilted his head back, seeking touch, looked like muscle memory. And of course, Izzy indulged him like he always did.

He caught Malone's pointed look but refused to acknowledge it, instead focusing on the couple before him. He didn't recognize either of them, but he certainly wasn't going to interrupt their scene to introduce himself.

Completely restrained, the sub was twined with ropes, knots dotting along their skin in a flowing web of organized madness. He didn't look like he could move an inch without resisting the ropes, but he didn't look like he wanted to, either.

It would have appeared almost non-sexual if not for the plug in his ass, with strategically placed ropes keeping it settled. From the low hum, it must've been a vibrator as well, and from the color of his cock, it had been vibrating for quite some time.

Do I want to see Rowes like that?

Aesthetically, Rowes would look amazing in those ropes, the red satin sheen to them only accentuating his beauty. But he much preferred Rowes at his feet, the strands of his hair silky between his fingers. He wouldn't have to restrain Rowes because he would stay still all on his own, Izzy's words stronger than any tether.

He went to pull his hand back, thinking better of it a second later. There was no one to judge them here except themselves, and he was so fucking done with that. They were never going to figure it out if they kept hiding, either.

"What do you think, Ro?" Izzy tugged softly until Rowes tilted his head back. His pupils were blown, his face flushed and his lower lip between his teeth. "That good, huh?"

Rowes only blinked before slowly turning his attention back to the scene. "How does he do that? It's stunning."

Izzy's mouth went dry at the soft words.

"A lot of practice," said Malone, stretching his legs out. The hem of his suit rode up, exposing his ankle. "Theo and Harry have been together for six months now, but Harry is one of the best Shibari Doms out there and teaches classes every few months or so. If you're serious about it, we could sign you up for one."

Rowes didn't shake his head this time, he only stared, licking his lips as Izzy peered over his shoulder. *I guess that's one thing off the limit list.* Rowes had made it clear in the car that everything was a limit until they figured some stuff out.

"What would you want when you were all tied up?" asked Izzy tenderly, moving his hand from Rowes' hair to his neck. Rowes' pulse thumped against his fingers, and he pressed against it, trying to slow it with his thoughts alone.

"I would just want to...I don't know — *be*." Rowes let out a huff, pulling his knees to his chest. "He looks so relaxed and happy, as if he doesn't have a care in the world."

"He doesn't," said Malone. "With his Dom taking care of him, all he needs to do is exist and give in. When he reaches subspace, it's a moment of pure exhilaration, trust and triumph for both of them."

Subspace was something that Izzy had never experienced, probably because he wasn't a sub. But he knew the feeling of calm when he helped Rowes — or touched him in the way he was touching him now.

Instead of pulling his hand back, Izzy leaned forward, so he could touch the base of Rowes' neck, wrapping his fingers around him almost like a collar. He didn't squeeze, even when every part of him begged him to.

"Maybe the toy, too," said Rowes, completely taking Izzy off guard as he swallowed, his throat bobbing against Izzy's fingers. "The toy looks like it would…" He trailed off.

No. Izzy applied the barest amount of pressure, reveling in the throb beneath his fingertips. Rowes wasn't getting off without an answer. "Like it would what?"

Rowes trembled, touching Izzy's hand with his own. "Like it would feel really good…maybe even better than the ropes."

Malone let out a soft chuckle, shifting beside them. Izzy didn't have to look to know that he was hard. He was in the same state, his traitorous cock threatening to steal his sanity as Rowes laid everything bare before him.

"Malone did that to me once," said Izzy, running his nose over Rowes' ear before breathing deep. He was the soft citrus of hotel shampoo along with a touch of Izzy's own cologne. Perhaps he'd grabbed the wrong one in their shared bathroom, or maybe it had been deliberate, set to drive Izzy insane.

"He cuffed me to the wall with my hands behind my back, a remote-controlled toy buzzing away in my ass." He clenched at the memory. It was still vivid to this day. "He sucked me off until I couldn't remember my own name."

Rowes let out a shuddering breath, his hand moving from his knee to his inner thigh as he spread his legs.

"Don't touch yourself," said Izzy, before he could stop himself. There was a darkness in his thoughts that had taken over, forcing his fingers just a tad tighter.

Rowes groaned, the vibration traveling up Izzy's fingers as he retreated to his knees again, snapping his legs shut.

"What else, Ro?" asked Izzy, glancing at Malone, who was watching them with dark eyes. *What am I doing?* He didn't know, and he didn't care.

"You would... I can't say it, Izzy, *please*."

Oh fuck. Rowes was imagining *him* tying him up, not some faceless Dom from the club. Jerking his hand away, Izzy forced his gaze to the plain black cushion on the couch. It was made of something slippery that was probably cheaper than leather and easy to clean while having a similar aesthetic.

"Isthmus." The sharpness in Malone's voice dragged away his spiral that was already beginning, steadying the rapid beating of his heart. "It's okay."

No, it wasn't. This had been the stupidest plan of his life that had been doomed to fail. Why had he ever thought that Unkinked would solve their problems? Their friendship had been stamped with an expiration date as soon as he'd watched that video and wondered what it would be like if Rowes was more than a friend.

"We aren't fucking," said Izzy, his voice almost a snarl. Rowes flinched, looking over his shoulder with wide eyes.

"I didn't mean—" Rowes started, but Malone cut him off.

"You did nothing wrong, Rowes. Isthmus is just struggling with something, even though he knows the right answer."

The right answer? Izzy wanted to punch Malone in the face and storm out at the same time, never looking back at this godforsaken club. But there was no way to burn the memories away.

"We had dozens of scenes in our time together, Isthmus," said Malone, somehow still looking relaxed. "Tell me... How many times did you get hard for me? How many times did you come?"

Izzy blanched, not expecting that question in the least. He thought back, worrying his lip as he tried to call on scenes other than the most vivid ones. Had it really been dozens? It hadn't seemed that way.

"Three times, Isthmus," said Malone, his gaze unwavering. "Three times, you got hard for me, and only one scene where I made you come — repeatedly. Do you remember how many times I fucked you?"

Sucking in a breath, Izzy clenched his hand into a fist. That one he knew. "None. We never did that together, even when I wanted to."

It had been one of the reasons they had broken up. Izzy had wanted something more, but Malone had refused, probably sensing that Izzy had been lying to himself about being a boy and a bottom. Malone had always been too smart for his own good, peacefully arranging their parting as *friends.*

Rowes seemed surprised at that one, his worry clearly starting to calm.

"Exactly," said Malone, turning his attention back to the scene. "You were my boy for six months and submitted to me almost daily, and yet we didn't fuck once."

Shit. Malone had a point — a big one. Izzy had been looking at this all wrong, fearing something that never existed and making a huge fucking deal about them. *Just like the videos. Well, all except one.* The D/s video was the only pure one in the bunch.

"Say it, Ro. I need to know." Izzy's voice was so much calmer than he thought it would have been. At least it was pure and steady, even when he was ready to fall apart inside.

"We would be just like this," said Rowes, biting his lip and wincing when he broke skin. "Me at your feet and you there, like we're meant to be."

"Fucking hell," said Izzy, grinning as he wrapped his hand around Rowes' throat again. They fit perfectly together, the contrast of Rowes' pale neck against his tanned hand like magic. "I think I figured it out, Rowes."

Rowes blinked slowly, his eyes shiny as he smiled. It was such a sweet, innocent smile, like there could never be anything amiss with the world. It was something no one ever got to see on set or in a scene. That was for Izzy alone.

"Yeah," said Izzy, tracing Rowes' pulse. It made perfect sense. "You're going to be my submissive."

Izzy wasn't sure if he'd ever seen Rowes look quite so shocked.

Chapter Eight

Rowes

He couldn't do this. On set with cameras and people everywhere, he'd never been so exposed, like they could see straight through his clothes to the vulnerable skin underneath. He might as well have had a sign on his forehead.

Submissive.

The word was like nothing he'd ever said out loud. It was a world unto itself, and a role unlike anything he'd done before. He could slip on a face and make an audience believe whatever he wanted them to believe — but being *real* had never been so intimidating.

"You're going to be my submissive."

Those words rolled in his mind over and over, corrupting his thoughts and slaking his strength. He'd been right from the very beginning. There was no going back from this.

But then he glanced over his shoulder and caught sight of Izzy and everything was…fine. He was whole, completely and utterly, when he looked to his best friend, the cameras and watchful eyes disappearing into nothing.

"You seem a little bit out of it today, Rowes. Everything okay?"

Skidding to a halt, Rowes turned to Lorena, her watchful eyes scraping him up and down and leaving him raw. She was amazing at her job, but that also meant she was the most observant person he knew.

"Did you check yourself for a fever?" she asked when he didn't respond, placing the back of her hand against his forehead.

Rowes couldn't help but glance toward Izzy, who was watching them with a concerned look. Was it okay that she was touching him? They hadn't spent much time at the club after Izzy's declaration, and they hadn't had much time to set down rules. But he knew Izzy was possessive of his things.

I suppose I'm one of those things now.

He wasn't sure what it was supposed to feel like to be wanted, but it sure as hell wasn't bad. He just hoped that their friendship wouldn't crash and burn like every one of his other relationships.

Not that they were in a relationship. Like Malone had said, they didn't need to fuck to be play partners. And getting hard had been a totally normal reaction. Rowes had woken up with Izzy's morning wood poking him somewhere more times than he could count. Usually they just made a joke and let it slide, Rowes covering his own erection as he hobbled to the bathroom.

"You don't have a fever," said Lorena. Rowes blinked. He had honestly forgotten she was there, even with her hands on him.

"I'm okay. Just tired." He eased away, clasping his hands behind him. She gave him a pointed look before glancing toward Izzy.

"Didn't get much sleep?" she asked, her voice calm, but her eyes fierce. "I hear you two are sleeping together again."

His hackles rose and he bit back his first response, which probably would have gotten him slapped. "We share a room. Is that a problem?"

He shouldn't have asked. With the way she narrowed her eyes and put her hands on her hips, it obviously was.

"As long as you aren't breaching any part of your contract," she said, her glare going soft. "You know why we had you sign that, Rowes. This show exists because of the fans, particularly our female fan base. Every woman in the world imagines themselves with one of you two. If you were together, where does that leave them?"

With that same imagination, probably picturing a threesome.

"We aren't having sex, Lorena. Please believe me," said Rowes, lowering his voice as a distraught-looking intern rushed by. "Izzy is my best friend, and I won't ruin his career or mine for three minutes of grinding."

A smile flickered over her lips. "Three minutes? That's it?"

Rowes snorted, covering his face with his hand. "That's what you heard out of all that? Man, you are worse than some of the fans." He touched her shoulder before giving into his need for contact and wrapping his arm around her. It wasn't nearly as nice as getting hugged, but contact always grounded him, especially when he was upset.

"Have some faith in me." First, he needed faith in himself. The line between sex and not was pretty thin, but the contract was fairly clear. As long as he didn't engage in intimate sexual relations, then he was fine. He'd just have to look up exactly what that meant.

Probably not a kiss, but maybe a blow job. *Why am I thinking about blow jobs?* He was not blowing Izzy anytime soon. *Unless he asks me to.*

"I do, Rowes," she said, squeezing him back. Her perfume was light and floral, teasing his senses. "As long as you have the same for me. And don't shoot the messenger. When I found out about the contract, I opposed it at first, but the producers made it very clear it was their way or the highway."

Well, that was news to him. He'd honestly thought that it had been Lorena's idea, because she had been the one to deliver it to him.

"Now, if you aren't okay, you can head back to your trailer for a bit," she said, referring to one of the spots on site for the actors. It was a good place to take a quiet moment or grab a drink or snack between scenes. "Today is gonna be chaos, and I doubt we'll get much actual shooting done."

The first day back on set was always hectic. Somebody would want to arrange the scene differently or change the script. Someone *always* managed to have a breakdown, although that was usually when they reached the ten-hour mark or so.

Rowes liked to be around, just in case Izzy needed him for prep or to get into character. He was a great stand-in for getting fake slapped, yelled at or hugged as Izzy practiced a scene before going in front of the camera.

"Well, here's a juice box. Let me know if you need anything else." Lorena grabbed the box from her purse, putting the straw into it for him before giving him one final pat and bustling away.

Izzy descended as if he'd been waiting for Lorena to leave a kill so the scavengers could move in. His gaze went from the juice box to Rowes' lips, anything but subtle in the crowded room.

"What was that about?"

He could not deal with two people in one day questioning his actions, especially if one was Izzy. Besides, it was a juice box — something that Lorena gave him on a sometimes-daily basis.

"She thinks I'm going into a diabetic coma or something," said Rowes, sipping at the juice. It was apple, which was his favorite, but unfortunately it was warm from being in Lorena's purse, which didn't bode well for the chocolate bar that was no doubt in there, too.

"You do get cranky when you're hungry," said Izzy, playing with the sleeve of Rowes' shirt. "I'm glad, though. I was starting to think you two were fighting, and I couldn't figure out why. You aren't leaving the show, right? My character would be nothing without his trusty sidekick."

"Not in a million years," said Rowes before taking another sip of his juice. Maybe he had been pale or something, because he could feel the juice filling him and leveling him out. "And I do *not* get cranky. It's only natural to be a little testy if I haven't eaten in a few hours."

Izzy was looking away, rolling his shoulders and clutching at his leather jacket that he'd donned for the scene. He was already in makeup, his hair styled to absolute perfection and probably nearly solid with the amount of product in it. There was a fake gash near the lower left of his lip—the result of a left hook from last season's finale.

They were picking up right where they left off—deep in enemy territory with only two bullets left.

"Okay, people," the director shouted, and Izzy instantly started toward the set. He glanced back to Rowes, motioning up and down his own body.

"You look great, but cut out some of the useless puppy act. You're a badass, so act like one," said Rowes, grinning as the persona slapped over Izzy's features like a shutter. "Perfect. Get'em, Kemble."

Watching the shoot was like having a front-row ticket to a shattered movie that made absolutely no sense. With the green screen in the back, Rowes had to imagine what the viewers would finally end up seeing. And the way they often shot out of order meant that he had no idea where they were starting or ending up.

Being behind the camera was different to being in front, though. Watching Izzy move like fluid grace was his middle name, even as baddies hurled themselves in and off screen, was thrilling. It looked like Izzy was in a losing battle, until Rowes got the cue that he was up next.

They were moving so much better than expected, lines and shots nearly flying by. It was the most productive he could ever remember being. It had only taken five seasons, but they'd figured it out.

Slapping his knee once, Rowes rushed past the camera, holding a gun in his hand and squeezing the trigger as he rolled. A baddie went down on the other side of the set as Rowes settled on his knees against the same dumpster as Izzy. He shuffled to the side, getting closer to his best friend before reaching into his waistband for the second weapon he'd brought for Izzy.

Only, it wasn't there. Panicking, he searched his back pockets, coming up empty. A bead of sweat rolled down his neck as he looked across the set to the path where he'd rolled. In the middle of the scuffed dirt, the gun rested with the barrel pointing their way.

Shit. It must've slipped from his pants during his roll.

"Cut! Reset!"

Breaking character, he offered Izzy a hand, lugging him to his feet as Izzy glanced toward the director in question. He always had trouble breaking character, especially in an unexpected cut. Rowes squeezed his hand briefly in an attempt to soothe him.

Doing stunts more than once was brutal, especially rolls when he gave it his all. Anything more and he usually had his double step in. He'd learned the hard way after jumping through a window in season one. At the rate they were going, his back was going to kill him in the morning.

"Sorry!" Rowes called out, trotting toward the gun and shoving it into his waistband, trying to tuck it deeper so it didn't fling free. It would have been easier if he'd had a belt, or pants with a little more room to them. His jeans were virtually painted on, which probably made his ass look great, but they weren't all that practical.

"Somebody get Rowes a damn belt!"

Rowes grinned, clearing out of the way as people rushed to reset the scene exactly the way it had been. Izzy resumed his spot, worry and intensity still fixed on his face. He couldn't slip in and out of character quite as easily as Rowes or Connley could, but he was still a damn good actor.

An intern passed Rowes a belt, and he quickly looped it in through his pants, securing the gun and tugging it tight. It would probably give him a bit of muffin top, but hopefully they would edit that out. Depending on how they shot it, a fan was bound to notice a continuity error, but he kept his mouth shut.

At the call of 'action', he burst into motion, his back screaming as he took the roll at full speed, almost throwing himself off with the strength of it. When he settled safely next to Izzy and reached for the gun, it was still there. He tossed it to his friend without a word, and Izzy grinned, fake blood staining his teeth.

"What took you so long?"

"And cut!"

Rowes heaved out a laugh, collapsing back to the dirt as Izzy stood from his crouch and passed someone his gun. Rowes was probably pissing off the wardrobe department by getting stuff dirty, but the dirtier the better, in his opinion. If women wanted a clean man, then they wouldn't be watching *Gunlover*.

Izzy held his hand out, helping Rowes to his feet with a grunt. "That last one looked like it hurt. You okay?"

Draping his arm around Rowes' shoulder, he pulled him closer, tilting their heads together as he ducked in. His eyes were sharp, some remnants of his character still there. Rowes shivered, casting his gaze around. No one was looking their way—too busy with everything else.

"Yeah." Rowes attempted to stretch, wincing when his back pulled in a very unfun way. "Let's hope there's a spa at the hotel, or I won't be able to move tomorrow."

Dropping his hand, Izzy rubbed along the aching spot, grazing low enough to rest just about Rowes' waistband. When he dug in his fingers, Rowes couldn't bite back his sudden yelp that could have come from a chihuahua getting stepped on.

Izzy pulled his hand away, his face etched with concern. "I thought you said you were okay. That didn't sound okay, Ro."

His voice had dropped into something Rowes didn't recognize, the edge of a growl rumbling in his throat. It was deep and dark, with the promise of *something* if Rowes wasn't honest. The hair on the back of his neck stood up as he looked around.

"I hurt my back," said Rowes, touching the aching muscles of his lower back. He hadn't even hit there, but he must've twisted the wrong way during the second round. It was a good thing that the directors looked happy with it, or he'd really fuck up his back trying it a third time.

"Then I'll take care of you. Don't hide your pain from me again."

Izzy's voice was low, but anyone could have heard him if they were paying attention. Rowes snapped straight in shock, letting out a second yelp at the movement. Lorena was bustling over to them, her forehead pinched with concern.

"Rowes hurt his back," said Izzy, cutting off anything Lorena was going to say. "I'm taking him back to our room. Can you see if someone has a muscle relaxant or something?"

"I'll get some for Rowes," said Lorena, "but you need to stay on set, Isthmus. You have at least two more scenes to shoot before we wrap up today. You can't just leave."

The momentary flicker of stubbornness was all Rowes needed to see. If Izzy put his foot down, he was going to piss somebody off, and nothing was worse than an actor making a fuss on set.

"I can wait," said Rowes, pointing to one of the chairs off to the side. "Izzy can take me back when he's done, but I can wait for now." He wasn't going to mention how uncomfortable he knew those chairs were and that he would be in absolute agony in ten minutes or so. He was good at breathing through the pain.

"It's not my first set injury, Izzy, and it's not like I broke anything. It's fine." *At least, I don't think I broke anything.* The pain was starting to spread around his sides, his ribs pulling tighter with every breath. He forced a grin on his face, bearing it.

Izzy pinched his lips into a thin line, working his jaw. Some of his character was still shining through, his fingers twitching like they would on his gun. "Lorena, take him back to our room. I'll be there as soon as I can."

"Okay," said Lorena, already reaching for Rowes' arm. "Come on. Let's get you into bed, and I'll find some meds."

"No," Izzy cut her off. "There's a jacuzzi in the room. Get in that until I get back. If you go to bed now, you'll just seize up."

Holy fuck. Rowes bit his lip. Izzy had been protective of him before, but this was on a different level. His gut bubbled, tingly and warm as he flushed. Lorena gave them both a strange look before she nodded.

"Okay. Good luck, Isthmus."

Rowes tried to recover, stretching out and wincing again. "Remember what I said, Izzy. You're a badass bitch. Act like one."

Izzy gave him a wink, not even looking to Lorena before he turned away, people parting around him as if he were a god.

He kind of is.

Chapter Nine

Izzy

The moment he heard the final 'cut', Izzy peeled his jacket off then tugged his shirt over his head as he stomped to the trailer they'd set up for makeup and wardrobe changes. He had to dodge Ainslie and Lorena, who had appeared shortly after leaving with Rowes, shutting his door behind him and stripping down to his underwear. His street clothes were barely back on, makeup still clinging to his face as he left, rushing straight to the hotel.

"Isthmus!"

Gritting his teeth in irritation, Izzy turned toward the shout. If it would have been anyone but the director, he would have ignored them. As it were, he liked the director, even if she was a hardass.

"Good work today. You going to check on Rowes?"

Another thing he liked about her was that she actually seemed to care about them. In season one, their director had almost ended the show, treating them more like objects than actual people. Things had been revamped with season two, and they hadn't had an issue since.

"I'm headed there now." He half-turned away, looking to the exit. He was almost there, so close that he could feel the freedom on his face.

"Good. I need to chat with him soon about his upcoming scene and to let him know that it won't be breaching his contract. We're going to shoot that next week, if he needs to do anything to prepare."

What? They were shooting scenes all the time, what would make one so different? His heart thudded with realization. *The kiss scene.* Despite their female fanbase, there really wasn't that much intimacy in the show, although there was a fair amount of suggestion.

And what did that have anything to do with his contract? As far as contracts went, Izzy's was pretty standard. He couldn't imagine Rowes' being that different.

"I'll let him know, and I'll help him with any prep he needs," said Izzy. The director flushed, which was something he'd never seen before. Her call of 'good' was lost as he spun on his heel out of the door with only one thing in mind.

The short drive and walk through the halls of the hotel were a blur, blood rushing through his ears as he tapped his key card on the door to their hotel room. Rowes was always one to put on a brave face, but his yelp was still echoing in Izzy's ears.

He could be stuck on the bed, unable to roll over or even get into the bath. Lorena probably wouldn't have been much help, always a stickler for not crossing the line into friendship territory. Or maybe he was close to passing out in the bath, the muscle relaxants doing their work. If he fell asleep, he could drown.

Nearing panic, he flung the door wide, rushing toward the bathroom and hitting it with his shoulder when the knob didn't turn fast enough. The door bounced off the wall as he hurled it open, probably leaving a dent for some poor cleaner to discover.

His heart stopped, only for his blood to pound in his veins a moment later, his gut going tight and his mouth dry.

Rowes was on his way either into the tub or out of it, but it looked like he'd gotten stuck, his face screwed up in his frozen position of half bent over and reaching for the handle on the edge of the whirlpool. Water dripped down his back, a few bubbles following the path and whisking the scent of lavender into the air. The candle at the edge of the tub flickered with the same scent, soaking the room and the steam that coated the massive mirror.

The stunts on set had left their mark with bruises on Rowes' back that were red and purple, and splotches of color on his otherwise-pale skin. The largest one had to be bigger than Izzy's hand, stretching along his side and his shoulder as well.

"Can you pass me a towel?" asked Rowes, halting Izzy's thoughts like a tree in the middle of the highway. "Sorry... I tried to get out when I heard the door, but you were too quick." He winced again as he twisted and moved to lift his leg over the edge of the tub, a little gasp pushing through his lips. The bubbles dripped lower, sliding down the curve of his ass.

Fuck. Izzy moved all at once as his limbs thawed, slipping on the damp floor as he lunged for Rowes. Gently grasping his waist and shoulder, he pulled

Rowes to him, supporting his weight and helping him upright. Rowes let out a pained groan before he held on, his limbs shaking with the obvious effort. "Can you make it like this?"

Rowes was trembling, the water nearly vibrating as he lifted his leg again, his body going tight at the move. Even with the heated air and the steam, he still looked pale.

"Fuck." Rowes let out a low groan, dropping his leg back into the sudsy water. "It didn't hurt this much on set." His eyes were red as he bit his lip, leaning his full weight onto Izzy. Izzy grasped him around his slippery waist, his fingers tingling at the touch.

"Hey, it's okay. That's why I'm here." Izzy moved both hands to Rowes' lower back, resting just above the swell of his ass in the dip where he fit perfectly. One side was rock-hard beneath his hand, the muscle spasming as he touched it. He'd had the same thing happen to him, and he knew just how painful it could be. "You pulled a muscle really badly here. Can you put your arms around my neck?"

Rowes nodded, tucking his head into Izzy's neck as he moved, and letting out a breath as Izzy slowly bent down, putting one hand under his knees and lifting. With the size difference between them, it should have been more difficult, but Izzy had apparently gained some kind of superpower. He reveled in it, doing his best not to jostle Rowes.

Lifting Rowes bridal style, he carefully navigated the wet floor of the bathroom, carrying Rowes to the other room before setting him on the bed. A few remaining bubbles soaked into the comforter, leaving Rowes shivering.

"I'm wet," said Rowes, clinging to Izzy as he laid him out. His hands were trembling, and every time Izzy moved him in the slightest, he let out a tiny whimper.

"I don't care, Ro. You could be covered in skunk, and I'd still be laying you out on this bed." Izzy eased back, lingering even as he glanced away. "Can you roll onto your front? I'm going to try to loosen up your back." He wasn't a professional by any means, but the thought of someone else touching Rowes in this state, even a professional, made him clench his jaw.

"Izzy…you don't have to. I'm sure the meds will kick in soon." His hair was leaving a halo of dampness on the sheets, the white comforter soaking up every drop. His face looked pale, his lips stark red and his eyes bloodshot and wet.

"Rowes," said Izzy, letting sternness slip into his voice. It was the same voice he'd used when Rowes had lied to him, and the reaction he got was the same. His pupils blew wide, his face relaxing and his mouth dropping open just enough for Izzy to see the pinkness inside.

Without a word, Rowes rolled over, clutching at the sheets and whimpering as he finally settled face down on the bed.

"Ro." Izzy smoothed his hand down Rowes' back, hissing as he brushed over the bruising there. "I don't want you to hurt yourself anymore tonight. I need you to tell me if you're in pain or if you need help. Promise me." His skin was so soft beneath his fingertips, still damp and floral from the bubbles. He probably tasted of lavender and the bitter sweetness of the bath.

"Are you asking me as my friend or as my Dom?" asked Rowes, his voice muffled before he turned his head to the side, blinking away the tears on his eyelashes.

"Is there any difference?" asked Izzy. The more he thought about it, the more he wondered how long he'd actually been Rowes' Dom without even knowing it. Taking care of him was one of the best feelings he'd ever had, and touching him was more satisfying than eating chocolate cake. He had to keep telling himself that just because Rowes was better than cake, didn't mean that he wanted to fuck him.

Tell that to this guy. Glancing down at himself, Izzy tried to squash the building warmth in his groin. His cock had started to tingle with the rush of blood as soon as he'd seen Rowes naked. He was only a man, though, and he couldn't fault his body for reacting to someone so beautiful. There was a reason Rowes had such a huge following, and why his shirtless scenes were some of the most watched.

"Is this where it hurts the worst?" he asked, touching the strained muscles of Rowes' lower back. They jumped under his hand and Rowes grunted, biting his lip between his teeth.

"Yeah. It hurts real bad, Iz."

He must've been bad. Rowes rarely called him 'Iz' until he was drunk, high or waking up from surgery. There had been a time that Rowes had insisted on calling him Isthmus, but that had stopped once they'd started living together.

"I'll make it better." Shuffling off the bed, Izzy rifled through his bag, ripping out heaps of clothing when he couldn't find what he was looking for. He touched something cold with his fingers, grasping it and pulling it into the light.

Lube was better than nothing, and he didn't exactly have massage oil floating around. At least it was unscented. He wouldn't have been able to do a good massage with strawberry or cherry, although peppermint might have done the job. He was never putting peppermint on his dick again, though, so he didn't have any in his bag. That was a lesson he did not need to repeat.

Stepping back to the bed, Izzy hesitated. If he sat off to one side, he would probably end up straining himself, or he wouldn't be able to work Rowes' muscles as well as he wanted to. But he didn't want to straddle Rowes and risk hurting him that way, either.

Touching the inside of Rowes' thigh, Izzy asked him without words to spread his legs, sliding between them and settling as close to Rowes as he could. *Don't look down.* He couldn't resist. He'd never seen Rowes' ass so up close and personal or his delicate furl between his cheeks.

"I'll probably have to help you into the shower again after," said Izzy, tearing his gaze away as he grabbed for the lube and drizzled some down the middle of Rowes' back. Rowes flexed, letting out another gasp that had Izzy chewing his lip. "Relax and let me take care of you."

This is such a bad idea. He knew after the first passage of his hands, that he wasn't going to end the night with his sanity intact. He'd always known Rowes was lean from his time in the gym, and he looked damn good without a shirt, but it was another thing to *feel* it.

With a deep shuddering breath, he worked his way over Rowes' back, starting at his shoulders and gently skimming along the blotched bruising covering his right side. Every gentle touch sent Rowes deeper into the bed, until the tension drained from his body with a few soft sighs. Once he was fully relaxed, Izzy touched the rock-hard muscle that was causing Rowes so much pain.

The groan Rowes released was pure bliss as Izzy touched him and curled his fingers as he worked the tight spot. He slipped over Rowes' skin, eased by the lubricant that was dripping onto the comforter. Izzy couldn't bring himself to care about the mess. He wasn't worried if they charged them an extra cleaning fee at the end of their stay, either. Every penny would be worth it.

Although, the cleaning staff would probably be wondering what they'd needed *that* much lube for.

"How is it?" Izzy leaned forward, putting more of his weight into his hands. He could feel each bunch of muscle releasing beneath him, until Rowes felt near boneless. He'd probably be fine.

Only, Izzy didn't want to stop. He grabbed the lube, pouring more on as some started to dry. It was tacky as it dried, which was the worst thing about water-based lubricants. Rowes didn't even respond as the cold lube touched his skin, his lashes brushing against his cheeks. They were long and darker than his hair.

"Ro?" Izzy asked softly, switching to his knuckles and kneading ever so gently. "Are you sleeping?" His imagination ran wild. If he could only have a moment like this every day to touch Rowes — to worship him when there were no interruptions or places to be. He could take his fill and look after Rowes at the same time.

"No," said Rowes, the muscle on his inner thigh tensing. Izzy dropped his gaze to it, his hands following.

Skimming over Rowes' ass, he dipped his thumbs between his cheeks, easing them apart for just a moment before he moved to Rowes' quads and started to knead. Rowes parted his legs wider, presumably to give Izzy more room to work.

Izzy bit his lip as he looked down, mesmerized as he continued. Rowes was hard, his cock pointed down along the bed and his sac resting to one side. It echoed his own cock, which was aching in his jeans, so squashed that it was painful. He made no move to release himself, moving his hands back to Rowes' ass unconsciously.

When he rubbed just right, slipping his thumbs between Rowes' cheeks, his cock twitched against the bed, a pearly drop gathering at the tip. The head was blushed red and shiny as Rowes let out a soft gasp. *What will happen if I really touch him?*

On the next pass, he dragged a finger over Rowes' furl, not lingering before he stroked lower to the soft seam of his perineum. Rowes' ass muscles jumped under him, his cock visibly twitching.

"Iz?"

"You're okay," said Izzy, repeating the exact same move just to see another drip gather at the head of Rowes' cock. It was nearly purple now, looking so uncomfortable in its trapped position. It couldn't be as bad as Izzy squashed in his jeans, though. "I'm not going to fuck you."

He wasn't so sure about that anymore. Rowes was so responsive, rocking into the next pass and arching his back. The meds and massage must've been kicking in, because he seemed painless, even with the dark bruises. Izzy let out a little chuckle, tapping his hand against Rowes' ass. "No moving. I don't want you to strain yourself again."

This time he lingered over Rowes' hole, massaging with his thumb in the same way that he'd rubbed his back into submission, only so soft that he was barely touching him. Rowes let out a gasp, tugging at the sheets as he clenched his fists. Izzy clicked his tongue, wrapping his hands around Rowes' wrists and bringing them over his head where they could rest on the pillow.

"Be still," he said softly, pressing his chest to Rowes' back as he leaned in to arrange Rowes how he wanted him. There was the perfect angle that wouldn't strain him at all, and once he found it, he lingered on his wrists.

Lube soaked into his shirt and skin, and even though it was unscented, they reeked of it. It brought an ingrained response to the forefront of his thoughts. Usually when he smelled lube from this position, he was already balls deep.

He squeezed Rowes' wrists once before tilting away. "If you can't keep still on your own, I'll tie you up. I bought some lovely blue rope after our trip to the club. It would look so beautiful against your skin."

Rowes let out a shuddering breath, going lax as Izzy rocked onto his heels. Peeling his shirt from his shoulders, he tossed the lube-soaked mess to the floor. *That's better.*

When he touched Rowes' hole again, he let his thumb rest there, putting the barest hint of pressure into it—not enough to breach, but enough for Rowes to really feel it.

"Iz," Rowes whispered again, his voice urgent. "Izzy, I'm hard."

Chuckling, Izzy leaned in again, until his naked chest was against Rowes' slick back. He nuzzled Rowes' neck, inhaling his scent until he caught the citrus beneath the overpowering lube. His hard cock was pressed against Rowes' ass, giving no question to his own state.

"You can be as hard as you want, but you're not allowed to come. That might cross a line," said Izzy, humping as Rowes sucked in a gasp. "You remember your safeword?"

Rowes nodded. "Red. Is this a scene?"

Is it? It certainly felt like it. They were both hard, even if they weren't having sex, and Izzy was so content he was almost high with it. There had been times with Malone that were so similar, only now Izzy was doing exactly what he had wanted to back then.

"I think we're past scenes, Ro." Izzy pulled himself to his hands and knees before he could strain Rowes' back from the weight. "We don't need a scene to do what comes naturally to us. Being on a set won't stop me from wrapping my hand around your neck."

He touched Rowes' neck with his slicked fingers, groaning at the pulse thudding beneath his fingertips. It was what had drawn him in the most when they'd watched the D/s fan video. Rowes looked perfect with Izzy's hand around his throat, so soft but steady. There was a trust to holding someone's life in his hands like that, and he cherished it.

"Izzy, I'm going to come," said Rowes, tensing beneath him. His cock was so dark and wet that it had to be painful now, much worse than a steady throb. Izzy couldn't dredge up any sympathy, purely fascinated as he watched. He could give in and let

Rowes come, but then the moment would end. He wasn't ready for that yet.

"Did I say you could?"

Rowes let out a high-pitched groan, biting his lip as he clenched his eyes shut. "No."

"Okay, just checking," said Izzy, resuming his massage as if he'd never stopped. He focused on Rowes' thighs first, giving him a break from overstimulation as he dug his thumbs in. His calves were next, the small amount of hair coarse beneath his palms. He reapplied lube twice until Rowes was completely slathered and dripping, the bedsheets ruined beyond repair.

Massaging his ankle with one hand, Izzy focused on Rowes' hole with the other, pressing his thumb against the furl that was calling to him. Rowes let out a whine before he started to whimper.

"Iz, *please*." His voice was nothing but a pained whisper as he trembled. "I can't stop it."

Izzy tugged his hand away, staring at Rowes' cock as it twitched. He had to be right on the edge, his gut throbbing and his balls tight. *Not yet.*

"You beg so prettily," said Izzy, tangling his fingers in Rowes' hair until he was sticky with lube. "I'm almost convinced, but not quite. I want you *desperate.*"

"I am." He raised his voice for the first time, tugging at the bed sheets. The bed groaned as he twitched his hips. "Please. *Please.*"

"Okay," said Izzy, this time pressing his thumb to Rowes' hole and giving a little push. His furl gave way but Izzy didn't force his way inside, massaging the tightness until it no longer resisted him.

Rowes let out a choked gasp, his cock pulsing against the bed as he started to shoot. His legs went tight against Izzy, his ass muscles jumping as his gasp morphed into a long groan.

It was the hottest thing Izzy had seen in his life. He'd had enough lovers to question if he was a bit slutty, but none of them had ever responded to him so seamlessly or beautifully, coming on command like a dream. No one had ever looked at him like Rowes did, either, or felt like him under his hands.

His chest heaved and he refused to blink, not wanting to miss a single twitch as Rowes finally stopped coming with an impressive puddle at the tip of his cock that slowly seeped into the comforter. His balls had drawn up tight, looking squashed and uncomfortable in their position.

"Izzy?"

He sounded so lost, with the edge of fear in his voice. It must've been the same uncertainty that was in Izzy's chest. He'd felt the crash before with Malone, when everything had been good up until the moment it hadn't been. He never wanted Rowes to feel anything like that or experience the crippling doubt that had haunted him for days, even with Malone's reassurances.

"You know," Izzy mused softly, "when I told you I wanted you as my submissive, I never suspected you would be quite so perfect. You always manage to blow my mind in the most wonderful ways, Rowes."

Rowes let out a sigh of what Izzy hoped was relief, relaxing against the bed as Izzy continued his massage, retreating to Rowes' lower back to make sure nothing had tightened up again. The lube had gone tacky with sweat, probably uncomfortable as all hell.

"We're good, then?" asked Rowes. He blinked his eyes open, but the lids looked heavy, barely opening halfway.

"So good," said Izzy. "Now let me get you into the shower, and I'll order room service for us."

Rowes bit his lip as he drew his legs up, slowly easing over until he was facing Izzy again. The move didn't seem nearly as painful as it had before, but that may have just been from the way his cock looked so sated. "But did you—you know—come?"

Sometimes Rowes was the sweetest guy. Izzy had tried not to wonder what kind of lover he would be, but it was obvious that he was a giver, even as a submissive. Izzy couldn't have asked for more.

Not that we're lovers. That was a line he wasn't sure if they would ever cross.

Grasping Rowes' hand, he brought it to his groin where he was still rock-hard and beyond uncomfortable. He was practically soaked with pre-cum, the zing of the touch almost too much to bear. Memories of his dream flitted over his mind as he pictured Rowes taking him down his throat, the damp warmth squeezing him so tight.

"Let me—" Rowes started.

"No." Izzy cut him off. "Tonight is about you." If he had his way, every night would be about Rowes. "Now, I'm going to go get the shower warmed up. I'll be back for you in a second."

Rowes had a silly smile on his face as Izzy left for the bathroom. He paused at the doorway, unable to resist looking at the naked expanse of beauty stretched out in his bed. He was never going back to what they had had, because for the first time in his life, he was sure of something.

Rowes was *his.*

Chapter Ten

Rowes

Despite a few twinges in his back, Rowes couldn't remember the last time he'd felt so good. Every moment of questioning himself had fallen away. Hell, his entire sexuality was being rewritten before him, his uncertainties obliterated with the best orgasm of his life. *Good riddance.*

His chest throbbed as Izzy pulled him closer, both of them half-asleep on the bed in a kind of mind-numbing stasis. He'd experienced something wholly different over the last few hours, and it hadn't been just the muscle relaxants. Maybe they had given him a little push, but they'd only ever made him sleepy in the past, not *floaty.*

Izzy had called it 'subspace', and it had brought back memories of the sub who had been trussed in rope at the club. *Did I look like that?* He'd been peaceful, the only worry his ability to stave off an orgasm that had encompassed his soul. And when Izzy had told him it was okay, a release like none other had sucked him dry.

The contract. He bit his lip, burying himself deep into Izzy's chest. He'd have to consult a lawyer soon to see where that line in the sand was drawn with the contract he'd signed with the studio. Sexual intercourse to him was fucking. But Izzy had almost been inside him, even if it had only been the very tip of his finger. It was more intimate than every encounter he'd had with a woman, and he'd experienced pegging with one particularly adventurous girlfriend.

No one had left him so satisfied and wanting for more to the point that it had hurt. And it wasn't just his cock. His chest, his gut and everything in between throbbed with a thick need for Izzy. He had to get closer and find a way to tuck himself inside Izzy, so he'd never have to face reality again.

"How are you feeling?" asked Izzy, his voice sleepy and soft.

Pushing up on his elbow, Rowes stared at his friend, grinning at what he found. Eyes slitted with sleep and hair tousled, Izzy looked like perfection. He'd kept his shirt off, washing himself with a cloth instead of joining Rowes in the shower. His jeans had stayed on, though.

He must've had the biggest case of blue balls ever recorded. Rowes had felt how hard he had been, throbbing through the thick layer of denim that had barely held him back. Rowes had been two seconds away from ripping the zipper down and taking matters into his own hands before Izzy had turned him down.

"About as good as you look," said Rowes, running his hand down the center of Izzy's chest. He knew for a fact that Izzy had had laser treatments to remove most of his chest hair, but there was still a bit there, coarse against his fingers. "Was anybody upset that I had to leave halfway through the shoot?"

It had been one of the many worries haunting him. The television and movie business was not a forgiving one, and just like his contract, if he fucked up, he'd be replaced.

The fans would probably react poorly to a replacement, but there was nothing keeping them from killing him off. It had happened to other characters before, and without Izzy, his character wouldn't have made it past season two.

He could only imagine Izzy's reaction if that ever happened for real.

"Everyone was worried about you," said Izzy, rubbing at his forehead before closing his eyes and letting out a sigh. "Even the director wanted to check in with you. She said something about your contract and that next week's scene won't be a problem. She wants you to practice, though." He snorted. "Not like you need any practice. You must've kissed lots of women, and men are not so different, I imagine."

It was probably supposed to be a joke, but it was the same as cold hands in the middle of his back. His mouth fell open as he stared at Izzy.

"She talked to you about my contract?" That shit was supposed to be confidential. He had planned to take it to his grave.

Izzy shrugged, reaching for him and clasping their hands together. "Yeah? Sorry if she wasn't supposed to. But anyway, I can help you if you want. Maybe you want pointers or something? She was cool with that."

Holy shit. He was going to hyperventilate. Izzy knew? He obviously didn't have a problem with it if he was so relaxed. Maybe he was fine with never being able to have sex with Rowes while the show was still spitting out seasons. It was kind of a relief to know they were on the same page.

"I can only imagine how cool she was with that," said Rowes, grinning as he let himself be nudged close again. "She's a big fan of 'boyslove' shows. I heard her talking about it to Ainslie one day. It's probably one of the only reasons that kiss made it into the script."

The thought of the kiss made his stomach drop right out from under him. Kissing had always been very intimate for him, and there was a big chance he was going to get hard from it. He wasn't even sure if his co-actor was gay or how the film crew would react to that.

They didn't exactly deal with that kind of thing in the series. There had been very few straight kissing scenes in the series so far, but lots of suggestions of more.

"You look worried," said Izzy, reaching to smooth the furrow on Rowes' forehead. "I told her I would help you as a friend, and I'm telling you I'll be there as your Dom." His gaze was soft and nowhere near the intensity from earlier.

"Yeah, but how?" Rowes scratched his chin where a hair was tickling him. He dragged it off, grimacing when he saw it was one of Izzy's. There was something about other people's hair that just made him itch. "You can't just *order* me to kiss this guy and have the scene come out great. It's going to be awkward as all hell, and what if he's gay? The next thing I know, he'll fall in love with me — and that would really be an issue."

"It's just a kiss."

As if anything about a kiss was 'just'. He turned his head away, spying their dishes from the room service that Izzy had ordered. He'd gotten fruit and toast for them, hand-feeding Rowes as they'd lounged together on the messy bed and watched a rerun on low volume.

"I don't like kissing strangers," said Rowes. He'd never kissed a one-night stand, too worried that he would grow attached to someone he would never see again. A date was different for him. Half the time, he was fine with sex on the first date, but that was after a conversation and a few basic questions. This guy would be a total stranger. It would be so unprofessional to ask him out to try to make things more comfortable for himself.

"Come on, Rowes. You can act your way in and out of anything. The kiss would just be an act, like everything else." Izzy helped Rowes lay on his chest as he winced.

"I can't. I'm not sure why I even agreed to it." He lowered his voice when he realized he was on the verge of yelling. He was great at agreeing to things, especially script revisions that put him in a tough spot—like a certain stunt that he was aching from.

"So practice," said Izzy, tucking his hands behind his head. His eyes were half closed, the picture of calm and satisfaction.

"With who? An escort? No thank you."

Izzy opened his eyes wide at that, pressing his lips into a thin line. "I already offered to help."

His heart thudded, blood rushing through his ears. There was no way. They couldn't cross any more lines than they already had. "But my contract…"

"The director said it wouldn't be a problem. I *told* her I would help you." Izzy rolled his eyes before wrapping his hand around the back of Rowes' neck and applying soft pressure. "Go ahead. Come up here and kiss me."

His voice had dropped again to the one that made Rowes' stomach flip and his groin pull tight. They hadn't even kissed, and he was already getting hard again. This was the worst idea. "Now?"

His voice came out husky and soft and not the protest he had been aiming for. Tangling his hand in Izzy's shirt, he leaned on his elbows so he could stare at Izzy's face. He wasn't flushed in the least, and that voice made him yearn for something that he wasn't sure he understood.

"Now."

Blushed red and plump, Izzy's lips look so soft, with a bit of shininess in the center where he must've recently licked his lips. Rowes had stared at those lips so many times, grinning along as he'd watched stories play out before him. He'd never looked with intent, though, or imagined how they would feel against his own.

"I'm waiting, Ro," said Izzy, his voice just a touch softer as he threaded his hand into Rowes' hair. He didn't pull or tug, instead resting his hand in the spot that made Rowes shiver. "It's easy. Just lean in and give me a peck. No tongue required."

No tongue was good. *Or is it?* God, he didn't know. He wasn't sure of anything anymore. His cock throbbed in the boxers he'd pulled on. Izzy had already gotten him off, so he shouldn't have been hard again so soon. It was embarrassing. He'd never been such a sex addict before, fine with getting off a couple of times a month with someone as long as he took care of himself in between.

Taking one last breath, Rowes leaned in, pressing his lips ever so softly against Izzy's. They *were* soft and smooth, and so warm that he almost groaned at the pure sensation that burned through him. It was nothing like kissing a woman — or anyone else, for that matter.

He tilted to the side for better access, applying just a hint of pressure. Izzy gasped, maybe feeling the same thing as him as his nerves curled to life, wrapping around him to settle in his groin. Izzy clenched his hand, applying the first hint of pull.

It isn't just a kiss.

Izzy moving his hand to his throat was the only thing that stopped him from deepening the kiss, easing him away before he was sucked under. They panted together, breathing each other's air. Rowes licked his lips. He could taste him, and it was nothing like he'd imagined.

Izzy's cheeks were flushed, his lips darker and wet as he traced them with his own tongue. Rowes stared, leaning against the restraining force at his neck as he longed to touch and taste. It wasn't an option anymore. There was one thing he needed in his life, and that was Izzy's lips against his again.

"I see what you mean," said Izzy, clearing his throat as his voice cracked. "Let's do that again — exactly the same... No, deeper."

Impossible. When Izzy released him, Rowes dove in like a starving man, lining up their lips immediately and groaning as they touched. He bit his tongue, keeping it between his teeth as Izzy grabbed his hair, tilting his head and returning the kiss with full force.

There was something magical about kissing his best friend when he'd been telling everyone that there was nothing between them. It was better yet that he was treading on the edge of his legal obligations with his contract.

It's not sex. The director said it's okay.

Izzy stopped him again, dragging him back by the hair. "Good."

His voice was breathless, his chest still heaving as his heart presumably pounded. Rowes could feel his own heart answering every pulse as he licked his lips in search of Izzy's taste. It was only a touch, but it was there. His blood thrummed, every ache forgotten.

"We should break for five minutes and try again," said Izzy, easing Rowes off him before standing from the bed. He didn't turn or look back as he marched to the bathroom, his step stiff and staggered. The door slammed behind him, rocking the single picture frame on the wall.

"Fuck." Rowes rolled onto his back, leaning into the pillow. Beneath his boxers, his cock was pointing straight to the ceiling, the spot at the tip dark and damp. He grabbed it, tilting it up and tucking himself into his waistband.

What is Izzy doing? Rowes couldn't hear anything over the fan that turned on automatically with the light in the bathroom. If he closed his eyes, he could picture Izzy's lips still red and soft as he bit them to muffle his shouts as he touched himself.

"Dammit." He closed his eyes, letting the image take over.

A door slammed and he sat up, grabbing the closest pillow and placing it over his groin. Izzy was standing outside the bathroom with the door shut behind him. His hair was wild, his eyes in the same state as he stared at Rowes with rigid intensity.

"I forgot to ask you something," said Izzy, his voice strangely calm. He looked almost high as he prowled toward the bed, the button on his jeans undone and riding low enough to show off the elastic band of his boxers. He didn't look hard anymore, but it was difficult to tell with the way the fabric shifted as he moved.

"I forgot to ask if you were the one kissing this guy or if he would be kissing you. I don't have the script for it yet."

Rowes shook his head, managing a half-shrug before he froze under Izzy's gaze. The tension between them was enough to fill the room, his contract the last thing on his mind.

"I don't know. I don't even know the name of the actor yet."

Izzy waved his hands, cutting Rowes off. "Then we'll just have to practice both ways. I guess that means it's my turn."

Dropping to his knees, Izzy crawled up his body, his gaze the only thing that was lingering. Rowes' entire body pulsed with longing for the impending kiss. "No tongue?"

Izzy grinned, licking his lips. "I don't need my tongue to break you."

As soon as their lips touched, Rowes was lost. Instead of sweet headiness and hesitation, Izzy took control utterly and completely, until the longing built in his soul. Izzy's hand at his throat made him tilt his head back and to the side, giving Izzy better access. At the same time, the hand on his chest made sure he didn't try to take control.

It should have been boring and flat. A kiss without tongue was no kiss at all, but Rowes was consumed by it. He cried out, parting his lips to try to beckon Izzy in.

Izzy pulled back, his eyes dark and his cheeks flushed. His jaw flexed as he gritted his teeth, the muscles on his upper body standing out. *Is he holding back?*

"Good," said Izzy, his voice a growl that sent shivers along Rowes' spine. "Now we will do that one again, exactly the same. I think we might need to practice this way just a little bit more."

Sealing their lips together, Izzy clamped his hand hard on Rowes' throat, cutting off his air with a single touch. His lungs burned in seconds, but Rowes didn't struggle, going lax as his Dom took complete control of every part of him. His soul was laid bare, and Izzy seemingly lapped it up, absorbing it through the kiss that was anything but simple.

"Good," Izzy whispered into his ear. "One more time, Ro."

Rowes was lost.

Chapter Eleven

Izzy

He'd never been so nervous prior to a shoot before. There was always the feeling he'd been born to be an actor, and it only grew more resolved when he thought of the spectators.

And meeting fellow actors was part of the gig. Most were fantastic, with a few assholes thrown into the mix. Others, he would gladly work with again if given the opportunity. A few shots were never enough to get to know someone well.

But he'd never had much to lose before. He was one of the stars of the show, and Rowes was always going to be right beside him on that. But here was the guy who was going to be kissing Rowes.

He'd never met a 'Clarke' before, but he was certain that it was the worst name in English history. *Clarke*. It oozed of pure douchebag energy, and the guy had the entitled air of someone who deserved to be there, touching Rowes as if they were *friends*.

Standing beside Izzy, Rowes seemed so easy and relaxed as he reached for the guy's hand to shake it, their touch lasting a moment too long for Izzy's taste. Izzy narrowed his eyes, reaching for Rowes automatically, and slinging an arm over his shoulder.

"This is Isthmus Linton, as you probably already knew," said Rowes, chuckling as he sent Izzy a grin. Their gazes lingered for only a moment, but Rowes flicked his stare to his lips before he looked away.

It was long enough for Izzy to know exactly what it meant. Rowes wanted to kiss him again, probably more than once. *Hopefully.*

It was strange to not be weirded out by that fact, but maybe he'd seen it all coming. As soon as he'd realized what their relationship could be, non-sexual had slipped away and buried itself back inside the closet.

"So good to meet you, Isthmus," said Clarke, clasping his hands together when Izzy made no move to offer a handshake. "I've been a huge fan of the show since season one, and it's super exciting to get the chance to be a part of the project."

"Yep," said Izzy, glancing toward the director to see if things looked any closer to being ready. The camera guys appeared prepared, but the set was still way off. The downside of shooting some scenes outside was that the weather always managed to wreak havoc. "It's great to have budding actors as the fodder. There's always the opportunity to try out new roles and get some experience."

Rowes shot him a glare, but Izzy just raised one eyebrow, grinning internally as Clarke seemed to wilt.

"*Fodder?*" asked Rowes under his breath, giving Clarke a pained smile. "Sorry, Clarke. Isthmus hasn't had his third cup of coffee this morning so he's extra grouchy."

Clarke looked between them, taking a half step back before holding up his hands. "No worries. I didn't realize you guys were together. I didn't mean to intrude or anything—just trying to do my job."

Izzy grunted as Rowes shot an elbow into his ribs. "We aren't together—not like that, anyway," said Rowes, the words turning Izzy's sour mood even darker. "I wanted to meet you, too. I thought I should at least introduce myself to the guy I'm supposed to kiss."

Gritting his teeth, Izzy moved his hand to the back of Rowes' neck, letting it rest there. With one move he could tug Rowes' hair or wrap his fingers around his throat. *Dealer's choice.* Rowes paused, giving him a pointed look before letting out a strained laugh.

"Yeah," said Clarke, scratching the back of his head as his cheeks tinted pink. "It's gonna be a lot of pressure to kiss a television icon. I hope I'm not too terrible at it."

Of course, he would be terrible. This guy's lips were thin, not soft and plush like Rowes'. And he was clean-shaven without any scruff. Everyone knew that kisses were always better if they were a little scratchy. And if he tried to slip Rowes any tongue, Izzy was going to cut it off.

The numbers on Izzy's watch silently counted toward the day's expiration as he worked his jaw. The director was still talking to one of the interns, the set looking no closer to completion. At this rate, they wouldn't get anything done today.

"Well, it was good to meet you," said Clarke, his gaze lingering on Rowes. "Both of you."

"Uh-huh—*ouch.*" Izzy winced as Rowes clamped down on his wrist, turning and half-dragging Izzy across the set. He was sweating beneath his leather jacket, which was much too hot for the summer's day. But in the movies, fashion always went above comfort.

The set was in a quiet part of town where a few streets had been sectioned off. Most of the buildings were old warehouses, with a few brick ones thrown in. People were few and far between except for fans trying to catch a glimpse or other members of the crew.

Rowes dragged him until they rounded a corner just short of where the trailers were. With most people on set, there was no one in sight, and no windows close by for people to spot them from.

Izzy turned his grip and twined his fingers with Rowes as they came to a stop beyond the edge of shouts of the set crew. "If you wanted to hold hands, you could have just said so."

Rowes tugged his hand free, shaking his head as he backed away. "You aren't subtle, you know. There are no less than thirty people over there, and every single one of them just watched you practically maul me in front of Clarke. I'm sure they wouldn't be surprised if you pissed on me next like some dog trying to stake his claim."

Good. Then they'll know who you belong to. Rowes must have been able to read his thoughts or something because his expression darkened.

"It's not okay, Izzy." Rowes took another step back when Izzy reached for him. "I love submitting for you and I see now that I've been doing it for a long time, but people wouldn't understand completely. They already think we're too close, and you're just pushing that boundary even more."

"I'll make them understand," said Izzy, closing the distance between them and backing Rowes against the closest wall. It was yellow brick and probably scratchy as all hell. There was barely a breath between them, his lips inches away from Rowes'. "Everyone in the world should know that you belong to me."

Rowes widened his eyes, glancing to the head of the alley where anyone could walk by in a moment. *Good. Let them see.* "What the fuck, Izzy? You can't say shit like that here. People are going to think we're fucking. I mean, what else could that mean to someone that overhears it?"

His lips looked even better than Izzy remembered, the lower one just slightly bruised from their repeated kissing. He'd always been a man who believed in perfection, and he'd insisted they keep kissing until it was absolutely flawless. In truth, the first time Rowes' lips had touched his had been pure precision, but it had taken a lot of repeats until he was satisfied that it was real and not a figment of his imagination.

"Let them think what they want. It doesn't change a thing," said Izzy.

Rowes pushed him away with enough strength that Izzy stumbled back, clutching at his chest where Rowes had dug in with his nails. His face was flushed, his eyes narrowed as he glared at Izzy.

"You are unbelievable. You won't be happy until you have a collar around my neck and a plug in my ass with your name on it. Take a walk and cool off before I punch you."

He'd never heard Rowes sound so furious, and he certainly didn't have a violent bone in his body, but Izzy didn't doubt him. That didn't stop Izzy from taking a step in and putting his hand on the wall next to Rowes' head.

Rowes looked to the side, suddenly blanching as he spotted something over Izzy's shoulder. When Izzy turned, he caught sight of Lorena at the end of the alley, her arms crossed and a scowl on her lips.

"Everyone is looking for you two. We're ready to go." Her eyes narrowed.

"We'll be there in a minute," said Izzy, turning back to Rowes. Rowes touched his chest with his hands, but didn't push him away, his chest heaving as he bit his lower lip.

"Iz," he whispered softly. "Not here. *Please.*"

Has he always begged so nicely? He must've done it before, when their relationship had been simple and the air wasn't charged between them like a bunch of firecrackers waiting to go off. Izzy couldn't remember for the life of him.

Izzy drew back, sending Lorena a bright smile that probably didn't reach his eyes. It was an expression he'd don for his character when Kemble eyed up a new gang member, already knowing he was going to shoot them in the forehead at the first opportunity.

"Can't keep the director waiting," said Izzy, grabbing Rowes' hand and tugging him away from the wall. "Come on, Rowes."

He'd never harbored a single negative thought toward Lorena. She was overbearing, but who wasn't in her type of business? It was her job to make sure everything was perfect, and that included being a hardass when one of them fucked up. But as she shot a glare at Rowes, Izzy narrowed his eyes.

"Is there a problem, Lorena?" Izzy growled, pausing next to her. Rowes' hand was clammy in his as he followed passively.

"Perhaps," she said, her face giving nothing away. "Before you two head out today, I'll need to talk with Rowes. The director wanted to speak with him about something."

When he glanced back, Rowes looked even paler, his lip between his teeth and his face blanched. He must've still been feeling off with his back. Izzy hadn't given him a repeat massage, but maybe he would have to. It wouldn't be a hardship.

"Good, let's go. Rowes, take a seat for a few minutes while we do the first shot. I'll check in with you before we get to your segment. We should be able to wrap up the episode today, hopefully." He'd checked on their progress earlier when he'd been going over his script for the scenes.

It wouldn't be long before they wrapped up the entire season again. Usually by episode eight, they were all exhausted beyond belief, and they didn't need much makeup to look grubby by number twelve.

Rowes didn't respond, ducking his head as Izzy led him to the closest chair. Lorena lingered, pulling a juice box from her massive purse before kneeling next to Rowes.

At least she was taking care of him. Maybe she wasn't so bad after all.

Chapter Twelve

Rowes

"Rowes." Lorena gave him a steady look as she passed him a juice box. His hands were trembling, and he could barely get the straw out of the plastic wrapper and into the little hole. Glaring at the floor, he sucked it down, wincing at the strong taste of artificial grape.

"Rowes," she said, drawing out his name.

"I know," he said as he took a breath between sips. "I *know*." He dropped his head into his hands as his stomach flopped.

Things were getting out of hand. Izzy had taken to Dominance like everything else in his life. Of course, he excelled, and Rowes loved him for it. He was also terrified about being good enough for Izzy. There had never been any pressure before, but this was something so new and exciting.

And he hadn't been kidding about the collar and the plug, either. He'd dreamt about them the night before and hadn't been able to stop thinking about them since. It had just slipped out.

But it could cost him his job.

He heard the distant call of 'action', and Lorena shifted closer, lowering her voice to a whisper.

"What were you guys doing? Anyone could have seen you, Rowes. It's one thing to share a room with separate beds, but what did I just see?" She didn't look pissed, only worried. It made sense, too. If he lost his contract, she would lose some of her income as his manager.

I'm finally being who I am. He couldn't say that. She wouldn't understand. Maybe some would, but not her. There was no freaking way.

"We were...um." He cleared his throat, then took another sip of juice. "We aren't fucking." He'd been saying that far too often lately, and it was getting old. He hadn't been penetrated at all, even if Izzy's finger had come damn close.

"Rowes." She let out a long sigh that was almost drowned out by the commotion on set. His part was coming up soon, and he needed to be ready.

Please stop saying my name. It was worse than getting scolded by his mother.

"Anyone could have seen you. Breaching your contract is a big deal."

He was very aware of that, thank you very much. He'd never been so aware of his contract in his life. "I didn't breach anything," said Rowes, hoping that the truth shone in his words. "We haven't crossed any lines."

"I doubt that," she said, giving him a knowing look. "If you guys are doing things like that in a public place, then I can only imagine what you do in private."

"Don't." He glanced to the audio crew, hoping he wasn't too loud. No one was looking their way, too focused on the scene, but it was only a matter of time before their whispers were noticed. "We already get so much speculation from the fans and some of the crew. We don't need that from you, too."

"Cut!"

Rowes jerked at the director's call, standing from his chair. He was still wobbly, but the juice had done some good. Lorena took the empty box from him, and he slapped his cheeks, trying to get some color back into his face. The makeup crew would probably descend on him in moments to adjust the hard work he'd just ruined.

As if summoned by his thoughts, Josie appeared, dabbing his sweaty face with a dark brush. Izzy was right behind her, squeezing his shoulder. He still seemed like Kemble, his gaze all too intense as he looked Rowes over. Izzy's gaze was so much softer than his character's, supporting Rowes instead of finding his weak spots.

"You good?"

Rowes nodded, biting his lip and forcing a smile on his face. Izzy must've believed him, because he looked relieved.

"I'd thought maybe I'd stepped out of line," said Izzy, scratching at a bit of dirt on his neck. He was filthy for the scene, his roll in the dirt as they escaped enemy lines taking its toll.

"No." Rowes held his gaze, refusing to back down. "I was serious about what I said, though."

He hoped Izzy would understand, and from the predatory look in his eyes, he did. Rowes' stomach twisted in the best kind of way, and he reached up to squeeze Izzy's hand that was still resting on his shoulder.

"Easy on the entrance this time, Ro." Izzy sent him a wink before he retreated to his starting spot. Rowes rolled his shoulders, giving him a thumbs up as Josie backed away.

"Got it."

* * * *

Rowes was dead tired by the time the director called it a wrap, pulling him to the side as the crew scrambled around set. For some of them, their day was just beginning.

"Lorena said we needed to chat about something. You injured?"

Always straight and to the point. Honestly, it was so much better than working with someone who beat around the bush for an hour before asking the question. It was probably why she was such a fantastic director.

"I'm good," said Rowes, only wincing a little as he twisted to the side. He was bound to be sore tomorrow, but Izzy had taken care of the worst for him, and the bruises weren't anything he couldn't handle.

Lorena was rushing over to them, her hair frazzled and her purse missing for once. She must've been surviving on energy drinks alone, but she still managed to look good.

"Okay?" The director looked to Lorena with one eyebrow raised. "So, what's the issue?"

Rowes shrugged, kicking his foot against the ground. The boots he'd been jammed into for the last scene fit terribly, and he already had a blister on his big toe. They looked nice, though.

"Rowes, don't try to deny it," said Lorena, letting out a sigh of frustration. "I caught you and Isthmus together in that alley, and you looked like you were just about to kiss each other — or had just finished."

Rowes was going to have to start looking for a new manager before he took a shower. He wasn't sure why she was being such a stickler, and getting the director involved was way offside.

"You said that earlier," said the director, shrugging her shoulders. "So what?"

Lorena blinked, her mouth opening and closing as she was struck momentarily speechless.

"You guys fucking?" asked the director, raising one brow. "Not that I care. It's kinda hot, if you ask me, but the PR team might have a shitfest."

"No, ma'am." Rowes had never called anyone 'ma'am' in his life, but this moment fit the bill. The director was a terrifying woman, especially when she could brush someone like Lorena off like that.

"Good. I gave Isthmus the okay to practice your scene with you anyway," she continued, sending another confused look to Lorena. "So what's the issue? Is it a sexuality thing? We can do a rewrite if that's what it takes, but Isthmus is right about supporting the LGBTQ community. It's about time."

Lorena gaped. "What?"

"Thank you," said Rowes, not stopping the smirk that slid over his lips as he sent Lorena a victorious look. He knew she was trying to look after him in her own way, but it was about time she got told. "I gotta get back before Izzy misses me. We haven't got the scene quite right, so I might have to do a little more practicing."

The director grinned. "This is going to be awesome. Too bad I couldn't convince them on more than one scene. If I had my choice, I'd have both of you two buck naked and grinding."

Rowes paused, touching his chest as his heart seemed to stop. "But I thought my contract changes were your idea?" What had Lorena told him? He couldn't remember.

The director snorted before rolling her eyes. "You've gotta be joking me." A stray intern tried to get her attention, but she waved them off. "The producers and Lorena were on point on that decision. I say you guys can fuck who you want, but I was only able to get it limited to a few of you. I'm surprised you even signed it. Most of the others lawyered up."

Well, fuck. His eyes burned as he forced the tears back, refusing to make eye contact with Lorena. How long had she been lying to him? But it didn't make any sense.

Unless she thought that he was the weak link that was dragging her down. It was better for her to smear his name through the dirt than drop a client unexpectedly. News like that spread faster than whispers of a secret pregnancy.

"Got it," he said, nodding as he bit his lip. He couldn't see Izzy anywhere, but he could almost feel him in his periphery, probably just out of sight. "I'll see you tomorrow bright and early."

"Sounds good," said the director. "And let Isthmus know that you guys both did good today. This season is going to be epic."

Rowes turned away, heading for the exit. He didn't look back.

Chapter Thirteen

Izzy

Something had happened. Rowes had beat him back to the room and ordered dinner for the both of them before he'd stripped down to almost nothing and sat on the bed. While aimlessly flipping through channels, he hadn't said a word since.

"What did you order for yourself, Ro? Hopefully extra croutons." Izzy's grin faltered when Rowes didn't smile, instead giving a simple nod. His bruises along his side stood out like dark paint against his pale skin. They would have been beautiful if they didn't look so painful.

"Ro?" Izzy slumped next to him on the bed, automatically reaching for him but pausing only inches away when Rowes flinched.

"When the director talked to you about my contract, what did she say?" asked Rowes as he closed his eyes. He was trembling, goosebumps all over his naked skin.

The only thing keeping his modesty was the thin pair of blue boxers.

"Not much," said Izzy, tilting his head in confusion. "Why? What happened? Did something happen between you and Lorena? If that bitch—"

"We can't have sex." Rowes cut him off, hanging his head low as his shoulders shook. "Apparently, I was the only one stupid enough to sign that fucking contract, and now we can't be together. Lorena said it was all the producers and director, but I can't believe her anymore. I don't know what to do, Izzy. I can't live without you, but I'm nothing without my career. What am I supposed to do? Wash fucking cars or something? Give the ladies someone hot and wet to stare at as I do a little dance in a club?"

What the hell is going on? Rowes looked close to tears with his eyes red and wet. It tore a hole in his chest. Izzy was supposed to protect him, not let him carry on by himself as he'd obviously been doing.

"What are you talking about? What contract? The director— I don't even remember what she said now, but something about how it wouldn't be a problem."

Letting out a heart-wrenching sob, Rowes turned into him, pushing his face into Izzy's chest. His cheeks were wet as he trembled. He looped his hands around Izzy's neck and pulled him in until his naked skin was against Izzy. It was the first time in the past few days that his mind didn't stray. Nudity didn't matter when Rowes was hurting.

"I signed a contract that said I couldn't have sexual intercourse with any members of the cast or crew. Fuck, I didn't ever think it would be an issue. It's always been easy to find a woman if I wanted one, and I never thought there would be anything like this between us.

You're my best friend, but now we're so much more and I *can't*." His sob cut him off as he broke down, curling into Izzy as he started to cry in earnest.

This is bad.

"Rowes, it's okay. I said you're mine, and I meant it," said Izzy, placing a kiss on the top of Rowes' head. "And I take care of what's mine." His heart was racing, his mind spinning. There was no way something like that was legal. Time constraints were one thing, but getting involved in someone's sex life? No court would agree to sue Rowes for that. "Besides, you haven't done anything wrong," said Izzy, plunging his hand into Rowes' hair. "You been perfect for me, even before we realized that we were meant to be more than just friends. You're supportive, kind, beautiful and the best actor I know."

Rowes smiled through his tears as he shook his head. "Connley is the best actor you know. Don't lie."

True. "That's not the point." Izzy moved his hands lower, skimming over Rowes' bruises until he found the knot in his lower back. Some of the tenseness had returned, a busy day and the tears probably not helping. Rowes let out a shuddering breath, and Izzy felt a hint of strain leaving him.

He could figure this out. He wasn't a lawyer, but he wasn't an idiot. They'd both been in the business long enough to know that it wasn't always *clean.*

"What exactly did it say?" asked Izzy. It was a good thing they had never shown him a contract like that, because he would have ripped it apart or set it on fire. *Why didn't you tell me, Rowes?* Even before they'd grown closer, he would have destroyed that contract on Rowes' behalf. No one deserved to be controlled like that and have their love and private life stripped of them.

Every contract had loopholes, no matter how airtight they seemed to be.

"Uh, I feel so stupid," said Rowes, wrapping his arms around Izzy's waist and squeezing tight. "I should have told you about it right away, but they said it was confidential, and I had a time limit to sign it. I didn't want to jeopardize the show or your career over a little clause."

"This may come as a surprise to you, Ro, but you are the star of a hit television show. They aren't going to fire you without some serious consequences for the ratings." Izzy took a deep breath, calming the rage that was curling under his skin. How long had Rowes been struggling with this on his own?

"I'm replaceable."

Izzy clamped his arms down until Rowes squeaked, trying to wiggle out of his hold. Rage like none other curled through his limbs, whisking his sense far away.

"*Never* talk about yourself like that," said Izzy, dropping his voice into a growl. He moved one hand to Rowes throat, squeezing just enough that it would start to hurt. "I love you, Rowes, but I can't sit here while you think about yourself like that. I'm not above putting you over my knee and spanking some sense into you. There is one thing that the fans have right about us, and it's that I'm nothing without you."

Rowes swallowed, his throat bobbing beneath Izzy's hand as his eyes went wide. Izzy tightened his grip, following the blush that spread over Rowes' cheeks as it presumably got harder for him to breathe.

As soon as he released him, Rowes sucked in a breath, coughing a few times. Even as his eyes watered, he didn't try to get away, clinging to Izzy with clenched fists.

"I'm sorry."

The apology thrummed through him, settling something deep inside. Cupping Rowes' cheeks, he placed a kiss on his forehead. "Forgiven. Now tell me about the contract."

"I have it on my phone, Izzy. I thought I should probably have pictures of it in case something came up that I had questions about."

Without leaving Rowes' side, Izzy reached for the phone, unlocking it with Rowes' password. He used the same code for everything, which made it easy to hack into any of his things to leave little surprises — like the time Izzy had changed his background to pink unicorns to make him smile. It had worked, and Rowes still hadn't changed it, even though it was months later.

He opened up the camera app, finding the finely printed contract between so many pictures of himself. He skimmed over it, growling under his breath as he read on. It was pretty damn airtight.

Sexual intercourse was off the books entirely, from what he could understand. There was a list of usual things Rowes wasn't allowed to do, like break confidentiality, leak images or scripts, but hidden among the normal was a section that hadn't been in Izzy's own contract.

His gut sank. He loved Rowes for who he was, no matter what, but they were both young and attractive. There should have been nothing to stop them from exploring each other, both as partners and lovers one day.

There was nothing like discovering a partner one inch at a time, tasting every bit and memorizing every part. The warmth of their skin, the way they tasted and the way they smelled would last in his memory long after the pleasure faded.

Some of the jargon was beyond him, which he'd expected. He wasn't alone, though, and neither was Rowes.

"I'm going to take care of this, but I need you to trust me," said Izzy, clicking the phone shut and returning both hands to Rowes' skin. He didn't pull away at the knock on the door that was probably their food arriving.

Rowes looked up at the sound, furrowing his forehead in confusion. "That better not be Lorena. I haven't decided if I'm speaking to her again or not."

"I'll take care of Lorena," said Izzy, the rage burning hot again as the knock sounded a second time on the door. There wasn't a dumpster out there that wasn't suitable for what was left of Lorena when he was done with her. "Answer the door and get our food. You can put the tray on the bed and sit on the floor."

Looking down at himself, Rowes' eyes went wide. "I'm practically naked." He reached for a robe that he'd left on the corner of the bed that morning, but Izzy stopped him with a hand on his wrist.

"And I want to show you off a little. No excuses at the door, just grab your food and give them a tip. You're beautiful. We've worn less on set in front of dozens of people. Remember the hot tub scene?"

That had been one of the most delicious moments of his life, now that he thought about it. He and Rowes had been in the hot tub in Speedos before they'd been ambushed by a rival gang. They'd fought them off nearly naked and dripping before Rowes had grabbed his gun and had taken care of the rest.

"Okay." Rowes sucked his lower lip into his mouth as he stood shyly. His gaze was on the floor, his cheeks flushed as he opened the door a crack and accepted the tray with as little eye contact as possible.

"Don't forget the tip," said Izzy, chuckling as Rowes reached for his ass cheek where his wallet would have been resting if he hadn't chucked his pants on the ground.

"Here." Izzy pulled a twenty from his own wallet, holding it out for Rowes. The door had swung wider as soon as he'd walked away, and the server looked like someone had just slapped her with a suitcase full of her favorite sex toys. Izzy waved at her. "Don't mind him. He's just tired from the workout we had today."

Izzy spread his legs wider, skimming a hand over the rumpled sheets of his bed. The other bed was made and completely untouched. She could think whatever the hell she wanted. Contract or no contract, he was done pretending.

Chapter Fourteen

Rowes

He never thought he'd be stepping foot back in the club again, especially not for a scene. Like before, Malone met them at the door, skipping the tour this time and taking them straight to the hall where the private rooms were. Rowes looked around curiously as they passed each one.

Izzy had called Malone from outside their hotel room, and Rowes hadn't even known they were headed to the club until they were in the car. Instead of filling him in, Izzy had spent the entire ride praising him. Some of the compliments had to be made up.

"I love your freckles. I dream about kissing each and every one of them..."

Rowes flushed at the memory. He had no idea how Izzy had managed to stay on the road in their rental car while Rowes had hardly been able to see straight. That hadn't even been the worse one, either.

"*Your lips are the sweetest thing I've ever tasted,*" Izzy had said, taking one hand off the wheel and touching Rowes' lower lip.

"*Well, I just ate chocolate,*" Rowes had huffed, crossing his arms, even as his cheeks burned.

"*That's not it.*"

At the next stoplight, Izzy had leaned over and kissed him in the daylight. Anyone could have seen them, but he'd done it. It made his insides squirm in a way that he was just beginning to understand.

"You okay?" Izzy's call pulled him from his thoughts as they passed by a couple who gave them a startled smile.

Even being in the kink club again somehow helped. There were people here just like them, who didn't ask questions or make assumptions. It was nice to be free.

Eyeing the engraved name on the door Malone had stopped in front of, Rowes narrowed his eyes. *Awake* was not very explanatory at all. If *Impact* was full of things for slapping and whipping, then what the hell was in *Awake*? Energy drinks?

"I'd like to blindfold you," said Izzy, pulling a thin leather strip from his pocket as he stopped at the door. It looked like he'd used one of his old ties from their promotion circuit and had reworked it into a blindfold. The gala he'd worn that to had been the opposite of this place, but Izzy had been there for him, his presence the only thing that had mattered. "What's your color on that?"

"Green." It was better than green. He'd only played with a blindfold once, and it had been amazing. The woman he'd been dating at the time had kissed him all over, every touch a surprise.

"If I may," said Malone, glancing at the makeshift blindfold. "I have one that will be a little more suitable. There are too many gaps with a tie, even if they do look pretty. You need to go for something padded and soft but not slippery. Unless this one has some importance to you."

"Sure," said Izzy, stuffing it back into his pocket with a shrug. "This trip was a little impromptu, and we're here to learn. It's just a tie."

Malone nodded before he disappeared into another room along the hall, and Rowes let out a soft breath. He wasn't sure if he'd ever met someone so intimidating except Izzy in his role as Kemble. Kemble was a powerhouse with both money and weapons at his disposal, and Izzy played him almost too well.

"This isn't a role, right?" asked Rowes, keeping his voice hushed in the hall. He had no idea how many people were behind those doors, and he didn't want to disturb them—especially the people in the 'wet' room.

"Put your hand on my chest, Ro." Izzy guided him to the spot over his heart, clasping their fingers together. He could feel the steady thumping of his heart that was just a little too fast to be normal and smell the sweat on his skin from the summer heat. "This here is real. Every part of the way I look at you and want to hold you tight is real and always has been."

"Your heart is going fast," said Rowes, pressing closer until he could almost hear it. If he could have, he would have crawled into Izzy's arms, then closer still, until there was nothing separating them.

"I'm nervous," said Izzy, shifting his feet along the floor.

"Nervous?" That didn't make any sense. Izzy didn't get nervous—not in front of the media or a thousand fans. He lived to be in the spotlight, and he did everything so well, that he never had to be nervous.

"I don't want to hurt you by accident or mess up," said Izzy, holding Rowes' gaze steady. "You're the most important person in my life, and I want to give you the world, but I need guidance. There have already been so many times I've screwed up without knowing it. That's why I've asked Malone for help."

That was another thing Izzy never did. He was the type of guy to struggle through lifting something on his own and pulling three muscles before he'd ever ask for help, not to mention directions. On their first trip to the club, they'd driven aimlessly for half an hour before Izzy had finally seemed to recognize a sign for the highway.

Izzy squeezed Rowes' hand as Malone returned. "I want to be as perfect for you as you are for me."

Malone grinned as he handed a new blindfold to Izzy. It looked to be some sort of soft fabric with a thick, fluffy lining. It was also about twice the size as Rowes had expected and would probably end up covering half his face.

"Why don't you just put me in a hood?" he asked as he reached for it. Izzy clicked his tongue, motioning for Rowes to turn around.

It settled against his face, even softer than he'd expected. It also cut everything out. There was no light at all and no cracks to speak of. The little slip of light at the bottom that he'd expected of the tie blindfold was gone.

Izzy secured it tight, sliding his fingers underneath the strap and against Rowes' scalp. He shivered at the touch, throwing his arms out as he nearly stumbled.

Izzy was there to catch him, pulling him back and off balance.

"That's not a bad idea, actually," said Izzy, Rowes jumping at his voice that was right against his ear. His voice had gone low again, in that tone that had a whole new meaning between them. "I could take all your senses away except taste and touch, then sample every part of you."

If he hadn't been on his way to hard already, the speed that blood filled his cock would have been even more painful. He'd never heard dirtier words, and it called to something deep within him that urged him to tilt his head back and fall to his knees. The world seemed to wobble, his balance thrown off as Izzy twisted them around.

He couldn't remember which way he was facing, let alone where the door was. He'd always had a terrible sense of direction, but now he was lost in a mass of darkness like a dream.

"Iz?"

"Right here, Ro. You doing okay?"

His throat clicked as he swallowed, and he reached for Izzy's hands that were on his chest. Letting out a sigh of relief when he found them, he rolled his shoulders, easing the tension away. He was just nervous.

"Still green. Don't let me fall, okay?" His legs were wobbly for some reason, something rushing through his veins that hadn't been there before.

"Never."

He caught the sound of the door squeaking a bit as it presumably opened, and their footsteps as Izzy guided him into the room. It seemed warmer, somehow—or maybe he was just more aware of his clothing. A thin T-shirt and shorts were all he'd worn, but they felt like too much with Izzy's hands on him, carefully guiding him into the room.

"Is Malone still here?" He turned his head back and forth, even though he was blind. There could have been twenty people and he wouldn't have known, but he trusted Izzy to keep him safe.

"I am. Because you are my guests, I won't be able to leave during the scene. If you need a moment, I can step outside." Malone was even intimidating when Rowes wasn't looking at him, his voice powerful in itself.

"Izzy?"

"Still here, Ro," said Izzy, just a touch of humor in his voice.

"Is Malone like a mobster or something?" he asked quietly. Normally, he would never ask a question like that, but his lack of sight seemed to have infused some confidence into his limbs.

Malone snorted before chuckling. "I'm a lawyer, kid, but I'll take that as a compliment. My boy is the only one who gets to see my soft side."

Rowes scrunched up his nose. Lawyers were right up there with mobsters in his bad books at the moment. But as long as Malone wasn't upset, then he wasn't worried. "Are you going to hurt me?"

"Did you want me to?" asked Izzy, trailing a finger down Rowes' spine. At least, he thought it was Izzy. He wasn't sure if Izzy would let Malone touch him or not. He shivered, his skin prickling.

"I don't know." He imagined the scene he'd watched on his phone alone, where Dom had paddled his sub. The sub had seemed so blissed out, even as his skin turned red. But he didn't like pain...at least, he didn't think so.

"Hold this," said Izzy, placing Rowes' hands on something smooth and hard that was at the height of his waist. Rowes grabbed it, holding tight as he slipped his fingers over the surface. It was stable and strong, supporting him as he leaned against it. It almost wasn't enough when Izzy's hands left him.

A slap rang out a moment later and Rowes jumped, almost letting go of his support as Izzy spanked him. It didn't hurt much through his pants, but it still tingled, leaving a warming bruise in its wake. His heart pounded, and he shuffled his feet.

"Did you like that?" asked Izzy, his voice coming from a different direction than the slap. Rowes turned his head, trying to track Izzy from the sound of his breathing. It was coming faster — excited and low, just like Rowes'.

"I don't know," said Rowes, shifting so his shorts rubbed against his ass. The sting hadn't lingered, leaving nothing behind but a phantom touch. "Maybe try again?"

He heard Malone chuckle. "He's hungry for it."

Maybe he was. Maybe he was starving for something other than just a simple touch or a loving hand. Maybe he wanted to be broken until he couldn't recognize himself in the mirror. If no one knew it was him, then there was nothing to worry about.

"Will you beat me?" asked Rowes, the question burning on his tongue. The need for it scorched through him in an instant, and he shifted his legs wider, inviting the touch.

A hand on his waist answered him and he jumped, expecting pain instead of a soft touch. Izzy's breath tickled the back of his neck and his ear before something hard pressed against his ass.

155

Oh fuck. Izzy was harder than steel, his cock digging into Rowes' ass as Izzy moved his hand to Rowes' pants and slowly pushed them down. Rowes sucked in a breath, lifting his legs one at a time as he was stripped of both layers, leaving him bare from the waist down.

His shirt went next, and he struggled to let go of his support as Izzy pulled it off his arms and presumably tossed it somewhere in the room. The whisper of falling cloth was the only tell that he hadn't folded it like he normally would have.

A hand came down on his naked ass a moment later, and Rowes tensed, yelping at the brutal sting of it. It was so much more without the layers of fabric protecting him, fire lancing across his skin before it settled deep. This one would definitely bruise and leave its mark for days.

"Where are the bruises from?" asked Malone, sounding slightly concerned.

"Rowes was injured on set." Izzy skimmed his hand over the bruises, keeping his fingers light. Rowes hissed at the touch anyway, leaning into it. They had never felt good before, not even when Izzy had massaged him — but now they did. "Are they feeling better, Rowes?"

"Green." Rowes nodded as he answered, moving his ass toward Izzy to try to get his attention back to where he wanted it.

"It's a good idea to ask about injuries or ailments before a scene starts," said Malone. "Once they are floating, a sub has no concept of mortality."

"Noted," said Izzy.

Why were they talking about him instead of doing something? He was naked, his legs spread wide and his cock dripping. Did they need an invitation or something? He arched his back, just in case, hoping that he looked more inviting. The move ignited the quiet spot in his back, but he pushed through it, gritting his teeth.

"A few rules, Ro." Izzy's voice came from the other side this time, far enough to be a few paces away. Why was he getting farther? Rowes stuck his ass out as much as he could, begging for another spank.

"Are you listening?" That was Malone this time, his voice even but somehow softer than before.

"Yes. Green. I don't know what you want me to say, but hit me again, Izzy." Rowes leaned against his wooden support, bringing his face to it. The blindfold was getting damp, his sweat soaking into it. He was too warm, even without clothes.

"I wasn't talking to you, Mr. Keppel," said Malone. "I never scene without my boy, and he's been very good and quiet so far. Say hello, Oliver."

"Hello."

Oh God, there were other people here. Rowes shuddered as he flamed hotter.

"I only want Izzy touching me," said Rowes, flinching away from the touch on his hip.

"It's me," said Izzy, following Rowes' movement before resting his hand over his heated skin. His palm was warm, making the nerves singe brighter. Rowes leaned into the warmth, taking everything he could get. "And that's rule one. Only I'm going to touch you, unless I check in with you first."

"Okay." Rowes let out a sigh of relief, most of his tension melting away. Without it, he could sink deeper into the feeling that was trying to overtake him. The pain faded away to something else as he panted.

"Rule number two," said Izzy. "If you want something you have to ask for it...nicely."

"Hit me, please," said Rowes, his back almost at its limit. It didn't hurt so much anymore, but he was shaking, his muscles barely hanging on. In all his time at the gym, he'd never felt so weak.

The slap was instant, ringing out louder than any of the previous ones. Gasping, Rowes waited for the pain to roll over him, trembling when it didn't. It was good, like the pleasant tingles of sitting too close to the fire, knowing that he would never be singed.

"Harder." He clung to the post, shifting his legs wider to prepare himself for the blow.

Izzy trailed a finger up his spine, leaving a shiver in its wake. He whimpered, heaving in his next breath.

"*Please.*"

Whatever had been holding Izzy back, suddenly disappeared as he brought his hand down over and over. Rowes took every blow, soaking up the sharp tingles that spread all the way to his cock. He was sure he was dripping and making a mess, but he couldn't bring himself to care. There could have been a camera pointed his way, and he would have smiled.

"If you have any more rules for him, tell him before he gets much deeper. He's very close to subspace right now," said Malone, his voice like a tether in the dark. Rowes clung to it as his hands slipped over the wood.

"Fuck." Izzy's voice was tight and strained. "How can you tell?"

"You see how relaxed he looks?" asked Malone. "And how his voice is slurring? His moans are more drawn out—longer, deeper. Ask him how he's feeling."

"Ro baby, how are you feeling?" asked Izzy.

Never in his life had Izzy called him 'baby', but it covered exactly what he was feeling. He was helpless yet comfortable. He wasn't sure if he could move his arms or legs, but they seemed to be working on their own, keeping him from keeling over.

"I dunno…weird." His voice *was* slurred like he'd been drinking. The strange thing was, he rarely drank, too worried he would spontaneously jump on social media and reveal every plot twist of an upcoming season.

"Wow." Izzy let out a loud breath, and Rowes felt him against his back, his cock still hard as he rubbed himself against Rowes' ass. The fabric of Izzy's pants against his ass was like torture.

"The rest of the rules, Ro." Izzy inhaled shakily. "I won't penetrate you, not even with toys. That will be a hard limit that neither of us will be pushing. I bought that plug for you—the one I want you to wear the next time you're on set. I want you to wear it now and all the way back to the hotel, so you get used to how it feels." He let out a heavy breath against Rowes' skin. "You have two choices."

Rowes nodded, his groin going tight as he imagined the plug. He couldn't believe Izzy had bought it for him. There were so many that he'd found online, with every shape and size imaginable.

"What does it look like?"

It was the first time he regretted not having his sight. He wouldn't move his hand to pull his blindfold off because removing it seemed almost wrong.

"It's big—maybe too big for some of the scenes in the script. You'll wear it, anyway, even if it makes you hard." Izzy caresses his ass, bringing a hiss to his lips. "That's not the best part. Instead of a jewel at the base,

I engraved my name. That way, if anyone sees it, they'll know exactly who you belong to."

Oh God. Rowes pushed his knees together as they almost gave out, leaning his full weight onto his hands and clutching his support.

"Do you like that?"

Nodding, Rowes' throat clicked as he swallowed dry. *"Please,* Iz. I need it. I *need* it."

"You have a choice to make, then. You can put it in yourself or ask Malone if his boy would put it in for you."

There was no way he could put it in himself. He needed a steady hand to play with his ass, and if he let go, he would end up on the ground.

"Malone, Sir? Could he—I mean—your boy?" He wasn't sure what the protocol was, but he hadn't been properly introduced, so he wondered if they weren't supposed to speak directly. It was the same way he loved when Izzy spoke for him, especially when he was feeling shy.

"Good."

Rowes expected a touch at his ass, but when he arched his back, Izzy spanked him again. The numbness from the repeated strikes had had time to cool, and the touch sent a wave of real pain through him. Letting out a groan, he scrambled to stay standing. Izzy's hand at his hip was the only thing that kept him upright.

"What's your color?" asked Izzy, caressing the spot that he had just struck. He slapped twice more before Rowes finally managed a whimpered 'green'. He moved to Rowes' ass, pulling his cheeks wide as something cool and wet slid over his hole.

Clenching at the feeling, Rowes tried to squirm away. It had been so long since he'd been penetrated, and Izzy had said it would be big. It would probably hurt like hell, too.

Not that he wasn't ready for it, but he wanted to struggle and have Izzy's hands hold him down as it was forced inside.

"Make me take it?" asked Rowes, reaching for Izzy's hand and turning into him. The move almost had him off balance, but he managed to hang on by grabbing Izzy's shirt. Izzy adjusted his grip, wrapping his arms around him and reaching for his ass to pull it wide.

Rowes squirmed, rubbing his cock into the rough fabric of Izzy's pants. He'd never thought denim would be so infuriating. It was enough to give him some stimulation, but he couldn't imagine coming from it. If Izzy touched his cock with a bit of skin on the other hand, he wouldn't be able to stop himself.

He wasn't even worried if that was allowed or not. His contract was the furthest thing from his mind, and he trusted Izzy to take care of it.

"This is a big one, Sir. Are you sure it will fit?" It was Malone's boy who asked, his voice so much softer than either Izzy's or Malone's. He sounded young, too, probably in his early twenties.

"Just do it," said Rowes, clutching Izzy tight. Izzy moved his hand from his ass only to give him three hard spanks that took his breath away.

"That was rude, Ro," said Izzy, giving one more hit that was stronger than all the previous ones. Rowes curled his toes, biting back a scream. It fucking hurt.

"I'm not sure what gave you the impression that you could order anyone around," said Izzy, squeezing his ass in a way that made everything ache. "You should apologize before Malone changes his mind and lets you try to put that plug in all by yourself."

"I'm sorry. I'm *so* sorry," said Rowes, leaning heavily against Izzy as his cheeks were spread wide again.

"Don't let it happen again," said Malone, the darkness in his voice sending shivers down Rowes' spine. "I'm very protective of my things, just like Isthmus is."

Rowes didn't even want to think if he would get some sort of punishment when what he was going through was already torture. His balls had never ached quite so fiercely, his cock probably purple with need.

"I'm sorry, Malone. It won't happen again, Sir. I promise."

He never broke his promises.

Gasping at the touch of something hard and cool against his rim, Rowes froze as he tried to figure out what it was. He'd been expecting plastic, but it felt more like metal, and so smooth that it slid in easily, despite his resistance. The head must have been very narrow because he hardly felt it until it suddenly grew wider, stretching him sharply.

It wasn't much, but it had been a long time. When he'd first started experimenting with pegging with a previous girlfriend, he'd learned to take a plastic cock hard and fast with minimal prep, but since *Gunlover*, he'd hardly explored himself that way.

"I'm not so sure. He's awful tight," said Malone's boy, pausing with only what felt like the tip inside. Rowes pushed against it, relishing the stretch as he took a bit more. It didn't hurt at all, sending a tingle directly to his cock. *I can take more.*

"Let me see," said Izzy, pulling Rowes' cheeks wider as he presumably looked. "Hmm, you might be right. Maybe I shouldn't have gone for the extra large. What do you think, Malone?"

"Try again, boy, and go slow. He looks like he has the ass of a virgin."

Wait. Rowes pushed back against the toy, but it moved away, barely sinking in at all.

"He's too tight, Sir," said Malone's boy.

Are they fucking with me? Of all the times for a mindfuck, Izzy had chosen now?

Izzy had always liked to keep him on his toes, on the set and off, but this was too much.

Usually, he got a tad frustrated and embarrassed before he chuckled. But now? It put him right on the edge of orgasm. He had to still his hips in order to not come on Izzy's leg, not knowing if had permission or not.

They were probably baiting him — *the bastards* — seeing if he would break down and yell at Malone's boy again. But he *never* broke his promises. He was, however, damn good at getting his way with Izzy.

"*Please*, Izzy. I want to come with it inside me. I've been so good for you, and I can take it. I want to hurt for you and feel your marks on my skin. I want the plug inside me every time I'm on set so I can feel it when I move. Can you imagine what it would be like if I have to dodge a bullet? I will probably come in my pants and groan for the cameras. When Clarke kisses me, all I'll feel is you inside me, and the memory of your lips on mine. All I'll think about is you, and when I get hard, it will be for you."

There was a beat of silence after Rowes trailed off, and he wondered if he'd pushed too hard. He had the habit of rambling when he got on a roll, and right now, his filter was lost, the blindfold only adding fuel to the fire.

"Give it to him," said Izzy, his voice so thick that Rowes almost didn't recognize him. "Give him the whole damn thing, and we'll see how well he can take it."

Oh fuck. In one motion, the plug was pushed inside him, the cold metal tip settling directly against his prostate. The brief stretch barely had a zing going up his spine, but it was heavy — so heavy that he clenched around it. That movement had it rubbing him on the inside where everything was so over sensitized that he could feel his orgasm building, already starting.

"*Please.*" Rowes grabbed Izzy by the waist, bringing their groins together. He was already shooting, the first few pulses probably ruining Izzy's pants. But he couldn't hold back.

Izzy reached between his cheeks, tapping the base of the plug, and Rowes choked as his prostate was nailed. His body jerked as his orgasm dragged on, sucking every ounce of energy from his bones.

Izzy caught him as he fell, slipping a hand behind his knees and picking him up bridal style as Rowes slipped away, letting the dark calm take over his thoughts. He could almost see himself from behind the blindfold as if he were watching from Malone's perspective and not his own.

"You got him, Isthmus?" asked Malone. Rowes turned into Izzy's chest as he was laid on something soft.

"That was so hot, Daddy."

Malone chuckled, followed by the sound of the door opening and closing. A quietness descended that hadn't been there before.

"You asleep, Ro?"

Rowes shook his head. Izzy sounded so fucked out, his voice thick and dark. His hand was grabbed, his palm pressing against something rock-hard and hot. *Izzy.*

"Come on my cock," said Rowes, the words like someone else had said them. He would never say something so filthy.

"Fuck, baby."

He caught the sound of a zipper, then Izzy's weight settled over him, naked flesh touching his spent cock. He twitched, his every nerve on fire.

"It's like you're inside me, Iz." Rowes rolled his hips, meeting Izzy's hard cock with his softening one. It was painful, but not as bad as his ass, which was burning against the bed. "You're touching me just right and hitting my spot every time I move. Your name is on me — in me. You own me."

"*Fuck.*"

Izzy dragged his teeth against his neck as something warm and wet landed on Rowes' cock. He groaned at the filthiness of it, reaching to smear it all over himself. Izzy couldn't fuck him, but he had been claimed one hundred percent.

Chapter Fifteen

Izzy

Malone had told him that *Awake* was the room of epic mind fucks where nothing was ever what it seemed, and looking back, Izzy had to agree.

The biggest object was a four-poster bed with a thick frame that Rowes had unknowingly leaned against for almost their entire scene. The bed itself was for anything but sleeping, with a dozen different restraints built into it where someone could be bound and edged for hours.

There were other things, too, like the needles that could be chilled or heated so they felt like they were cutting, and the endless number of hoods and gags. The speakers built in could shake the room, which could be useful in a sleep deprivation scene, and the cage in the corner had probably never seen a dog.

But Izzy didn't expect his own mind to be just as fucked over as Rowes. He was holding onto himself— barely— his hands shaking with an energy that came from nowhere. He felt like he could fuck five people and still get it up for more, but at the same time, he never wanted his hands to stray from Rowes' skin.

"You okay?" he asked Rowes for what was probably the fourth or fifth time. He'd taken off the blindfold almost as soon as he had laid Rowes on the bed, and it had been soaked with sweat and tears. Rowes was still crying in slow, lazy drips that curled down the sides of his face before falling.

Rowes only nodded, swallowing as he reached for Izzy's hand and squeezed tight. Izzy had tried to pull away once to grab them some water, but Rowes had clung to him like a leech, refusing to give way.

"Did I hurt you?"

Rowes shook his head, curling his lips into a smile. His breaths were slow and soft, as if he were on the edge of sleep, and he had yet to open his eyes.

"Why are you crying?" Izzy wiped away another set of tears as they built.

"I feel too good not to cry." Rowes nuzzled into him, only wincing when he wiggled his ass on the bed. "How long until we have to leave?"

Glancing to the closed door, Izzy let out a contented sigh. Maybe he could convince Rowes to stay here forever. The bed wasn't as comfortable as his back home, but it was better than the hotel one. They could leave the show and live in the club without contracts or questions between them.

The whole idea of it was so tempting that Izzy almost suggested it. It was really too bad that they both loved their careers.

"I'll give you two options," said Izzy, smoothing his hand down Rowes' chest just because he could. Those abs belonged to him, and so did his nipples. Every little bit was his, even the hole he wasn't allowed to touch.

"One, we see if Clint has a room here and stay the night. I still have to talk with Malone about a few things, so we need to hang around for a bit." He touched Rowes' sides, tracing the bruises that were on their way to healing. "Option two, we head back to the hotel now and we crash in the jacuzzi. I'll have you play with that plug of yours and see how many times I can get you to come."

Rowes giggled, kissing Izzy's pec in a way that was all too natural. A month ago, it would have been just as natural for them to have been this close, but they would have had clothes on, for sure, and they wouldn't have kissed.

"I don't think I could come again if I tried," said Rowes, motioning to his soft cock. It was filthy, with dried cum that must've been itchy as hell.

At the knock on the door, Izzy grabbed the closest blanket, tossing it over Rowes. It seemed strange, when Rowes had just been naked in front of two other men, one of them a stranger, but Izzy wasn't letting anyone see his property without permission.

"Come in," he yelled. He wasn't sure if they would hear him or not, because Malone had mentioned that the rooms were mostly soundproofed. The door cracked a moment later regardless, and Malone's boy stuck his head inside.

His cheeks were flushed, making his boyish looks appear even younger. His eyes seemed old, though, catching everything he saw, including the little cues Izzy and Malone had given him throughout the scene. If Izzy had his guess, he was probably a similar age to Rowes and himself.

"Hey." He waved from the door, slowly taking a step inside before carefully shutting it behind him. "Daddy said we have to leave soon, but that you needed to talk to him. He didn't want to interrupt your aftercare."

Which was thoughtful as hell. Izzy was feeling exceedingly possessive, but Malone's boy was also one of the most unthreatening people he'd ever met. He almost wanted to hug him.

"How are you feeling, baby?" asked Izzy, looking to Rowes, who had finally opened his eyes. His tears had stopped, but his eyes were still bloodshot and his nose swollen. He also looked relaxed as all hell.

"So good. Less floaty, but super happy." He grinned, even as he said it.

"There's a Zen room, if you wanted to chat there instead. I can take care of cleaning this room and the laundry after I show you there," said the boy, ducking his head when Izzy looked his way again.

"Okay—just...I want to clean Rowes up a bit first." He pulled away from the bed for the first time, fastening his jeans as he strolled to the nearest sink and grabbed a cloth. Rowes furrowed his forehead but didn't react otherwise when Izzy wiped the crusted cum from his groin.

After Rowes' donned a robe, Malone's boy led them a short way along the hall, to a door that looked almost identical, except for the *Zen* engraved on it. It was much more clear-cut than *Awake*, with a lavender scent diffuser, soft music and comfy couches. Malone was the only other person in the room, reclined on one of the couches as he sipped from a bottle of water.

Izzy would have killed for a drink. Nothing was better after good sex than a finger of hard liquor—and that had been some amazing sex.

Malone's boy slipped back into the hall as they settled on a couch across from Malone, soundlessly closing the door. Izzy grabbed the nearest blanket, wrapping it around Rowe's shoulders. His sub was wearing a robe that he'd found in the room because he'd winced at the sight of his pants, but the robe was silky and not at all warm.

"You two look happy," said Malone, giving them a smile that spoke volumes.

"Very," Izzy replied, just as easily. He'd never been so fucking satisfied in his life. "Your guidance was much appreciated. The next time we're both free, we'll have to schedule a repeat."

Malone nodded, his eyes sparkling. "It would be my pleasure."

Reaching into his pocket, Malone pulled out his phone and a pair of glasses, perching them on the end of his nose as he looked to the screen. "I read over the contract you sent me. Unfortunately, it's pretty clear-cut, except for what we talked about before. The only way out is for the contract to expire or for a new one to be proposed and approved. It's not exactly my area, but things like this usually can be renegotiated...at a cost."

Rowes perked up in his arms, instantly tensing. Izzy hushed him, squeezing him through the blanket. "Relax, baby."

"Which part of it is clear-cut?" asked Rowes, moving closer even as he turned to face Malone fully. "Sir," he added as an afterthought.

Malone smiled. "You don't have to call me 'Sir', Mr. Keppel. 'Malone' will do."

"Oh." Rowes pursed his lips. "Then call me Rowes."

"Thank you, I will." Malone glanced back at his phone. "So, as per the contract, you cannot engage in sexual intercourse with Isthmus or any of the other cast members. That's the part that's clear-cut."

Izzy could see the panic on Rowes' face as he looked at himself, then back to Izzy, his eyes going wide. "But what we just did…"

"Was intimate, but not *intercourse*," said Malone. "Legally, intercourse involves vaginal or anal penetration by anything from a finger, tongue, penis or object. Oral sex is actually deemed a separate act by legal standards, so that wouldn't count in your contract."

"But the toy…the plug," said Rowes, reaching for his ass and gasping as he shifted on the couch.

"*I* can't put it in, baby," said Izzy, grasping Rowes' hand and bringing it to his lips, "but any other non-cast member can. Like, let's say, Malone's boy — or yourself, if I asked you to."

Rowes gaped, his eyes shimmering with fresh tears before he threw his arms around Izzy's neck, hugging him tight. "You guys are geniuses."

His voice was muffled by Izzy's shirt, but Malone still chuckled.

"We can really be together?"

Izzy had never seen Rowes so hopeful, not even when he'd gotten the part in season one.

"There's no one on this planet who could stop us, baby. I want to prove that to you." Izzy reached into his pocket for the thing that had been hidden there all along. Throughout the scene it had been burning him through his pants, reminding him that it was there with every movement.

It was heavy, with interlocking metallic links that mimicked a tight chain inlaid with jewels. The jewels themselves were black, polished and cold to the touch. At the center, the chain met with a small O-ring and a charm shaped like a heart. Hidden within the heart was a small lock that held the entire thing together.

"There's only one key," said Izzy, holding the bracelet where Rowes could see it. It sparkled in the light, and his chest went tight. He'd bought it as soon as he'd become Rowes' Dominant, and the custom piece had just arrived the day before.

"It's beautiful," said Rowes, touching the locking charm. His hands were trembling, his eyes wide as he admired it for the first time.

"This means everything to me, Ro, the same as you do. Never take it off." Fumbling for the key, he unlocked the chain, wrapping it around Rowes' wrist. "Are you willing to accept it and me?"

"Do you even have to ask?" Rowes blinked rapidly, his eyes going shiny again. "I want to spend the rest of my life by your side, no matter what that means. Even if it meant never kissing you again, I wouldn't leave. I could never give you up."

Izzy locked the clasp, letting out a heavy breath as his own eyes burned. He'd never thought of buying a ring for someone, but the makeshift collar seemed more significant somehow. It wasn't just sharing a home and a life with someone. It was sharing every part of his soul.

"Oh no, I missed it!" Malone's boy cried from the door as he slipped into the room. He knelt next to their couch, leaning as close as he could to Rowes' wrist without touching him. "It's so beautiful. When Daddy told me Mr. Linton was looking for a collar for you, I was so excited. It's more gorgeous than I imagined." He touched the collar at his own throat, his eyes brimming.

"Come here, boy," said Malone. "Give them some space. *Jesus*." He held out his hand as he stood. "Keep in touch, Isthmus, and talk to Rowes about what to watch for with the drop. I'll only be a call away if something comes up."

Izzy turned back to Rowes as the door shut, cutting off a whisper of noise from the hall. "You look so beautiful, baby." He touched the charm before bringing it to his lips. "If the director has a problem with you wearing it on set, I'll chat with her. It's discreet enough that it should blend in, for the most part."

Rowes leveled him with a look that brooked no argument. "Problem or not, this is *never* coming off."

He closed his eyes, stroking the jewels. When the day ended, they would go back to their lives and the set, but everything was going to be different. There wasn't a thing in the world that could stop them.

Chapter Sixteen

Rowes

His heart was pounding as he clutched the wall, Clarke moving closer to him with every passing second. Time seemed to slow as he stared at the lips he was moments away from kissing, terror ricocheting through him as he contemplated running.

It wasn't the cameras or even the threat of a hard cock that was so petrifying, but the idea of kissing someone who wasn't Izzy. Izzy had done everything he could to ease Rowes' worries before getting on set. When the morning of the planned scene had arrived, Izzy hadn't given him a moment to think about it, not letting him leave their room until he'd kissed every inch of him.

It wasn't enough. Those kisses had cooled, and now there was a new pair of lips headed his way.

The plug that he'd put inside himself as Izzy had watched from across the room, jerking his cock as Rowes had moaned, was one claim. The collar on his wrist was the second, tucked safely beneath his sleeve and out of sight of the cameras.

But his lips were Izzy's, too, and now he had to loan them out to another man. It just didn't feel right. Visually, Clarke looked like he might be a kissable guy, with a rugged jawline and crystal blue eyes...but he wasn't Izzy.

Clarke sent him a concerned look, pausing when they were just inches apart. They couldn't speak with the microphones ready to pick up every sound, probably already catching Rowes' pounding heart.

They hadn't practiced before the cameras were ready to roll. There was no way he'd make Izzy watch that, and Rowes' may have convinced himself that he was ready. *I'm not ready.* Would he get fired for pissing himself? Because he was getting pretty close.

When Rowes glanced to the side, he caught sight of the camera and the director, the latter looking way too eager. She motioned her hand, urging him to get on with it.

"You okay?" asked Clarke. It was only a whisper, but it was enough.

"Cut," the director drawled, leaning forward on her chair and resting her cheek on her hand. "Okay, Rowes, can you look a little less terrified? It's a kiss, not a grenade."

Clarke snickered, ducking behind his hand as he circled back to his starting position. Rowes clutched the wall, unable to move as his knees trembled.

"But I'm behind enemy lines, right? I should be terrified." He didn't mention that his character Salem would never kiss the enemy. He was far too loyal to Kemble for that. It was a plot hole that was going to piss off a lot of fans.

"You guys have been going out for months on the sly and just happened to catch each other in the middle of a gunfight. Think surprise, disbelief and longing. There's too strong of a connection between you to let bullets get in the way."

"Okay, got it." Rowes rolled his shoulders, bringing his hand up so his gun rested against his chest. He was pretty sure he'd shot enough baddies for it to be empty three times over, but sometimes things happened like that on screen.

"Action."

Clarke rushed in, gun drawn, only to stop two paces away, his mouth open in shock. Rowes slipped into character a second too late, bringing his gun out before he realized just who he was looking at.

The man before him was his lover, on the other side of a gang war, like Romeo and Juliet. His heart pounded as the gun fell from his grip, Clarke dropping his own weapon before moving in close.

Rowes flickered his gaze to Clarke's lips, licking his own as he mustered every bit of arousal that he could and pushing longing into his gaze.

"Asha." The name fell from Rowes' lips, and he could almost believe his tone. He let the questions play over his face. *How? Why? What?* Clarke closed the distance between them, cupping Rowes' chin.

"Salem." Clarke breathed against his lips, the whisper like silk as he tilted his head. Rowes shuddered, clutching the hard brick against his back as he fought with himself. *Not here. Not now.* Kemble could be anywhere.

He gasped as Clarke's lips touched his, the softness and the warmth almost startling. Something stirred in his gut, like an electric jolt singing his nerves. His lips had always been sensitive—more than any part of his body.

Izzy.

Rowes opened his eyes instead of shutting them, trying to look for Izzy past the haze of Clarke and the cameras. His body went taut against his will, and he touched Clarke's leather jacket, ready to push him away. The lights burned his eyes, making them water as he caught the shimmer of the camera lens.

"Cut." The director let out a sigh, rubbing her forehead. She'd been getting more frazzled as the day progressed, her hair starting to go astray. "Okay, that was better, but Asha isn't electrifying Salem with a taser. This is a kiss after a long reunion, so less shock and more 'oh it's so good to see you'."

Clearing his throat, Rowes looked away, grabbing for his gun as Clarke took a step back. His hand was trembling as he touched the handle, tucking it into his palm. It was realistic enough to trick the cameras, but it was a useless replica. They only used real weapons when there was no risk of accidental injury. "Got it."

He could feel Izzy's eyes on him, and when he looked up, he couldn't hold his gaze. Izzy's face was unreadable on the outside, but the tension in his jaw and the way he was holding himself were huge clues for Rowes. He was pissed—furious, even.

Biting his lip, Rowes shook out his free hand, trying to sink back into his character. But instead of aligning his thoughts with Salem's as the director called 'action' again, all he could think of was Izzy.

He could close his eyes and pretend, but Clarke's kiss was nothing like Izzy's. How many shots would the director allow before she called it?

It turned out seven was not the lucky number, and as the director called 'cut' again, Rowes knew he was in for an extensive talking to. Izzy beat her to him, taking him by the wrist and squeezing. The collar dug into him, the metallic chain completely unforgiving as Izzy squeezed it through his shirt.

"What's going on, Rowes?" asked the director, keeping her voice low as she crossed her arms. She looked just as frustrated as he felt, a few strands of hair defying gravity and sticking straight up. Izzy's hand was steady on his, and it was the only thing that was keeping his tears back.

"I…" He trailed off, looking to Clarke. It wasn't just his ass on the line. Clarke was just starting out, and they could fire him easier than swatting a fly if they thought it was his problem.

Izzy leaned in, whispering directly into Rowes' ear. "Is it the plug? You can take it out if you need to."

Rowes widened his eyes, glancing at the director who was looking between them. "I'm good. I swear. I'll shake it off and try again. This will be the last shot, director. I promise."

Izzy went to pull away, but Rowes turned his hand, grasping him and holding tight. He was shaking, the bubbling of nerves in his gut more intense than anything he'd felt on set before. Tugging Izzy a step closer, Rowes stood on his toes to whisper to him, glancing around but ignoring the gazes on them.

"I want it to be you."

Izzy narrowed his eyes as he stepped back, his pupils blown wide. He only squeezed Rowes' hand once before he pulled him in for a hug that was much too brief. People parted for him as he retreated behind the cameras, still wearing his gear from his earlier shoot. The intensity from his character was still in his gaze, burning into Rowes as he retreated to his starting position.

Readying himself, Rowes brought his gun up, pressing it against his chest as he leveled his back against the wall. The call 'action' was a distant one, and the next thing he knew, Clarke's lips were on his.

He felt himself clamming up, the tension rolling through him like an unstoppable force. He clamped down on it, but it slipped through his fingers, numbing his character to a bumbling idiot who couldn't fucking act. He was going to get them all fired, and it would be all his fault. No one would ever hire him again—not even for a toothpaste commercial.

"Hey!"

Clarke jerked back, turning to Izzy, who had settled against the opposite wall on set with his gun leveled at Clarke's chest. He had his jacket on again, his makeup perfect after a day in grime. His eyes were glimmering in the set lights, Kemble in his every move. It was beautiful.

Izzy closed the space between them in a few short strides, the cameras tracking him like it had been the plan all along. The director bit her lip, leaning forward in her chair as she let it go on.

We're rolling with it, then. Clarke seemed to catch up a second later as Izzy grabbed him by the shoulder, twisting him away and nailing him with a punch to the face that looked a little too realistic.

Clarke dropped to the ground with a groan, stilling as he settled in the dirt. His lip was shiny with blood, a smear of it on Izzy's knuckles as he grabbed Rowes' jacket, pinning him to the wall with a move that was all strength.

"You're doing it all wrong," said Izzy, licking his lips and grinning. "No one touches you but me."

There was more than just his character behind his words, the pure possession silencing everything but Rowes' beating heart. Wrapping a hand behind Izzy's neck, he pulled him in, dragging him in for the only kiss he'd ever wanted.

He couldn't stop the moan as they touched and Izzy possessed him, ripping his strength from his grasp and taking control. There was no easy pressure or careful thoughts, only teeth clacking and the taste of blood as Izzy pushed his tongue into Rowes' mouth.

Fuck. He was hard in moments, and hopefully, the camera didn't catch it as Izzy explored his mouth, touching and tasting every bit. And as he tried to draw back, Rowes held on, deepening the kiss and drinking down Izzy's moan.

It was everything he'd ever dreamed about, with their friends and the cameras looking on and every single one of them silent. Right now, no one was judging them or bitching. They were enjoying it as much as the fans were bound to.

He was panting by the time Izzy forced their lips apart, leaning their foreheads together. His heart raced, his lungs burning for air as he closed his eyes, trailing his hands down Izzy's back and hugging him tight. They were already flush, but he didn't want to risk Izzy pulling back. The cameras would pick everything up, including the way he was throbbing.

"What do you say we get out of here?" asked Izzy, giving Rowes one last peck before he reached for the gun at his waistband.

Rowes nodded, barely able to play along as he scrambled for his own gun, subtly adjusting himself as he bent over. *I'm on set and I'm so fucking hard.* He hoped his jeans were forgiving enough not to completely give him away.

Izzy turned, kicking Clarke as he strolled past the camera like a predator. Clarke groaned softly, curling up as he hopefully exaggerated the hit.

"You coming?"

Licking his lips, Rowes nodded, tucking his gun away and running after Izzy to keep up. As soon as he reached him, he slung his arm around Izzy's shoulder in exactly the way Salem would do to Kemble.

"Cut."

Rowes stumbled as soon as the director said it, almost hyperventilating as his breathing picked up tenfold. Izzy touched his hand, sliding his finger under the links of the collar and tugging.

"You okay?" asked Izzy, putting himself between Rowes and the director as she strolled toward them followed by a half dozen or so other people. Clarke was picking himself off the ground and shaking off the hit, sending a grin their way as he sucked the blood from his lip.

"Why couldn't you do that on the first take?" asked the director, scratching the back of her neck. Her face was flushed as she looked between them with glowing eyes. "I'm glad all that practice paid off, but we're in for one hell of a rewrite if the producers okay it. We'll call it a day so I can show them what we've got. You want to take a look?"

Rowes didn't want to see it. He *couldn't.*

"If you're giving us the rest of the day off, I'm going to take it," said Izzy, grinning at the director. "I don't think that's ever happened before." He winked, his usual calm self in place.

Rowes didn't know how he could do it. Acting was one thing, but this was something else entirely. He couldn't just will away an erection, although it was starting to go down with the taste of Izzy dissipating. He licked his lips, catching the last remnants of it.

"I might change my mind," said the director, looking over her shoulder. "If the producers don't go for this, we'll just end up reshooting it all. I'm not deleting that bit, though. No siree!"

If they stayed any longer, Rowes was going to die of humiliation. Using Izzy as a shield, he adjusted himself again so he'd be less conspicuous, conscious of the many eyes on them. The rules about no cellphones were fierce but he'd already seen more than one set shot pop up in a fan video online.

"Let's go," said Rowes softly, his voice sounding much too weak. Izzy nodded, clenching his jaw. He may have looked calm, but Rowes knew the signs. His pupils were dilated, sweat gathering in his hairline, the grip on his false gun much too tight.

In the trailer, they changed quickly, Rowes managing to keep his hands to himself as Izzy watched him, his dark gaze catching every wince when the plug rubbed him just right. It felt bigger than it had on set, every nerve alight as it shifted, and the heaviness making him work to keep it inside.

"Does it hurt?" asked Izzy, already in his street clothes and leaning against the door frame. Thank goodness Rowes had been avoiding looking his way as he dressed, because he looked delicious, even in clothes, with the bit of dirt and makeup from set clinging to him and his hair styled to perfection. They never would have gotten out of the trailer if he'd spotted him naked.

"No," said Rowes, letting out a small laugh. "Not at all." It wasn't even uncomfortable. He didn't want to brag or anything, but he felt like he'd been built to wear a plug—or maybe it was that Izzy had picked the perfect one.

"Why do you keep flinching then?" Izzy stopped Rowes with a hand on his naked hip, his pants still around his ankles where he was trying to fix them because he'd realized he'd put them on backward in his rushed state. "You don't have to put a brave face on for me, baby."

"Every time it moves, it's like you're fucking me," said Rowes, laughing as Izzy pressed his lips together. Two could play at the game Izzy had been doing all day, but Rowes was determined to win. "And if I relax, it slides out just a bit, only for me to suck it back inside when I clench. It's getting me really worked up, just like you would."

"Am I a good fuck?"

Laughing, Rowes tugged his pants up before wiggling his ass and letting out a little moan. He tilted his head back, licking his lips as he let his eyes slide part-way shut. "Yeah, Iz. That's the spot."

Izzy curled his hand around Rowes' shirt, pulling him off balance. "You're playing with fire, Rowes."

"I know." Rowes smirked, glancing toward the door. Right now he was *safe* and ready to push some boundaries. "What are you going to do? Push me up against a wall and make me come? You almost did that already."

He hadn't really been close to coming, but Izzy didn't have to know that. He'd been too scared at the time to be anywhere close, but now? He was on top of the world.

"You're a fucking tease," said Izzy, grabbing him by the back of the neck and tugging him toward the door. "You know you're going to get it when we get back to the room."

Rowes giggled, turning to kiss Izzy on the neck before he could open the door. Lingering, he dragged his teeth over his pulse, licking the sweaty stretch of skin before he pulled away, giggling as he pulled the door wide and stepped outside.

There were people moving all about, most sticking around as they set up for tomorrow or for other scenes that day. There were way too many people around for Izzy to do anything too obvious, and it only spurred Rowes on. *I'll show you a tease.*

When Rowes looked to Izzy, he swallowed, his throat clicking. Izzy's eyes were dark, his face unreadable as he stepped after him, his body moving with purpose. "Push me, Ro. See what happens."

Is that an invitation? It certainly sounds like one. Rowes grinned, clasping his hands behind his back. "I would *never.*"

There were only a few people brave enough to interrupt them on their way off set, but Izzy plowed through the conversations at record speed, dragging Rowes along by his hand. His grip was tight, his thumb roaming the space beneath the bracelet and tugging on it. It was on display for everyone who cared to look, but even if they did, they would only see a fancy piece of jewelry.

"I'm surprised you didn't want to watch the playback," said Rowes, slowing as they reached the cusp of an alley they'd nearly kissed in before. There were only a few people outside, and it was getting dark, the sun peeking just over the edge of a few low buildings.

Some of the scenes had to be shot at night, and they were just getting prepped for that, but luckily, they were done for the day. Maybe everyone else would be on pause until the director had her way.

Leaning against the brick, he dragged Izzy to a stop. The rugged blocks were warm from the last of the summer's sun, keeping any possible chill from the impending night away. "I thought you would have wanted to watch yourself fuck my mouth with your tongue." He licked his lips with exaggerated slowness. "I can still taste you."

"Fuck." Izzy's grip went tight enough to bruise as he cast a look over his shoulder before dragging Rowes deeper into the alley. There were no lights in the spot, and most of the daylight was blocked. Their company was a single dumpster that reeked of piss and rotten fruit. The cricket beneath their feet went silent as Izzy pushed him against the wall, his hands rough.

"What are you going to do?" Rowes should have been looking for people, but he was caught in Izzy's gaze. He'd never seen him so frazzled or close to his limit. And he couldn't help but wiggle his ass and push that much more.

"Get on your knees."

Rowes bit his lip, peering at the ground as Izzy flipped their positions and pushed Rowes between his legs. He was hard, his loose jeans doing nothing to hide the evidence.

I did that. Rowes grinned, reaching for the zipper on Izzy's jeans and running his nail down it. His cock jumped at the touch as if it could spring free and touch him on its own.

"Strike one. Get on your *knees*. I won't ask again." Izzy's voice was strained as he clenched his hands into fists.

"What are you going to do if I don't listen? Spank me?" Rowes giggled softly, a rush of adrenaline going straight to his head as Izzy wrapped a hand around his neck, forcing him to his knees with brute strength alone. When he hit the gravel, Rowes barely felt the sting of contact.

Rowes rocked as he was released, shuffling ahead until Izzy's zipper was only inches from him. Licking his lips, he held Izzy's gaze, dragging his tongue slowly back and forth.

"Strike two," said Izzy, gripping Rowes' hair and jerking his head all the way back. He was bent over, his position every bit as Dominant as he was. "I should get you another collar so I can tie you to the bed and make sure you never leave." He touched the bracelet with his free hand, pulling it harshly.

At this rate, Rowes was going to have permanent bruises on his wrist. The tug stung, but he relished it, letting out a moan as something sparked within him. He'd been off all day, but now he was high and floating, Izzy consuming every bit of his thoughts.

Something crashed beyond the alley and Rowes jerked back, moving to his feet as Izzy straightened. Their surroundings flitted into awareness as Rowes huffed, the smell of garbage and old piss suddenly overwhelming.

"Not here."

Nodding, Rowes swallowed, adjusting himself the best he could as Izzy did the same. The walk back to hotel was going to be so fucking awkward. He tugged his T-shirt down as far as it would go, and it just barely covered his bulge.

"When we get back to the room, you're mine," said Izzy, slinging his arm casually around Rowes' shoulders as they stepped out of the alley. He had the sense to nod at a nearby intern who was bustling around so quickly that her cheeks were flushed from the heat.

"I'm looking forward to it."

Chapter Seventeen

Izzy

He had Rowes stripped and sprawled on the bed in under a minute, grabbing both of their cellphones and putting them on silent. He didn't give a shit if the director called them all back for a reshoot. As far as he was concerned, eight hours of filming had been enough.

Rowes giggled, bringing his knees to his chest before letting them flop wide. The view showed off his hard cock that was bright red and his plugged ass with Izzy's initials at the base. Seeing his name there made him throb. He owned that part of Rowes — every part.

"I should have got you a cock cage instead," said Izzy, putting a false amount of anger into his voice. The truth was, Rowes acting like this — all brave and slutty — was like crack, but it was fun to pretend to be angry and ignite that fire that made Rowes burn hotter.

"What's that?" asked Rowes, stroking his cock from base to tip before letting out a little moan. He was insatiable. "Sounds fun."

His sweet, innocent Rowes. He hadn't realized how inexperienced he was until they started talking kink. It was hard to set limits when you'd barely explored yourself in the vanilla world with a steady partner. Luckily, Rowes was a fast learner.

"It does, doesn't it," said Izzy, locking the door and slipping the chain into place before he strolled to his suitcase. Malone had recommended a few things for them if they ever scened in a place that wasn't soundproofed.

Among his clothing, he'd stashed a gag. With black straps and a red mouthpiece, it was an intimidating device. Rowes wouldn't be able to spill more than a muffled scream past it.

Grabbing the gag, he set it on the bedside table in clear view. Rowes stared at it, his eyes going wide, even as he stroked himself.

"Do you remember your non-verbal safewords?" asked Izzy, trailing his fingers down the middle of Rowes' chest. Rowes shivered at the touch, goosebumps breaking over his skin as his eyes fluttered shut. "Not so brave now, are you? Are you afraid that there might be consequences to your actions?"

Izzy had made a list of rules for himself that he wouldn't cross with Rowes, and he'd almost broken one. He was never doing anything in public again, except for simple touches or a planned kiss. Even if they weren't breaking Rowes' contract, there was a line that he wanted to keep from the public.

Except for that kiss. He'd had Rowes' first kiss between them in the privacy of the hotel room, and no one would ever get to see that. The kiss in front of the cameras was all he was willing to share.

"I tap you, knock something twice or snap my fingers," said Rowes, swallowing as he looked back to the gag. "Is that going in my mouth? I can just stay quiet."

Chuckling, Izzy reached for Rowes' cock, squeezing it as hard as he imagined a cage would. Rowes let out a high whine, grabbing at Izzy's hands.

"Hurts."

"Are you tapping out?" asked Izzy, easing his grip a tad.

"Fuck no." Rowes got the same look he'd had when he'd yelled at Malone's boy. His lips pressed together as he clenched his jaw and narrowed his eyes. Through it all, he groaned, the sound louder than a television would be.

"I don't think you realize how loud you are, baby," said Izzy, clamping down again and letting Rowes' whimpers wash over him. "The entire hotel will be at our door, calling the police because I'm giving your ass a little slap. I don't want to end up on the cover of some tabloid. We'll talk about caging your cock another time," continued Izzy, releasing him and giving the head a little flick that made Rowes twitch his entire body. "For now, put that gag in your mouth, and I'll buckle it up. I don't want it too tight—just enough for you to feel it."

After staring at it like it was some sort of alien protoplasm, Rowes finally pushed it into his mouth, his teeth grazing the rubbery surface as he pulled his lips back and grimaced.

"It can't be that bad."

Rowes slipped it out of his mouth and licked his lips. "It tastes like plastic."

"Does it hurt your jaw at all?" Izzy asked, waiting until Rowes shook his head. "Put it back in, then. Next time, I'll come on it for you first, so you'll have something to suck on." He chuckled as Rowes screwed up his face even more.

"Not a fan of cum?" asked Izzy, reaching for the buckle, pulling it just tight enough so the gag wouldn't slip around and carefully keeping Rowes' hair out of the clasp.

Shaking his head, Rowes touched the thick strap, trailing his fingers along it until he found the buckle.

"There's a quick release here if you feel like a non-verbal safeword isn't enough." He moved Rowes' hands to the clasp. "If you have any trouble breathing, I need you to safeword right away, okay?"

Rowes nodded, giving him a thumbs up.

"Excellent. Now get on your hands and knees with your legs together, and push that cock of yours through your legs so I can see it." Izzy licked his lips as Rowes followed his orders, tucking himself so his balls and cock were easily accessible from behind.

The teasing at the set had gotten Izzy riled, but Rowes following orders was the real drug. Every movement was for Izzy, and every breath was his to control. He tried not to let it get to his head.

"You already had your warmup on set, so I'll start right in." He brought his hand down on Rowes' ass, smirking as he jumped and let out a muffled yelp. Rowes widened his stance, probably to make himself more accessible, but it let his cock slip too far forward and out of Izzy's spanking reach.

"See this?" Izzy grabbed Rowes cock from behind, tugging it back into position before tapping Rowes' hip. He didn't let go until Rowes' legs were back in place, his cock tucked behind them where it was supposed to be. "If you let it slip again, every spank will be on your balls. I won't be pulling my hits, either."

Rowes shuffled his legs even closer, wobbling a bit as Izzy moved on the bed.

"Good boy."

He watched the shudder that went through Rowes at those words and the way his arms trembled. His cock twitched, too, a drop of pre-cum making its way along the back of his thigh. Izzy watched it fall until it was caught in the little dip behind his knee, pooling there like milky pearl.

"You like that," said Izzy, watching fascinated as the plug twitched when Rowes clenched around it. He would have given anything to tug that plug out and guide his cock inside bare, fucking Rowes hard as he screamed through the gag.

Letting out a shaky breath, Izzy turned away, rolling his shoulders as he gave himself a moment to steady. Malone had warned him he could get in over his head and push himself or Rowes too far if he didn't read the signals or if he let his cock get the best of him. He could already feel it happening—his desire for Dominance overtaking his rational thought.

"I liked your ass better when it was painted red," said Izzy, flexing his hands as he focused his gaze on Rowes' ass. There was still a lingering bruise from his last spanking on the lower part where Izzy had focused a lot of his attention. "Let's start there."

He didn't give Rowes time to adjust or breathe, laying five spanks in quick succession in the same spot.

His hand tingled as Rowes jerked his hips, his ass slowly starting to flush as Izzy stepped back, his chest heaving.

The color started slowly at the center where the first hit had been, flushing darker as the mottled look grew until a wavering replica of his hand was imprinted on Rowes' flesh.

"I own you, Ro," said Izzy, dropping his voice into a growl. "Inside. Outside—every fucking part." He raised his hand, doing the same to the opposite cheek and watching the color flow. Rowes was groaning steadily, his voice a muffled sob as one elbow gave out. He scrambled upright again before reaching to re-tuck his cock.

"So fucking good for me."

There were tears on Rowes' cheeks, his eyes bloodshot and big. "What's your color? Nod for green or shake your head for yellow or red."

There was no hesitation as Rowes nodded, a bit of drool dripping from his lower lip. The only thing that would have been better was if Izzy had gotten a gag with a see-through ball so he could have watched Rowes lick at it as he struggled not to drool.

Or even better, a spider gag to hold his mouth open while Izzy slowly worked his cock inside. He'd have to take his time—Rowes had never taken a cock in his life, and Izzy wasn't exactly small. But every minute of slow patience would be worth it.

He could call Rowes good all fucking day if it made him look like this. Izzy's cock throbbed at the sight, and he reached into his jeans to adjust himself before thinking better of it and popping the button then dropping the zipper. Sighing with relief, he leaned closer, biting into Rowe's ass where his cheek was still hot and flushed.

Rowes let out a squeak, tensing as Izzy lingered and sucked, blood blooming beneath the surface in a purple hue. He let go with a wet smack, moving to the other side and doing the same thing.

"You look good—so fucking good." How could he resist any longer with Rowes' cock right there and leaking? "Don't come."

That was all the warning he gave before he grasped Rowes' cock, tilting it back an extra few degrees before sucking it into his mouth. *Fuck* he tasted good. Sweet and salty in all the right ways, with that lingering thickness that Izzy knew he'd be able to taste even after he'd brushed his teeth.

Whimpering, Rowes squirmed, trying to pull away as he kept his thighs slotted close. Izzy held tight, making sure Rowes wouldn't be able to pull away, even if he tried.

"You taste so fucking good, baby. Why is every part of you so perfect?" Izzy went to work, moving on his side for a better angle and kissing up and down Rowes' shaft. Every time a drop of pre-cum beaded at the head, he licked it away, savoring the taste with a moan. Rowes twitched his hips almost constantly, his steady stream of cries muffled behind the gag.

Izzy hadn't been exaggerating. Without the gag, they would have had more than one interruption by that point. But those muffled yells were music to his ears.

Licking his lips, Izzy sucked Rowes' cock back into his mouth, tapping his balls in the imitation of a slap, only a much softer version. Rowes squeaked, his legs trembling as he jerked forward and almost out of Izzy's grasp.

"Are you close?" asked Izzy, circling the base and squeezing tight as he repeated the motion, holding Rowes' orgasm off as he nodded frantically and tugged. Izzy dragged him right back by his cock, never ceasing his sucking. "You asked for this, Rowes," said Izzy as he pulled back, easing off the bed. "When you asked me to kiss you on set, then taunted me in that alley, you asked for it."

He wished he knew what Rowes was thinking. Maybe where and when the next hit would come or if he'd take the gag out, only to push his cock inside next. That had been his own thoughts originally. *But no.*

When Rowes turned to him in question, his face flushed and streaked with tears, Izzy pulled his own cock out of his pants, jerking hard and fast. Pleasure crashed over him, Rowes' gaze sending him beyond the moon as he started to shoot almost immediately. He'd been waiting too long to hold back.

He clambered up, aiming his cock at the bruising handprints as he started to come, shooting over the marks in thick ropes. Before he could finish, he thrust his cock between Rowes' cheeks, painting the base of the plug. White dripped over the engraved initials and the narrow neck that was holding Rowes' open just enough that he could hopefully feel it.

"Perfect." Wiping his hands on Rowes' back, he turned from the bed, heading to the small sitting area where there was a second television. It didn't take long to find the remote or the typical action channel that cycled through the same ten movies. "What do you think? *The Mummy* or *The Bourne Identity*?"

He loved them both and had seen them enough that he didn't even need to watch the screen to picture what was going on. If he had anything to say about it, there would have been more movies in both franchises, even if some of the fans thought they were better left without additional sequels.

"I'll order some food for us, too. And I'm thinking a cheesecake for dessert. We have to celebrate that awesome script rewrite today." He grinned, glancing to Rowes, who was looking at him with absolute disbelief. "You can take the gag out and sit on the floor here." He pointed at his feet.

Rowes grabbed the buckle of the gag, pulling it off and wiping his mouth with his arm. "Aren't you gonna get me off?" He splayed his legs as he sat back, letting his cock spring forward with a sigh. It looked painful, the flush at the tip nearly purple.

"Nope," said Izzy, grinning as Rowes glared. "And you aren't going to touch yourself, either." He added as Rowes' hand twitched, and he looked to his cock. "You were naughty today, so you don't get to come. Me, on the other hand? I'm just getting started."

God, he loved taking Rowes off guard, and he responded so well to it. He looked half like he was relaxed in subspace, while tittering with a frustration that was nearly palpable. Izzy had zero sympathy.

Chapter Eighteen

Rowes

Izzy was driving him insane. Truthfully, his sanity had snuck out of the window what felt like hours before, and since that time, he'd been nothing but a moaning, whimpering mass of pure nothingness. It was almost simple to be in this state, except for the side of infuriating longing.

"How is your fruit?" asked Izzy as he pressed another strawberry to Rowes' lips. He'd fed an entire bowl of the stuff to him, pushing his fingers inside with the fruit and sometimes stroking his tongue a few times.

"My cock hurts, Iz." Rowes took the berry, digging his fingers into his thighs. He'd been so hard for so long that he was almost dizzy with it. Even when their food had arrived, Izzy had left him kneeling at the couch, hardly letting him move at all. He'd only been sheltered by the couch, so close to discovery that it was maddening.

Snapping or coming. One of them would happen, but he wasn't sure which. When he did come, he was pretty sure he was going to pass out from it — or maybe his cock would fall off. Either way, he was fucked.

"That's a weird answer to my question. I didn't come on the strawberries, Ro. That's just white chocolate. Are they not good?"

Is it possible to hate someone just as much as I love them?

"They're delicious. Thank you." Rowes rolled his eyes as he said it, putting every bit of sarcasm he could muster into his voice. He took another as Izzy pressed it to his lips, chewing quickly before swallowing.

"Are you being ungrateful?"

Blanching, Rowes looked up, worrying his lip as he caught Izzy's gaze. He looked a little unimpressed. *It's not my fault. Just let me come.* He was sure he would get another spanking if he said *that* out loud, and that would *not* help his situation.

"No," said Rowes, ducking his head and rubbing at his thigh. This was a part of their new relationship that he loved the most. Izzy had always looked after him, but Rowes had never gotten the chance to push back at all and have some fun. He'd been too worried he would ruin their relationship. "I'm never ungrateful."

"Okay," said Izzy, scratching at his chin. His own meal was a fancy salad with bits of chicken that he occasionally slipped to Rowes. His lips glistened with dressing and one random poppy seed. "Come here then."

He patted his leg, leaning so Rowes would have room before he set the dishes with the remnants of their foot to the side. Rowes surged into his lap, wincing as he moved his legs for the first time in a while. He'd kept shuffling and moving a bit as he'd sat on the floor, but apparently, it hadn't been enough.

His toes tingled, his calves aching and weak as he settled into Izzy's lap, facing him so their groins were together. The fabric of Izzy's jeans scraped against his oversensitive cock, and he flinched away before it could become too much.

"You know, you'd be much more comfortable without pants." Rowes wiggled his hips, his cock waving back and forth from the movement. "See? Super comfy."

"You're a brat," said Izzy, grabbing Rowes' hips and guiding him so there was more space between their groins. When he reached for his zipper, Rowes perked up with a grin.

"You won't regret it, Iz." He licked his lips as Izzy slowly exposed his cock to the air. He was hard again and so fucking beautiful that Rowes just wanted to kiss every inch.

"You're right, this is nice...airy," said Izzy, fisting his cock and stroking it from base to tip before leaning it so their cockheads touched. Rowes shuddered at the touch that was like a thousand needles of pleasure.

Our cocks are touching. Oh God. They were one step away from grinding.

Izzy started jerking himself in earnest, running his thumb over the head before squeezing the base of his shaft, his cock going harder and harder as he sped up. Rowes licked his lips, fascinated as he watched the pre-cum well up before Izzy polished it away.

"Do you want me to get it wet for you?" asked Rowes, unable to tear his gaze away or even reach for himself as he throbbed. He preferred a wet jerk himself, but he'd heard some guys like it dry. Wetter was better, in his opinion.

"No need," said Izzy, a groan behind his teeth as he inched his hips off the couch. "All I need to do is look at you, and I'm already close to coming. That pretty cock of yours is so hard and lonely. Fuck, it makes me want to come."

Izzy let out a groan, tilting his head back as he breathed sharply through his nose. "Fuck yeah."

He aimed his cock as he started to shoot, his cum coating Rowes in a way that was so reminiscent of their scene. It was as if Izzy wanted to mark him — claim him — and make sure every man would know he was already taken.

"You like that, baby?" asked Izzy as he recovered, reaching for Rowes' cock and slicking it with cum. "You like it hard and fast, I bet. Just you wait. By the time I'm done with you, you won't remember your own name."

"Oh fuck." Rowes was so close, teetering on the edge as his cock was coated and jerked with the perfect amount of pressure. He curled his toes, biting his lip as his orgasm drew close enough to taste. "Fuck, I'm gonna come."

"Thanks for letting me know," said Izzy, pulling his hand away as if he'd been burned. "Good boy."

His chest heaved, his cock throbbing and aching as his impending orgasm was interrupted yet again. Izzy even had the audacity to wipe his hand clean on Rowes' belly, grinning as he did it.

"Back on the floor, Ro."

"Fucking hell." His legs were trembling as he tried to step back, his cock so hard that he was sure he was going to explode. "Iz, *please*."

"Did you need a pillow?"

He'd never taken Izzy for a sadist. He'd been so fucking wrong about a lot of things, though — like how much he liked it.

Tears rolled down his cheeks before he could stop them, and he let out a sob as he dropped back to his knees next to the couch. His legs hurt like hell, but it was nothing to the ache of his cock. It was actually painful, something that he'd never experienced just from being hard.

"How about you sit cross-legged? It will be easier on your knees, especially with you shaking like that. Did you want a robe?"

"No!" Rowes almost shouted. Was he shaking? He touched his leg. His whole body was vibrating, his muscles so sore that fresh tears streaked down his cheeks. His teeth chattered.

"What's wrong, baby?" asked Izzy softly, carding his fingers through Rowes' hair.

"Let me come," Rowes whispered, pleading with everything he had. The carpet was rough against his sore ass, offering no relief as the plug shifted inside. He squeaked as it rubbed against his spot that was so sore and sensitive.

"Anything but that. I'll give you the world, but you don't get to come."

A sob broke free of his throat, his shoulders shaking as he started to cry in earnest. The fog that had been creeping at the corners of his thoughts swept in, taking control of everything at once.

The throb dulled, the tears on his cheeks going warm as the fresh ones kept coming. Something loosened in his chest, and suddenly, he was breaking down.

Izzy's warm arms were around him, laying him on the soft bed as he was cradled and cuddled like the most precious thing in the world. Every worry faded away with his tears, Izzy taking the burden that had been weighing him down since he'd signed the contract.

"Are we gonna make it, Isthmus?" His voice was shaky—barely understandable.

"Of course."

How could he be so fucking calm? His voice so steady and sweet? He must've known for sure to be that confident.

"First, I want you to come for me." Izzy wrapped his hand around Rowes' cock a moment later, and Rowes couldn't hold back. Three strokes later he was jerking uncontrollably, spilling into Izzy's palm as his vision darkened away.

"I'm never leaving your side."

Chapter Nineteen

Rowes

He'd silenced his phone once already on the way from their hotel room, but it rang a second time as Izzy guided him across traffic to their cab, an arm slung over his shoulders.

"Who is it?" Izzy asked, lifting his hand to block the sun from Rowes' face. The gesture put a smile on his lips, the warm feeling in Rowes' gut only spreading. Scenes were one thing, but it was the little things that he really loved. Hand-feeding was probably at the top of that list.

"The director," said Rowes, accepting the call and putting the phone to his ear. "Hello?" Hopefully, she hadn't been trying for too long. Izzy and him had been busy for quite a while.

"Have you heard from Lorena?" asked the director, straight and to the point like she always was.

Rowes blinked. "Uh — no?" The last time he'd talked to her she had glared up a storm and had basically called him a liar—that, and bringing up his closeness with Izzy with the director. That had been way out of line, and he still hadn't decided how he was going to handle it.

"I was on a wild goose chase of phone calls this morning trying to track you down. She wouldn't answer her phone, and neither would you or your boy toy." She let out a sigh.

Boy toy? That was as perfect a term as Rowes had ever heard. He snickered, elbowing Izzy, who looked at him in confusion.

"Anyway," The director continued, "Don't go to the location today. Just come straight to my office, and I'll meet you there."

Her office? She couldn't have been talking about the production company's home base, which was hours away by plane. She probably meant her temporary office that she'd set up out of her hotel. Apparently, she'd managed to get one of the board rooms where there was lots of space for meetings and whatever else she got up to. Rowes tried to keep his attendance to mandatory things only.

"It sounds like bad news," said Rowes, his stomach dropping. They were probably doing a script rewrite or something, but he usually wasn't called in for those. The director and producers had the final say, and as far as he was concerned, he was fine with following orders.

But Izzy had thrown a wrench in the season and the show itself.

"We'll see." She hung up with a click and Rowes stared at his phone as Izzy opened the door for him and he slid into the back seat of the cab.

"What sounds bad?" asked Izzy as he slid into the opposite seat. He was bouncing his knee, but he didn't look nervous. If he was feeling anything like Rowes, then he was brimming with energy.

"Not sure," said Rowes before turning to the cab driver. "Can you take us to the Fairmont?"

Izzy's frown deepened as he slid into the middle spot and buckled his seat belt. The cab driver pulled into traffic, heading the opposite way that Rowes had expected when he'd woken up in Izzy's arms.

Shrugging, Rowes looked out of the window, trying to shake off the sinking feeling. It wasn't just the call, either. He'd been high on Izzy for days, and he was coming down...hard. Izzy had talked to him about it and explained what a drop would feel like, but it was still different to go through it.

He'd expected sluggish thoughts and maybe having a harder time smiling, but he was a touch nauseated. That, and there was a headache brewing at the base of his skull.

"They probably want a reshoot," said Izzy, leaning back and looking like the picture of comfort. "That kiss was way too smoking hot, and it melted the film. Or they want it from a different angle where it'll look less like I'm trying to suck your soul out of your body."

Rowes let out a sigh, unable to convince his lips to smile. He'd felt low before and had been a little lost after their first scene, but it seemed to be kicking his ass extra hard today. He clenched his hand on his thigh where he knew there was a bruise. It was almost numb, even as he dug deep.

Weird. An hour ago he'd been concerned about breakfast and kisses, but he was pretty sure he would never be able to eat again. And the sunshine flitting through the window was way too bright, making his headache flare.

"Ro?"

Blinking, Rowes looked to Izzy, not knowing if Izzy had been talking to him or if that was the first time he'd tried to get his attention. He sank a little bit deeper. After everything Izzy had done for him, he couldn't even pay attention.

"Are you feeling okay?"

Rowes shook his head. His gut was tight, nausea crawling up his throat like he'd eaten something off at breakfast. And fuck, did he ever want to cry. If there was a death of a family member scene he needed to film, today was the day.

"I think you're dropping," said Izzy, leaning closer and speaking quietly so the cab driver wouldn't hear them over the radio. He was their usual driver, so he was used to their clinginess. And he'd mentioned that he didn't watch much television, so that was always a plus.

"I was fine this morning," said Rowes, scratching at a hole in his jeans. Everything seemed to be wearing thin, even his clothes. Then again, they were a designer brand that had been made to look like he'd just gotten sweaty fighting off a wildebeest or something.

"I don't feel like myself." He rubbed at his chest where a persistent ache was setting in, almost stronger than the nausea. "Last night I was more me than I've ever been, but now?" He dropped his face into his hands, doing everything he could not to let the tears go.

"What if that wasn't me? And it was all just another persona, like the ones I throw on every time I'm in front of the camera. It's like I'm going to wake up and find that you are just a figment of my imagination." He tried to pull away from Izzy, but his Dom held him tight, steadying him.

"You know what I love most about you?" asked Izzy, his voice soft as he stared out at the passing cars.

His lashes were long, touching his cheeks each time he blinked. Rowes had never taken the time to really look at him, his presence steady and constant.

"No." Rowes sniffed, wiping at his cheeks. There wasn't much to love most days. He was a placeholder in a lot of his life — something for fans to look at, put on their desktop computers or talk about at work.

"I always know," said Izzy, a smile touching his lips. "When you're acting, you enthrall people, and they can't see the real you behind the character. That's never happened with me. When I watch you in front of the camera, it's almost like seeing double. I see your character, hear their words, but underneath, it's all you. The little smiles, the sparkle in your eyes when you really think something's funny, it blows me away. You never could fool me."

Izzy chuckled, leaning over to rest his head against Rowes'. "When it's just you and me, there is no double. Last night, that was all you. Every whimper, every tear was all you, and it was so perfect that I could never doubt you. I just hope your ass isn't too sore for today."

This time Rowes did chuckle, his chest aching for a whole different reason. Izzy always seemed to know the exact right thing to say and when to say it.

"Feel better?" asked Izzy, seemingly ready to risk a kiss as he dragged his lips against Rowes' hair.

"You aren't just saying that, right?" He couldn't see double when Izzy was acting, but he thought he knew the real Izzy. Izzy's character was him, only with a gun with a heaping pile of excessive intensity.

"I could write it down if you don't trust it," said Izzy. "I could send it to you in a card every day until you believed it. You know I can't lie to you. I'm not as good as Connley."

That part was the truth. Izzy was a shitty liar at the best of times. Some of his most frequent retakes were when he was lying on set. Connley was the opposite, though. He was on a whole different level he was so good. He would probably be able to fool a polygraph with ease.

"True," said Rowes, biting his lip as he looked from under his lashes.

Izzy chuckled, pushing at his shoulder. "You weren't supposed to agree with me."

The cab rolled to a stop and Izzy unbuckled both of their seatbelts, helping Rowes out of the car. Rowes took his hand with a grin that felt much more real. Touch had always helped him, but touching Izzy was the best part of his life.

"I'm not going to keel over. I'm fine." When Rowes said it, he realized that he actually meant it. He felt so much better than he had when the director had called. That had been like sugar crashing after twelve hours of filming.

"You let me know if you're feeling down again," said Izzy, tilting his head back to stare at the hotel. It was a step or two above theirs, with a chauffeur and what looked like a guard next to the entrance. "I'm on the wrong side of the camera."

After asking the doorman where they should go, they were ushered directly down a set of hallways to what appeared to be a boardroom. The door itself looked like someone had painted over rich wood, dabbing some gold paint on each bit of trim so it looked expensive. The original wood probably would have looked nicer, but Rowes was the type to keep a scrubby pad for his dishes in a little green frog holder, so his opinion probably didn't count.

As they approached, the director stepped out of the room, letting the door fall shut behind her. She was shaking her head, her hair even more frazzled than it had been after the multiple kiss retakes.

"Rowes," she said as soon as she saw them. "And Isthmus." She bit her lip, tapping her chin with one finger. "Maybe it's good that you're here, too. Maybe someone with an extra appendage can get a point across to these idiots." She let out a huff. "Good luck."

With one last shake of her head, she turned away, strolling toward the exit with her running shoes squeaking on the floor as she went.

Rowes watched her retreat, clasping his hands together. There could still be sexism within some of the filming companies, but he'd never heard the director point it out quite so bluntly. It made the dread and guilt so much worse.

But it wasn't as bad as before. The feeling from the car was just out of reach, Izzy's presence seemingly enough to keep it at bay.

"What the hell was that about?" asked Izzy, following Rowes' gaze. "I thought this was about a reshoot."

"Me, too," said Rowes. "What else could it be?" His mind instantly jumped to the worst. When he hadn't listened to Lorena, had she gone straight to the top? He refused to think that way. She was a good woman, even when she was angry.

"Mr. Keppel." The voice greeted them as they Rowes stepped through the door, swallowing when he caught sight of the producers for *Gunlover*, as well as a man and woman he didn't recognize. They were sitting at a rectangular table, papers and a few bits of equipment pushed to the far end. Each of the producers had a coffee in hand, while the other two people only had a stack of paperwork and a tablet.

"And Mr. Linton." The executive producer seemed a little startled by Izzy's presence, looking to the others before he slid his hands across the tabletop. "Isthmus, your presence isn't required at this meeting. It is only for Mr. Keppel, his manager and a legal representative of his choice."

"Then consider me his lawyer," said Izzy, his hand never leaving Rowes' arm. "Or a stand-in, at least. He's working on hiring one at the moment."

This sounded bad...like fired *bad*. All his years on the show flashed before his eyes. The gags, the wasted shots when he messed up, that one time he'd accidentally smashed a ten-thousand-dollar piece of equipment...it all added up. Sure, all that stuff was replaceable, but so was he.

"Okay. If that's how you want to do this," said the executive producer as Izzy guided Rowes to his seat. "This is Mr. Votch and Ms. Sassen. I'll let them proceed with the agenda for today."

Rowes swallowed, fighting the urge to reach for Izzy and hold his hand tight. His thoughts were whirling, blood rushing through his ears as he wavered. Grabbing the back of the nearest chair, he held on, begging for the moment to pass.

Mr. Votch was more attractive than Rowes had noticed at first, clean-shaven with a well-fitted suit and aviator glasses perched on top of his head. He reached for the tablet, typing in a password before clicking something on the screen. Passing the tablet along the table toward Rowes, he hit play on the video he had cued up.

"Can you identify the persons in this video?"

Rowes' hand trembled as he grasped the tablet, barely hanging onto it as the video started to play. There was a whooshing sound like poor audio quality, before a cheesy song cut in.

This is not going to be good. He recognized the app as the same one where he had found the D/s video that had changed his world. The user who had uploaded it was the same person, too, but it was the title that was a dead giveaway.

"I can't believe it! Rowes Keppel is a confirmed submissive and his Dom is none other than Isthmus Linton."

The title scrolled across the screen and Rowes' mouth went dry as he looked to Izzy. His heart was racing, his palms sweaty as he gripped the tablet.

Someone at Unkinked? It had seemed so safe and tight-knit, but there had been a lot of people there — some of whom he hadn't even spoken to. Clint had seemed so starstruck, even if he didn't seem like the type to sell out. Meeting someone famous did strange things to people.

Fresh words appeared on the screen as a low beat started up. It was a heavy song, filled with as much potential as something that could be heard in a sleezy club. Rowes blinked away the tears that were already starting, trying to read them before they could disappear.

"This doesn't even need an explanation, so I'm just going to let it roll."

"Sit," said Izzy, helping Rowes into the nearest chair as he wavered again. Izzy sidled behind him as soon as he sat, resting his hands on Rowes' shoulders and presumably staring at the same thing Rowes was.

The room went from hot to cold as the first clip played, an iron ball settling in his gut. Whoever had caught them had taken the video in slow motion, enhancing it until it was very clear as to what was going on.

The alley looked different than Rowes remembered, but it didn't seem real without the scent of garbage and piss. Even in shadow, his silhouette was all too familiar as Izzy forced him to his knees with a hand around his neck.

It could have been anyone in low light like that. They used stunt doubles, and their faces were mostly obscured.

But then they were pulling apart, Rowes jumping to his feet when they'd heard that noise. The person taking the video moved until they were tucked away out of view while their lens captured everything.

His hopes that they hadn't been caught clearly came crashing down as he left the alley with Izzy, a smile on his lips and both of their faces in full view. The other things that were apparent were the obvious erections in their pants.

Swallowing, Rowes looked to where Izzy's hand rested on his shoulder, his tanned fingers dark against his paler skin. He had that same urge to pull away and deny everything that he'd had when Lorena had first accused him. Only at that point, he hadn't done anything wrong. Now, he wasn't sure if that was true.

"The people in the video, Mr. Keppel?"

Izzy was silent behind him. Rowes wanted to reach for him so badly, but his heart broke instead as Izzy pulled his hands away, taking a step back and putting space between them.

If there was any time in the world that he needed touch it was now. Rowes shivered in his chair, trying to find Izzy through the tears. He was only a little way away, but far enough for it to be monumental.

"Myself and Izzy—Isthmus," said Rowes, clearing his throat as he clasped his hands together. The video had continued on, showing some older clips in a whole new light. He looked away, rubbing his throat where the memory of Izzy's touch burned bright.

"And what exactly were you doing?" asked Mr. Votch, retrieving the tablet and pausing the video. The song cut off abruptly, leaving Rowes with the sound of his racing heart.

"Fooling around," said Izzy, his voice cutting. "We'd just finished an epic retake and we were a little wound up." He'd crossed his arms, his face going dark.

"Two hundred thousand hits and counting on this video and it was only uploaded two hours ago," said Mr. Votch, setting the tablet on the table and returning to his seat. "By the time the video has been taken down, it might be close to a million."

"So?" asked Rowes softly, glaring at the polished fake wood of the table. It may have been an expensive hotel, but it seemed that the fittings were just as false as some people in the industry. "There are so many fan videos out there about us. What's one more?"

"Not only have you violated your contract, Mr. Keppel," said Ms. Sassen, speaking for the first time, "but the suggestions made in this video lead us to believe there is some kind of BDSM relationship between you and Isthmus that would be contrary to the studio's views."

He couldn't breathe. The air was right there in his lungs, but it felt as if he were underwater. Reaching for Izzy's hand, he only found air.

"As you can imagine, we don't take this situation lightly," she continued, reaching for one stack of papers and sliding it his way. "Here is your notice of termination. Have your lawyer review it before you sign it."

Termination? The paper moved before his blurry eyes as Izzy tore it off the table.

"You can't fire Rowes," said Izzy, his face filled with disbelief. "He's a main character of *Gunlover*. You'll lose thousands of fans." The paper shook in Izzy's hands, the corners curling as he fisted it.

"He *was* a main character until he met his tragic end at the hands of a rival gang. The fans will still have Kemble, and they'll rally for him as he goes through the loss of his best friend."

His throat had never been so dry. Lorena had been right about everything. *Everything.* She'd only been trying to look after him while he'd been flirting with Izzy like an idiot. That kiss on set had probably sealed his fate, even before the video was released.

"You can't do this," said Izzy, hissing through his clenched teeth. "I won't shoot another scene without him."

Rowes reached for Izzy's thigh, squeezing hard. He didn't want to take Izzy down in his train wreck of a life.

"Let me put it this way, Isthmus," said the executive producer, tenting his fingers. "Rowes goes quietly, or he will never work on a set again. Even low budget horror casters won't take him after I'm through. If you'd like to align your fate with his, then please continue."

"Sorry I'm late."

Rowes flinched, whirling at the sound of Lorena's voice. She was behind him, holding the heavy wooden door wide as she pulled the heel of her shoe back into place. One strap of her dress had fallen down her arm, and her hair was an absolute disaster.

"Funny thing," she said, making her way to the only empty chair and taking a seat. She was breathing fast, but she smoothed her dress of the few wrinkles it had gathered. "I found out from the director that you were meeting with my clients. It's strange that I wasn't notified. I'll assume this was an accidental oversight."

The executive producer was glaring, but the two lawyers at least looked a little apologetic.

"So, what were we saying?" asked Lorena, spotting the tablet and reaching for it. The video was still paused, frozen on an old picture of Izzy whispering something into Rowes' ear, and Rowes with his eyes half-lidded.

Scrolling back to the start of the video, she played it again. The same music started up. It was no better than the first time, the scene condemning him a second time.

"What am I looking at?" asked Lorena, tilting the screen and squinting her eyes. "Is a little spoiler alert really worth a meeting with the execs?" She chuckled, stopping the video and tossing it back to Ms. Sassen.

"This is an obvious breach of contract—" Mr. Votch started.

"My clients had explicit instructions to practice the upcoming scene, contract or no." Lorena picked at her nail, flaking off a bit of red polish with a raised brow.

"This video was shot after that scene," said Mr. Votch, scrolling back to the video and pointing to the bottom corner where there was a date and time stamp of all things. "Mr. Laurie's termination is final. The company can't support these types of activities."

"I see." Lorena, steepled her fingers, leaning in. "I would *caution* you on that. *Gunlover* is in the top three ranked shows on late-night television, with hundreds of millions of dollars in profits. If the entire cast was fired, a fan or two may notice."

The executive producer's glare turned fierce. "I'm not going to be manipulated here. My show is an action series involving *straight* men."

Izzy snorted.

"I thought you would know your audience a bit better after so many seasons," said Lorena, shaking her head. "Why do you think Isthmus has so many fans? The only thing better to women than one hot man, is two — preferably naked and together. When this season is released with that scene, I guarantee you will have higher ratings than any other episode."

Mr. Votch scoffed before he slapped the table. "I think we're done here. Review the paperwork and sign it — or consider your career over."

Lorena tilted her head back, inhaling deep through her nose. "Ah, the smell of blackmail always gets me going." She grinned.

Rowes was mildly worried for her sanity. No one took on lawyers and producers with a *smile*. She'd always been a kick-ass bitch, though.

"I didn't think you'd respond well to threats, but here we go," she said, rubbing her hands together. "If you fire Rowes, the show is finished. Every dime you've spent on this season will be down the drain, and once news gets out as to why, this company won't be far behind. Rowes won't have to say a word. People talk, and let me tell you, no one will take your side."

"Have your lawyer take a look, Mr. Keppel. I'll be in touch." Ms. Sassen gathered the tablet, pushing her chair out.

"We aren't done here." Rage rolled off Izzy in waves, red creeping up the collar of his T-shirt and his eyes wild.

"Yes, we are," said Lorena, slowly standing and regarding the producers.

Rowes followed almost numbly, clutching the table as he wobbled. For his entire career, he'd dreaded this moment. He wasn't the best actor out there or the most attractive. Izzy was everything he wasn't, on and off the screen. As long as they had Izzy, the fans probably wouldn't notice his absence too much.

He touched the papers in Izzy's hand, slowly taking them from him. The edges were crinkled, some of the printer ink smudged from Izzy's sweat. He couldn't look at them and read the words that condemned his career, along with everything else he was. But he couldn't let anyone else make the sacrifice for his screw up.

He was numb as he left the office, Izzy at his size and Lorena following with a click of her heels. Someone tried to stop them out front, asking Rowes for a signature, but for once, he brushed them off. His signature would be worth next to nothing soon. He could fight it, but what was the point?

All he could wonder was how they were going to kill him off. They had enough saved footage that had never rolled in order to do it with some serious editing. He'd taken a few bullets over the seasons, survived a poisoning as well as an alarming number of stabbings. Being Kemble's best friend had come with some downsides.

"Hit by a car, maybe?" he mused, sticking his hand out to hail a nearby cab. It slowed to a stop as Izzy came up behind him, still stomping and fuming.

"They can't fucking do this!" A few glances turned their way, and Rowes pressed a finger to his lips, staring down the road as he opened the cab's door.

"They *won't*," said Lorena. "Rowes, no one is going to sit by and let this happen. I can speak for Izzy without asking, and Connley and Ainslie wouldn't need much convincing."

Izzy looked close to tears, carding his hand through his hair violently as he stared back at the hotel. When he turned to the cab, he widened his eyes in surprise. "Where the hell do you think you're going?"

Rowes' lips moved, but he could barely comprehend what he was saying. He blinked, shaking his head as he tried to focus. He pulled the cab door shut before Izzy or Lorena could get inside.

"I'm going to head back to the hotel and call my lawyer. You're going to head to the studio." He pointed over his shoulder, which was the opposite direction of the hotel. "And before you say anything, yes, you *are* going to shoot today. The show must go on, right? No one is giving up the show because of me. I'm not going to let that happen."

Clenching his fists, Izzy nailed the top of the car. The driver squeaked in protest, giving Izzy a dirty look. "Don't be so fucking ridiculous. Get out of the fucking car."

Rowes rolled up the window, turning to the driver and giving him the directions back to his hotel. The car lurched ahead as Izzy brought his fist down again, Lorena looking on with concern etched into her features.

"That was intense," said the driver, shooting Rowes a look through the rearview mirror. "I never thought he was such an asshole in real life. I'm a big fan of the show, but *shit*."

His hackles rose immediately, but Rowes bit back his automatic rebuff. It wasn't the first time someone had called Isthmus an asshole to his face, probably digging for dirt, but it was the first time he didn't plan on defending him.

Why can't he see? If he took Lorena's route, he would be ruining the careers of dozens of people. He was just one guy—a replaceable one at that. Why didn't anyone else see that?

His phone buzzed against his hip, and he jumped, grabbing for it as he made a non-committal sound to the cabbie. When he looked at the screen, he saw Izzy's name in neon blue, the buzz almost violent as he held his phone.

"Hello?" He wasn't not going to answer. No matter what they had been through, he always answered.

"What the fuck, Ro?"

Rowes winced, holding the phone away from his ear and quickly turning the volume down.

"There's no need for you to be so upset, Isthmus," said Rowes, biting his tongue as he said Izzy's full name. He hadn't called him that since they'd first met, long before they'd auditioned for *Gunlover*, when Rowes had spent his days at tryouts for numerous roles and Izzy had posed for art classes on the side.

"Are you serious right now?"

Izzy was pissed—no, beyond pissed. In all their time together, he rarely raised his voice, but apparently, he'd snapped. Maybe Rowes leaving him on the street had pushed him too far. Lorena was there, though. She could summon a driver with the snap of her fingers.

"I need you to calm down," said Rowes, sharper than he'd intended. "If not for me, then for yourself." The way Izzy had pulled away from him at the meeting flashed through his mind. He had probably just been trying to make the situation look better, but it had fucking stung.

"And I need you to get your ass back here. We aren't done talking yet—not to each other or the producers."

"So you just want your career to crash and burn," said Rowes, running his hand through his hair. His cheeks were wet, but every time he wiped them, it didn't seem to make a difference. "I, for one, don't want to see that. I want to see the show do well, actually. You've put so much time and effort into your role—years—and the fans would never forgive you for backing down now."

He cast a glance to the cabbie, who seemed way too invested in his conversation. This was why he liked to stick with his usual driver who never leaked a thing about their conversations.

"He's prepping for a difficult scene right now. Sorry. Just giving him some feedback." He covered the speaker on his phone as he said it. The driver gave him a slow nod before turning his gaze back to the road.

"It's like you don't even fucking care," said Izzy, the disbelief in his voice obvious. "I'm trying to help you—stick up for you—and you're acting like you want nothing to do with me."

"That's not true." Rowes bit his lip, reaching for his wallet as the cab pulled in front of the hotel.

"You left me on the street, Ro." Izzy took a breath. "I had to watch those lawyer assholes walk by me all high and mighty while Lorena called her driver."

"I left you because you need to go to the studio. I'm a big boy, and I can look after myself. This has *nothing* to do with you, so carry on and stay out of it. I'll talk to Lorena later." It was a pathetic excuse, and Izzy seemed to catch on right away.

"If you want to play that way, Ro, then so be it."

The line went dead, and Rowes pulled the phone away from his ear, wiping his tears away one last time. Tapping his card against the machine to pay, Rowes stepped out of the cab.

"That seemed like a pretty intense scene he's working on there," said the driver, rolling down his window and leaning out of it as Rowes headed for the hotel.

He looked back, mustering a smile. "It's going to be an epic season. The best one yet."

Chapter Twenty

Rowes

Maybe he was permanently numb or something. Rowes looked at his hand where he'd accidentally gotten a papercut. A few drops of blood had welled up, but he still hadn't felt the sting. *What the hell is wrong with me? The drop?*

Something in the practical side of his mind told him that was the case, but what the hell was he supposed to do about it? Izzy had pulled away from him before he'd gone on a rampage. If Rowes called him now, there was no telling what he would do. Not to mention, Izzy would be on set, hopefully doing his best.

It sat strangely on his tongue, the thought of endless days of nothing stretching before him. Somewhere along the line, *Gunlover* had become his life. Without it, he was a 'has been', but not even that. He would still be known as Kemble's sidekick.

He'd tried watching a few fan videos, wondering if the sight of Izzy would spark his frozen nerves. He hadn't gotten far before frustration had overwhelmed him. What he saw wasn't real. Until he'd stumbled on a stream of comments.

Every video they'd watched together, he found comments under someone with the username 'Linty'. It was a terrible name, but one he had given to Izzy when they'd started living together and he'd discovered that Izzy had to clean out his belly button lint on the daily.

"So hot. I bet it's even better in person."

The first comment caught his eye before he skimmed the comments of another video, finding Linty's hidden among the ones from the last few days.

"They are so beautiful together. I wish they could be like that all the time and not be worried about upsetting people."

Was it Izzy? Is that how he really felt? Rowes tried to care, but he was so numb and cold, his body frozen.

The words and videos weren't the same as the taste of Izzy on his lips or the warmth of his palm in Rowes' hand. There was no morning breath or sweaty socks after a long day at work together as they made television history. No hand-feeding while he sat at Izzy's feet, either, because it was over—all of it.

Would he ever feel the same way he had before? He'd been so innocent, each touch just friendship with none of the heat or expectation there was now. There was no contract to stop them now…nothing holding them back. He should have been ecstatic. He should have run to Izzy's side and pulled him in for the hottest kiss of his life before getting fucked against that same brick wall that had sealed his fate.

But there was nothing. His heart was still beating, breath filling his lungs, but otherwise it was an abyss. It was too much to shake off by himself.

He whirled around as the door clicked open, swinging wide seconds later. His heart stopped when he saw Izzy standing there. *You can't be here!* He wanted to scream it, but he couldn't because Izzy was already wrapping his arms around him and pulling him close.

The papercut throbbed to life as everything came crashing down. Terror stuck him to the core, his future a dismal stretch of emptiness without Izzy beside him every day.

"You can't be here," said Rowes, clutching Izzy's shirt. He smelled of sweat and sunshine, his chest still heaving. Had he run the whole way?

"Where else would I be?" His voice was breathless.

"The set. You need to finish four scenes today, not to mention the reshoot from yesterday. You can't be here. *You can't.*" Rowes pleaded, pushing at Izzy with one hand while he held him close with the other. "Get out of here. *Go.*"

"Holy fuck, Rowes. Do you know who you're talking to?"

Blinking, Rowes looked to Izzy's face. He was pissed — beyond pissed — still wearing his anger on his face as sweat beaded on his forehead.

"Please don't yell."

Sighing, Izzy took a step back before seemingly thinking better of it and leading Rowes to the bed. There were two queens, but the sheets were completely unruffled in one, still smelling of fresh laundry and bleach while the other was neatly made but smelled like them. Housekeeping had already come and gone, the tip missing from the little tray by the phone where Rowes had set it.

"I'm not going to yell," said Izzy, looking much calmer as he sat before pulling Rowes between his thighs. "I shouldn't have in the first place, and I'm sorry. I was just... No, there's no excuse. I lost my temper—the one thing I promised I would never do with you. Probably best that you left me there, and I had to run halfway across town before I managed to catch a cab. Lorena thought I was being ridiculous."

"That didn't bother me the most," said Rowes, his heart still aching at the memory of Izzy pulling away from him. He didn't have the right to be upset about it. He'd pulled away on countless occasions under Lorena's disapproving stare, but this had been so different.

"I should have listened to Lorena," said Rowes, shaking his head. "She tried to warn me that we were getting too close on set. If I wouldn't have agreed to that kiss, then we wouldn't be here."

"Do you regret it?" Izzy drew back, his face blank as he caught Rowes' gaze.

"No." *Not for an instant.* Without that kiss, they would probably be right where they had been—just friends floating through life, confused about who they really were to each other. "Not for me, at least. I just don't want to see this happen to you, Iz. You have to go back to the shoot. *Please.*"

Pressing his lips together, Izzy shook his head. "You really don't get it."

What was there to get? Izzy was going to be ruined if he quit now—if they fought back. How could he not see that?

"First things first, though," said Izzy, clasping Rowes' hands in his own. "I shouldn't have belittled our relationship, and I'm sorry for that. I should have just told them straight up that we're in a D/s relationship."

"Yeah, 'cause that would have gone well." Rowes rolled his eyes, his knees shaking at the memory of the board room. "They already thought we were getting freaky, but they'd probably change their minds and..."

"And, what?" asked Izzy, his voice sharp. "Judge the fuck out of us? News flash! They already do. Every critic, fan, producer, director — it doesn't matter — are going to judge us, no matter what. So we might as well tell the truth. I'm not ashamed of who I am or who I love, and nobody is going to convince me to change my mind."

Rowes let out a groan, looking to the ceiling for help. The light on the fire detector blinked green and red, but it was of no assistance at all. "I don't want you to be tainted by this — by me."

"Ro, baby." Izzy leaned in, touching his forehead to Rowes' chest. "I know you're upset, so I'm gonna let that one slide, but never speak about yourself like that. You aren't a burden or a freak. You're *you*, and I fucking love you for it."

It was official...he was never going to stop crying. Not if Izzy kept saying things like that.

"What about *Gunlover*? That show is your life. You can't lie and say it's not."

Nodding, Izzy bit his lip. "It's very important to me, but no job is worth losing you."

Rowes cupped Izzy's chin, placing a soft kiss on his lips. "Iz, you aren't going to lose me." A fresh wave of tears rolled over his cheeks. "I'm your number one fan, and if you don't finish this season, I will be severely disappointed. Please do it...for me."

It broke his heart to think about the days alone with Izzy on set without him, but Izzy's smile at the end of the day would be worth it. He loved acting more than anything, and without it, Rowes knew Izzy would be more lost than him.

"I want you there, baby," said Izzy, looking out of the window where the sun had almost peaked. The work day was already dragging close to the halfway point. "I need you. You're my muse."

"We're going to figure this out," said Rowes. "A few weeks from now, we're going to look back and have a laugh about all this."

"But are you okay? You aren't dropping?"

"Not anymore." Rowes shook his head. He felt almost back to normal—at least a lot closer than he'd been before. "It had just been too much at once, and I got overwhelmed. I should be fine now."

"You're sure?" Izzy cupped his chin, his gaze searching. "I'll stay right here forever if that's what you need."

* * * *

Izzy

It was after midnight by the time Rowes peacefully fell asleep. Izzy rolled his shoulders, trying to shake off the stiffness of Rowes sleeping on him. Lorena had called them twice, and Izzy had taken it both times, things getting progressively bleaker with the news she had.

He hadn't expected it to be easy, but he wasn't budging. The show was over as far as he was concerned, his passion for it already dwindling.

He looked up at the sound of a knock on the hotel door, carefully extracting himself from a peaceful

Rowes. Glancing over his shoulder to make sure Rowes was still sleeping, he pulled the door open.

"Isthmus."

Izzy rubbed his eyes as a blurry Connley appeared before him. How anyone looked that put together when it was so late just wasn't fair. But Connley wasn't top-tier for nothing.

"Lorena called me," said Connley, inviting himself inside and lowering his voice as he caught sight of a sleeping Rowes. He made one quick glance to the second untouched bed but didn't make any comment.

Grabbing a robe, Izzy tossed it on and rubbed his hands together. The room was chilly without Rowes next to him and so dry that his lips were chapped. He grabbed a bottle of water, offering a second one to Connley.

He wasn't sure if Lorena's call was a good or bad thing. Connley was completely unreadable at the best of times, and Izzy had never seen him angry. Still, they were asking a lot.

"So what's going on between you and Rowes? I don't usually pry, but it's hard not to notice some things. The new script I was handed today was a big clue. He's not in a single scene." Crossing his arms over his chest, he stared steadily at Izzy.

This is not a conversation for midnight. But maybe now was better than Sunday brunch. He grabbed an armchair, motioning for Connley to take the second one. Rowes was still sleeping, his face peaceful in the lamplight.

Izzy ran a hand through his hair as he sat, finishing off the water bottle and tossing it toward the bin. "You know anything about kink?"

Connley's eyes widened a fraction for a split second...more than Izzy had ever seen him act surprised. "No way, man. I thought that shit was all for the cameras."

"Maybe it was at one time," said Izzy. He'd never admit it to Rowes, but early on in their relationship, he'd always added a bit of extra affection because of the way that the crowds reacted to it. Instead of nudging Rowes' shoulder, he'd wrap an arm around him, and instead of raising his voice, he'd whisper directly into Rowes' ear.

Fans loved it. Like Lorena had said, the only thing better than one hot man was two. And who cared if they were together? As long as the fans got to see their abs. It had been frustrating that everyone always assumed that they were in a sexual relationship, but Izzy *had* played it up.

Then things had changed. Maybe it was habit, or maybe he hadn't wanted to go back to brief touches or accidental glances. Rowes had become his clingy teddy bear with a sweet soul and an attitude he saved only for Izzy.

After that, things had really changed.

"We were just friends up until a few weeks ago, but then I asked him to be my submissive. He already kind of was before, but I wanted something more between us," said Izzy, scratching his chin and lowering his voice as Rowes mumbled and rolled over.

"I didn't know you were into that kind of thing," said Connley, sitting in his own armchair just a tad stiffer. "We could have chatted if I had guessed."

What?

"No way, man." Izzy looked at him in disbelief. He wasn't *that* blind. Connley didn't read as a Dom or a

229

sub. He hardly read as sexual at all, despite his good looks. He flitted between personalities so quickly that Izzy could never keep track, and he could be an emotionless wreck. "I never pegged you for a kinky bastard."

Connley shrugged. "Well, Ainslie pegs me as often as she likes. She's my Domme."

Holy shit. He cracked up, muffling his laughter behind his hand as Connley sent him a glare. He couldn't help it. It was almost euphoric.

"If you've got a problem — "

"No," said Izzy quickly. "I'm laughing because the cast is made up of a bunch of kinky fucks, when the producers are trying to fire Rowes for misrepresenting the studio. If only they knew." He shook his head. They would need a hell of a lot more than two lawyers if they tried to take them out.

"So Lorena wasn't pulling my leg," said Connley, looking to the side as he nodded. "I thought they might try to do something after that kiss on set. That shit was awesome. It was the first time I wondered if there was really more than friendship between you guys. You've always been touchy-feely, but not 'hands down the pants' touchy."

"I still haven't figured out what to do," said Izzy, rubbing the back of his head. "I can't imagine it here without him, but Rowes is right. There is more on the line than just me or him. I'm just as lost as Kemble would be. I should just walk away…"

Never seeing the lens of a camera looking at him was one of the worst things he could imagine. Television was what had made him, but it was also the only thing he wanted to do. Without *Gunlover*, who knew? There were always places to go. All that really mattered was Rowes.

"If we fight it, Rowes and I are going to find a lot of closed doors," said Izzy. "But I can't just roll over and take this." It was his job to protect Rowes. Maybe 'job' was the wrong word. It was his everything.

"What did Rowes have to say about it? I'm sure he was upset." Connley picked at his nail where a speck of fake blood looked to be dried on. He'd probably just come from the set—at least, hopefully. Hopefully, it wasn't real blood from Ainslie and himself sceneing.

"Not really." Izzy shook his head. Rowes had seemed shocked, but no more than that. At the hotel room, after an initial cry, he had smiled, his eyes sparkling. He hadn't looked angry at all. "He wants me to keep shooting. Some 'the show must go on' bullshit. He should know that I'm the one who takes care of him, not the other way around."

Connley snorted, a smile touching his lips. "I'm guessing you're pretty new to this Dom business, even before Rowes."

Shrugging, Izzy looked away. "Kind of. That still shouldn't matter."

"Rowes isn't just a submissive. He's also a person— a very smart one. It's one thing to care for him by offering your support and comfort, but its another to belittle him or not listen. Respect goes both ways."

Izzy was silent for a long time, looking at his hands. He was so tired that they blurred before his eyes. He couldn't remember if he'd showered or even washed up since running across town.

"Maybe I'm not cut out to be a Dom. I'm certainly not a submissive." Izzy shook his head. That was something he didn't even have to think about.

Connley sent him a glare before smacking him on the back of his head. "If I had a dime for every baby Dom who doubted themselves, I wouldn't have to work again. Just 'cause you fucked up once, doesn't mean you're a bad Dom. Hell, Ainslie fucks up all the time."

Connley glanced over his shoulder before dropping his voice. "Don't tell her I said that. She's perfect, but she can be really sensitive, too." He leaned back in his chair once he saw the coast was clear. "Do you have a mentor?"

"Yeah, Malone. He's a member of Unkinked outside of town here," said Izzy, running his hand through his hair.

"Then call him. He'll help walk you through this kind of thing better than I can. The best advice I have is sometimes you have to shut your mouth and open your ears. Communication only works if you're ready to listen."

"Oh my God." Izzy let out a groan, chuckling as he lowered his face into his hands. "Stop with the preaching, man. You're going to start spouting proverbs in a minute if you don't quit it."

Connley laughed. "You Doms are all alike." He paused as Rowes grumbled in his sleep, kicking a leg out. He was probably dreaming about a fight scene or something. He was so adorable. "We should get to bed. Early start tomorrow."

"I know...if we even show up. If Rowes goes down, then so do I."

Connley raised one eyebrow. "If Rowes goes down, we all do. We are with him — all of us. I'm calling the producers as soon as I leave your room. I just wanted to talk to you first."

"Really?" Izzy perked up, the tightness in his chest loosing.

"You are so fucking dumb sometimes." Connley patted him on the shoulder before standing from his chair. "Night, Isthmus. I guarantee that everything will be worked out by morning. Actors who aren't working are hella expensive, and people move fast when a franchise is on the line."

Chapter Twenty-One

Rowes

The director practically cackled when she caught sight of them strolling onto the set together. It only lasted a moment before she was back to business and barking an order at a passerby. People scrambled around the set, rushing to make sure everything looked exactly as it should.

Lorena looked just as smug as she should, a grin on her face and her arms crossed as she watched the crew. When she caught sight of Rowes and Izzy's arrival, her smile widened to something almost predatory.

"Don't let it go to your head," said Izzy as they stopped in front of Lorena. Her smile didn't dim in the least.

"It's the biggest win of my career," said Lorena, motioning around the set. "The show goes on sans a singular scene, your contracts are amended and everyone keeps their jobs, including me."

It wasn't a complete win, which Izzy had been very prompt at pointing out. After Connley had approached the executive producer and let him know that Ainslie and he were goners if they terminated Rowes, things had changed pretty quickly.

With the loss of one cast member, the show would have gone on, but the entire main cast? There would be no recovering from it. And there was too much at stake to let it become just another canceled show in television history.

Lorena had jumped on that vulnerability right away, getting their contracts reworked in a way that gave Rowes more freedom than he'd had in months. The only kicker had been the kiss scene.

The planned kiss scene had been cut, and the one between himself and Izzy had been tossed in the trash. The rest of the season had been rewritten as if the event had never happened. But the innuendos had been left in place, the teases and snippets there to tantalize the audience.

There was no time to think before the scene was set and Izzy was doing his first take in front of the camera.

"Think more dangerous," said Rowes, as soon as the director called cut and everything was reset. "You're out for blood, and you don't need a gun to shed it," said Rowes. Izzy slid right into character until Rowes struggled not to take a step back from the sheer intimidation of his look. He was surprised that the camera didn't burst into flames on the next take. The director certainly looked a little ruffled.

* * * *

"You good to go?" asked Rowes, yawning behind his hand as he snuck a package of gummies from Lorena's purse. He didn't have any more shots, and he was beyond tired. They had been shooting for hours straight, and it was way past time for bed. They had a lot of catching up to do after the pause in the show.

Izzy looked around the set, slipping into a chair beside where Rowes was as few of the crew bustled about. Rowes had such a profound respect for them, setting up every day and taking things down every night. It would get easier once they were doing indoor shots, but they couldn't exactly leave cameras outside. What if it rained?

"Not yet," said Izzy, letting out a sigh as he leaned back in his chair.

"Not yet, what?" Rowes yawned again, rubbing his eyes with his free hand. He handed Lorena's purse back to her as she headed home for the day, his stomach grumbling from the lack of a real meal for dinner. "What are you talking about?"

"You asked me if I was ready to go," said Izzy, chuckling as he patted his knee.

"Did I?" He could barely keep his eyes open, and there was still so much to do. Eventually, he'd hit a point where he got used to the lack of sleep, but the first few days back were always the worst. The limbo had spoiled him.

"You did good today," said Izzy, creeping his hand up Rowes' thigh.

That had him wide awake, pulling away and standing as he blinked at the people around them. It was already a little too late. The director had spied them, giving them a smirk and a little wave as Rowes flushed.

"You're a tease," said Rowes, setting his bag on the ground and fanning his face. "The contract is gone — but have a little decency." He couldn't believe he was actually saying it. This was their chance to go all the way, and he was dragging his heels.

Is it nerves or something else? Maybe he was more tired than he thought. He was horny, so it couldn't be that. He couldn't wait to have Izzy, but maybe not in public?

Izzy shrugged. "Like a little contract could stop me. You're mine, Rowes, and now everyone knows it." Tugging Rowes back into his chair, he settled his hand on his knee, squeezing once.

"Lorena told me about a bunch of calls she got today," said Rowes, his jaw cracking as he yawned. "Two were television interviews—I said no to one because I figured we'd still be shooting—and one was radio. Undecided on that one. We're television stars, not rock stars."

"Sounds good," said Izzy. He looked unreasonably wide awake, without a single blemish besides the smudged makeup from his last scene.

"Do you want me to order dinner?" asked Rowes, closing his eyes and picturing the warmth of hotel food. He wavered, his mouth watering.

"First, come here," said Izzy, patting his thigh again.

Rowes glanced around. There were still a lot of people moving about, including Connley, who was smiling at them for some reason. Izzy's hand on his back felt too good to protest, though.

"What are we waiting for?" asked Rowes as he sat, letting out a sigh as he leaned into Izzy's chest. It felt so amazing to be held after a long day, and Izzy smelled so good. He was still in some of his wardrobe, the scent of leather clinging to him from his jacket that he'd discarded at some point.

"Are you wearing the plug?"

Rowes almost shot right back up again, but Izzy held him firm, whispering into his ear. "I was wondering all day. Was that a limp I saw, or did you just lose your footing for a second? I thought I saw you wince once or twice, too. Did it hit your spot?"

"No." Trying to squirm out of Izzy's arms, he gave up after a moment or two, giving in to the beautiful feeling of utter powerlessness. "I didn't wear it today. I didn't know what today would be like…and the wince was when I got stung by a bee. Almost ruined one of your shots."

The truth was, he'd worn it for short stints on set before, but he'd been so stressed about how it would go today that he hadn't been able to bear it. As for ruining the shot, he'd almost screamed his brains out when the hornet had stung him twice consecutively.

"Where?" Izzy grasped Rowes' hand, placing a kiss on the tip of his swollen finger. It still smarted, and it was almost completely red to boot. Hornets were the worst.

"It's fine." Rowes looked over his shoulder. There were only a few people left, but they were sending an awful lot of glances their way. Soon, the only ones left would be the security crew, who would keep an eye on the area after everyone was gone. "Stop it."

"You safewording?" asked Izzy, taking his hand right back and kissing along his wrist.

"No," Rowes kept his voice low, a thrill running up his spine at the same time. *Holy shit. We* are *doing this.* "What are you doing?"

"Well, first I was going to give you another kiss," said Izzy, placing a kiss on Rowes' other wrist, "then I was going to ask you if you wanted to stay behind on set and maybe christen that wall over there."

He waggled his eyebrows, glancing at the same wall that he'd kissed Rowes against. His heart pounded as Rowes stared at the brick. The hottest kiss of his life had happened there. It needed a plaque or something.

"Maybe you could fight it a little," Izzy continued, his eyes going dark. "Pretend you don't want it and try to get away. Maybe it would be fun."

He was going to hyperventilate if Izzy kept this up, which was a strange sensation when he was hard. They'd talked about more limits after their last scene, and consensual non-consent had come up as a possible interest. It almost seemed a little rough for Izzy, though, who was careful with Rowes to his core.

Could he admit that it thrilled him? The thought of being pinned and struggling against Izzy's hands had him going even harder. But how far would they go? Even after everyone was gone, there would still be security guards, although they probably wouldn't be in the exact vicinity.

He'd never pictured their first time as something overly romantic. At this rate, he'd wondered if he'd have to climb on Izzy's cock himself in the middle of the night and wake up his Dom with a nice surprise. It would be different not to be treated as if he were made of glass, though.

"What if I fought a lot?" asked Rowes, tucking his face into Izzy's neck. His neck strained from his position as he lowered his eyelids, trying to give off relaxed vibes. "What if I screamed?"

"You could try." Izzy's voice was unreadable. "I'd love to see it, baby. You're strong, but I'm way stronger."

Rowes narrowed his eyes. Was that really what Izzy thought of him? He was pretty sure Izzy was the stronger of the two of them, but he spent his fair share of time in the gym. It just wasn't fair.

Is Izzy fucking with me again? He slowly pulled away, leaving his empty juice box by the chair and strolling to the wall in question. Izzy tracked him with his gaze, his eyes going even darker as Rowes leaned against the wall, running his hands over the brick.

One of the crew members shot him a strange look before packing up some complicated sound equipment. *Let them see.* Maybe he was done hiding their relationship. It was time to live in the limelight.

The surface was rough under his hands and hot from the summer sun that had faded long ago. The area itself was fairly open, considering an entire film crew had to set up there, but it was still off the beaten path. The dumpster down the line was real, with a few additional holes in it to replicate the bullets that had flown around during their firefight.

The whole alley and a nearby warehouse were the set for two-and-a-half episodes, so they'd already spent a hell of a lot of time on it. People lined up outside the sectioned-off area every day, trying to catch a glimpse of their favorite stars. They didn't stay long when they realized they couldn't see or hear a thing and they weren't going to get a part in the show just by spending three hours being annoying.

It also made their continuity checkers all the more important. There were 'no parking' and 'no trespassing' signs everywhere to keep a lot of the public out, but it would be easy enough for someone to mark the wall with graffiti and completely ruin their next shot without some serious editing. Their security guards were good, but there were usually only two at night, and they had fair amount of ground to cover.

Rowes tugged at the button on his shirt, popping the top one as he let out a sigh. It was too easy to tilt his head back, swallowing and bringing up his foot to rest on the wall. It was the best seductive posture he knew, and from the way Izzy leaned forward in his chair, it was working.

"What are you going to do about the security guards?" asked Rowes softly, licking his lips and grinning as Izzy cleared his throat.

"I took care of it."

That sounded ominous as all hell.

"No one to hear me scream." A straggler jolted, nearly dropping their case.

"Sorry, just practicing for a role I'm auditioning for." He raised his hands in surrender, but the person was already moving on. It was crazy how many people believed that line. He could probably get away with murder if he used it right.

Not going to happen. He'd never had the desire to delve into the darker parts of his mind that he had to display so openly on set. He'd never thought about fighting back during sex either, though.

"You think I could get away with murder?" asked Rowes, touching his lip as he waited for the last person to get the hell out of their play space. There were so many surfaces and still a fair amount of equipment strewn around. What would Izzy do? There was no way he'd just push him up against the wall and have his way.

"Absolutely." Izzy leaned his chin on his hand. "But you're too sweet to hurt anyone, let alone murder somebody."

"I don't feel sweet." There was something in his gut that wasn't sweetness at all. It was almost gritty, sliding through his veins and bringing dark thoughts along with it. "I feel like I need to be punished."

That got Izzy's attention right quick. He stood from the chair, crossing the distance between them in a few short strides.

"Let's get something clear right now, Ro. This" — he wrapped his hand around Rowes' neck — "isn't punishment. You wouldn't like your punishment or get hard from it. You would *hate* it. I have a feeling that you are gonna love what we do on the set."

Things were so twisted and confused in his mind that he let out a giggle, leaning into Izzy's hand. It cut off his breath just a tiny bit, so his face felt strange, but he could still breathe.

"What's funny?" asked Izzy, tightening the pressure for a moment before he relaxed again.

"Everything is so backward." Rowes grabbed Izzy's hand, tightening his grip when he thought Izzy might pull away. "I love the things people tell me I shouldn't — spanking, the plug, the humiliation. They should be punishments, but I love them. I feel like I'm losing my mind. I can't imagine something you could give me that I wouldn't want."

"So sweet, but so naïve," said Izzy, pulling his hand away. "There are many things I could do to punish you, but I'll give you one example, just so you get the picture."

"If it's spanking, I'm game," said Rowes, quirking his lips at Izzy's glower. They were close, but the coast was officially clear. Hopefully, no one would come back for something they forgot. They would get a big surprise if they did.

"How about you sleep in your own bed for a month—or better yet, you don't get to come. I would still fuck you, tease you and come on your face, but you wouldn't get to...for a whole *month*."

Now they were getting into serious territory. *A month?* His balls would probably shrivel up and die in that amount of time.

"I'll be good," said Rowes, moving his hands to Izzy's hips and resting them there. "I won't even be a brat."

"I like when you're a brat," said Izzy, leaning his forehead against Rowes'. "It reminds me not to take things too seriously. You're a lot of fun, Ro. Never change that."

He was more than a little confused, but that was nothing new. This entire journey together had all been about confusion and discovery. There was so much for him to learn, and they had all the time in the world.

"What are you going to do to me?" asked Rowes, pushing at Izzy's hips when he felt their hard cocks meet. If they started grinding, he was going to come in his pants before they even got to the good part.

"What's your safeword?" asked Izzy, never moving his hand from Rowes' neck.

"Red. I'm green right now, Iz." Rowes rolled his hips ahead, grinding into Izzy's for a brief moment. He still could believe that they were doing this...in public, even if the area was guarded and deserted.

"You know this is the same spot you kissed Clarke," said Izzy, drooping his hand and taking a step back.

"You were such a slut for it—mouth open, licking your lips and clenching on that plug in your ass."

It was the first time he'd even been called a slut in his life, but he could see it becoming an addiction. Was that really what he'd looked like? It felt like it had happened so long ago. "I didn't mean to."

"No?" Izzy crossed his arms, his gaze going dark. There was sweat on his neck, his T-shirt damp between his pecs. He was probably filthy from such a hard day of work, but Rowes loved it. He wanted to lick every dirty inch. *Where is that coming from?*

"You moaned for him," said Izzy, clenching his jaw as he pointed to the side. "I was waiting there for you, watching as you humiliated yourself and moaned as he kissed you. Did you get hard for him?"

What? Rowes sucked in a breath. "What? No!"

Gripping the wall, he stood to his full height, energy zipping through his limbs. What the hell was going on? Fear shivered up his spine, his muscles snapping taut.

"What's your color?"

Izzy's question slammed into him and the fear drained away in an instant. "Green. I just thought—"

"Try not to think too much," said Izzy, cutting him off. "And don't lie. I saw that hard cock of yours and so did every camera on this set. Did he slip you some good tongue and you just had to offer him the whole package? You *did.* Such a slut."

He'd never imagined a scene would be anything like this. It was almost as if Izzy were trying to start a fight. How far would he go? *Well, if you want to play like that.*

"Yes," said Rowes, biting his lips as his face flushed. "I wanted him. I got hard for him, too. I wish he would have pinned me here and pulled my pants down, fucking me where everyone could see. The director would have kept rolling, selling our tapes to the tabloids so everyone could see how much I wanted him."

He deserved an academy award or something. Izzy looked ready to hulk out, minus the CGI. "What's *your* color, Izzy?"

Izzy smirked, his slipping control back in an instant. "I'm so green I don't know if you'll be able to handle it. I'm also wondering how I missed how much of a slut you are. Would you let him come in your ass?"

Rowes shuddered, goosebumps prickling over his skin. "Yes."

Taking a step closer, Izzy touched the wall above Rowes' head, boxing him in.

"Then I'd get on my knees and suck his cock. I wouldn't want to waste a single drop."

"Shit." Izzy closed his eyes for a moment, licking his lips. "Turn around so I can fuck you just like that."

Rowes crossed his arms, turning his head away. There was only a small amount of room between them, and it was so hard not to give in and do exactly what Izzy wanted of him. "No. I said I'd do that for him, not for *you*."

"A cock is a cock, slut." Izzy moved one hand to Rowes' hip, urging him to turn with a nudge.

"I said *no*." Rowes stood firm, leaning as far away as he could as Izzy grazed his lips over his throat. "We're out in the open. Anyone could walk by. And maybe I'm all fucked out. I went to his place after that scene together, and he gave me a hand as I sucked him off. I—"

Izzy's lips on his cut him off, stealing his breath all over again as he was pinned to the brick wall. Only this time there were no cameras, just him and Izzy beneath the hazy alley light that had nothing on the set lights. Relaxing into the kiss, he almost let himself get swept away until Izzy tightened his grip on his hip.

The kiss was too sweet for what he really wanted at the moment. There would be other times for exploration and kisses, but for now, he wanted something *hot*.

Jerking his face to the side, he broke their connection. "Can you taste his cum on my lips? I still can." He ran his tongue over his lower lip as if he were searching for the little bit of white gold.

"Fuck." Izzy grabbed him by the chin, but Rowes resisted, pushing against Izzy's chest. He wanted to prove himself. He could be more than just Izzy's sweetheart. He was a motherfucking brat when he needed to be.

Izzy staggered back, reaching for something at his waistband and tugging it free before pressing it to the side of Rowes' head. His heart stopped when he caught sight of what looked like one of the prop guns on set.

It's not loaded. His heart pounded as he struggled for real, jerking to the side only to have Izzy drag him back, the gun tracking his every move. People had *died* on movie sets from guns that had gone off accidentally or from a blank at close range.

"Yellow."

Izzy drew back, the darkness dropping from his face and morphing into concern. "The gun?"

"Yeah." Rowes looked at it as Izzy pulled it away. It wasn't a set prop at all, but a cheap plastic replica that Izzy had probably bought at the dollar store. Now that he could see it, he spotted a bit of orange peeking through where it looked as if Izzy had blacked it out with a permanent marker.

"I'll put it away," said Izzy, slipping it into the back of his waistband. "Sorry."

"No, it's okay," said Rowes, grabbing it and putting it back into Izzy's hand. "I thought it was a prop gun, and you nearly gave me a heart attack. You know how dangerous those are."

"That's why I got this beast," said Izzy, flicking the plastic with his fingernail. "All the intimidation, none of the risk. Besides, you know how closely they guard the prop weapons. You okay? You want to stop? I have some amazing aftercare planned for us, and we could jump straight to that."

"No. We're doing this," said Rowes. "With the gun, too. Next time, just give me a heads-up. I trust you, but I was scared—and not in a good way." It had been like meeting a bear in the woods, freaking out, only to realize it was just someone's really big dog that had wandered off. It wasn't the good kind of adrenaline that he'd gotten from previous scenes.

"You sure?" asked Izzy, biting his lip as he adjusted his grip on the fake gun.

"Yeah. Green. Call me a slut again. I'm still hard." Rowes nudged Izzy with his cock to try to get the point across.

"You *are* a slut," said Izzy, slipping back into the scene in seconds. Rowes could see the change in his features and the sudden flicker of anticipation in his eyes. "And for the record, I couldn't taste his cum on your lips. I think it's best you get on your knees for a refresher."

Rowes glanced to the ground where gravel was strewn throughout. His knees would be bruised to hell if he did. He could picture admiring those bruises as long as they lasted.

"You won't shoot me," said Rowes, shaking his head and putting a quiver into his voice. It didn't take much. Adrenaline was rushing through his veins, giving him a high that was sure to be exultant.

Grabbing him by his shoulder, Izzy spun him violently, planting his arm across the back of Rowes' neck as he fumbled with his pants. He must've stashed the gun for a moment because he seemed to get them down all too easily as Rowes struggled. Before he knew it, Izzy had dropped them just past his ass.

Something cool and hard pressed between Rowes' cheeks and he went stiff, grappling with the brick. It was the gun, Izzy sliding it against his hole like a threat. He flushed hot, his cock going so hard that he had to struggle not to come.

"Who said anything about shooting you? I have much better things I could do with this baby." Izzy pressed harder, until he ached from the pressure on his hole. "I could see how loose he fucked you open — how wet you still were from it."

"Fuck, yes." Closing his eyes, Rowes leaned into the touch, groaning as his hole burned. The gun disappeared, a slap ringing out a moment later that almost had him in tears. It was so fucking good — and exactly what he needed.

"I think I should film this," said Izzy, his grip going light. "All the fans get to watch you anytime, but I need something just for me. Not even Clarke will get this."

Rowes hissed, starting to look over his shoulder as Izzy's grip loosened.

"Move and you won't come for a week. Nod if you understand."

Rowes nodded, sucking in a breath as Izzy let him go. *Is he serious?* He had to look like a mess with his pants now around his knees and his legs spread as wide as they would go. It probably didn't help that he was panting exactly like the slut Izzy had called him.

"There we go."

He wanted to look, but he wasn't willing to face Izzy's punishment if he moved to see the camera. He needed to come as soon as possible. A week would be torture, especially if he had to watch Izzy on set, probably touching the wall where he was currently splayed out.

"And here you go," said Izzy, suddenly pressed against Rowes again. Slick fingers were at his entrance, pushing inside before Rowes could register what was happening. Izzy must've grabbed lube at some point, because when he nudged two fingers deep, there was no burn, only the zing as he found his prostate immediately.

"Fuck, Iz." Rowes turned his head into his arm, trying to muffle his cries. The sounds were ricocheting off the brick, probably traveling way too far. The security guard would hear him, then all hell would break loose.

"Two fingers and you give in already? So easy." Izzy dug his teeth into the back of Rowes' neck before sucking hard. He would probably leave a bruise, marking Rowes in a place he couldn't even see. It was too hot for a scarf, and he couldn't exactly wear a turtleneck.

"Don't." Rowes twisted. He wasn't sure if he was saying 'don't' to the mark or to the third finger pressing inside, but it didn't really matter. He wanted them both more than he'd ever wanted anything.

"He must've had a small cock, because you're still pretty tight. Good news for me, but not for you," said Izzy as he settled the third finger deep.

It was so much. If not for the plug that he'd worn on and off lately, it would have stung something fierce. But it would be nothing to Izzy's cock. Rowes knew intimately the girth and length of it, and taking it would be no easy task.

"Don't fuck me. *Please*." Rowes played into the part desperately, struggling even as he rolled his hips into the touch.

"I'm gonna fuck you raw." Izzy groaned as Rowes clenched around him. "You *like* that? Such a cum-slut. I want to see you dripping after."

"Oh God. Oh *God*." He was so close to coming that he had to sneak his hand down, clamping around the base of his cock to stave off his orgasm. His cheek scraped against the brick, probably scratching him raw. He barely felt it.

"I'm not going to have much to watch later if we stay like this," said Izzy, his voice light. "I've got a better idea." With a tug, he jerked Rowes away from the wall, spinning him around before forcing him to his knees.

Rowes dropped like a rag doll, stones stinging his skin as he landed. Before he could recover, Izzy pressed on the back of his neck, until he touched his hands to the ground.

Oh. Before him was Izzy's phone, the reflection of his own face looking back at him. Tears were streaked down his face, one cheek bright red with a drop of blood near the middle. Along the bottom of the screen was a red circle next to a timer that was slowly climbing higher.

Izzy *had* started filming them. He'd been certain it was just a play — tying into the constant judgment on film. But this was something nobody but Izzy was going to judge.

Reaching past him, Izzy adjusted the screen so Rowes' face was displayed, along with his cock that was purple and dangling between his legs. Next, Izzy tugged his pants the rest of the way off, folding them and tapping Rowes' hip. "Lift your knees one at a time."

He slid the folded pants under his knees, the uneven ground instantly more forgiving. Rowes let out a sigh of relief. He hadn't been about to safeword or anything, but the fact that Izzy was still caring for him, even in the midst of a scene, filled him to the brim.

"Next time, I'll have a few cameras so I can watch myself fuck your hole on one, and your facial expressions on the other. You won't be able to hide a thing from me." He knelt behind Rowes, returning his fingers to his hole. Thrusting three in at once, he stole Rowes' breath.

"Next t-time?" Rowes struggled to keep up as his elbows wobbled. Every time Izzy touched his prostate, his arms turned into jelly.

"Every day after we film, I'm going to set you up just like this. It doesn't matter where it is— I'll have you. Maybe I'll invite the sound crew around so they can hear every moan and gasp. Maybe Clarke will come so he can see exactly what he can't have."

His skin prickled, his cock throbbing as pre-cum dribbled from the head. His brain was officially offline, and there was no way he could do anything but go along with whatever Izzy whispered in his ear.

"Yes. *Please*. Every day. I don't care if it's in the middle of main street. I want everyone to know that you own me and that you can do whatever you want to me."

He nearly sobbed as Izzy pressed his cock against his hole, so blunt and hard that it was sure to hurt. The pain was bliss as Izzy pushed his way inside, though, claiming Rowes in the final way he craved.

How could he have ever thought they were just friends? Izzy angled his cock over his prostate and Rowes sobbed, dropping to his elbows as his muscles went weak. He needed to come so badly that it hurt, his cock the single point of pain in a mass of pleasure.

"Get up," said Izzy, grabbing him by the hair and tugging his head back until Rowes scrambled back onto his hands. He let out a shaky breath, trying to stay steady as Izzy picked up his pace, slamming into him so his knees almost left the protective cushion.

His rim ached, the lube easing the way but not the stretch. He wasn't sure if he'd ever expected a cock like Izzy's — as persistent as it was hard, with no sign of stopping.

"Look at yourself," said Izzy, his voice strained and dark.

Rowes had hardly looked away. His own face looking back at him was mesmerizing. It didn't even seem like him. It was someone else whose cheeks were wet, their eyelashes clumped together with tears. His cock wagged back and forth with each touch, dripping pre-cum every time Izzy nailed his spot.

Izzy's breathing picked up, going harsh as he started snapping his hips that much harder. He was mostly hidden from view, except for the brief glances when Rowes dipped lower on the screen at a particularly hard thrust.

"Stay still while I come in your ass," said Izzy, pressing something to the back of Rowes' head. It was the gun, gleaming black in the low light and looking so real that Rowes could almost taste the acidic stench of sulfur.

The second Izzy stilled his hips, Rowes started to shoot hot cum. He couldn't wait for permission or for a hand on his cock, the choice was taken from him, his balls emptying on the ground as Izzy pulsed inside him. He struggled to stay upright, watching his cock spurt, some of the dampness soaking into the pants beneath his knees.

He fell to his elbows, lowering his head to the ground as he sucked in huge breaths, his lungs screaming from the exertion as his ass ached, with Izzy's cock still inside, huge and rigid.

"You with me, baby?" Izzy reached past him, grasping his phone and stopping the recording. The timer was much higher than Rowes would have expected. It felt like it had been over in an instant.

"Uh-huh." Rowes turned his face into his arm, trying to smother all the noises that were trying to escape. He'd stopped crying at some point, which was a bonus, but he was still raw.

"I'll get you cleaned up at the hotel, but for now, let's get your clothes back on."

He was still wearing his clothes except for his pants, which were probably filthy and full of rips now. He had no idea how he was going to move, though.

Hissing as Izzy pulled out, he slowly went limp until he was lying on his side on the ground. The gravel digging into him was almost pleasant as his skin buzzed.

"Ro?"

Rowes only grunted, closing his eyes as a peace like none other washed over him. He wasn't sure how Izzy did it, but by the time that calmness started to retreat, they were back in their hotel room, the jacuzzi jets humming around them and Rowes leaning into the naked chest behind him.

"Iz?"

Izzy moved his hand down the center of Rowes' chest. "I got you, baby."

Chapter Twenty-Two

Izzy

"What a shit show," said Connley, nodding quietly as he spoke into Izzy's ear. The other actor, who was rarely rattled by crowds, seemed on edge, his eyes darting around as he took in every screaming face. Maybe it was because Ainslie had come down with a bug and was stuck in the hotel, but he'd followed Izzy around for the last two hours.

It would have been cute if it had been Rowes doing the following. But Rowes was staring at the crowd with wide eyes, just as rattled looking as Connley.

Premiere night was always a little nuts, especially with the way the *Gunlover* producers did it. They'd set up a massive screening in something like a huge theater, with the cast members at the front and a few chosen fans at the back. The areas were separated and sectioned off, but the fans would still get to see their favorite characters react to each scene.

Izzy had already seen the whole season himself, and he could understand why they were so excited. It was epic, despite his losing the kiss scene with Rowes.

It was better than what could have happened if they hadn't fought back. The fans seemed to know something was amiss, though. The trailers had been strange, especially since footage of the kiss had been mysteriously released to the public.

Connley tugged on his arm, dragging his gaze away from Rowes and the only thing he wanted to see that night. Izzy had had just about enough. Connley was driving him fucking insane.

"Call your Domme," said Izzy, leaning close as he wrapped an arm around Connley's shoulders. "She'll pick up for you, and she'll help talk you down from whatever's going on in your head right now."

He patted Connley on the back, who grinned back sheepishly and strolled over to his own manager, who presented him with a phone. The cameras flashing were almost blinding in their multitude, as if it were an awards ceremony and not their sorry little crew.

"Hey," said Izzy, throwing his arm around Rowes' shoulder and tugging him close. "You're gonna miss the party if we don't go in now." Even Connley had finally dragged his heels in the door with his cell phone to his ear.

"I just can't believe this many people are here," said Rowes, looking to one of the camera people. They were sucking up the interaction, camera rolling as they caught everything for the entertainment news that would probably air in a few hours.

"I'm calling it, and you are coming inside," said Izzy softly, reaching into his pocket with his free hand.

"I—" Rowes' voice cut off with a yelp as he bit his lip, his face flushing a few shades as he widened his eyes.

"You were saying?" asked Izzy, clicking the remote in his pocket a second time to ease the vibrations of the plug in Rowe's ass. It would still hum away, but at a much lower setting that Rowes would be able to take a lot easier than the jolt Izzy had just given him.

"Sorry. I bit my tongue there. Weird," said Rowes, putting his hand to his mouth as if he were checking for blood. "Let's head in."

There was no 'do you think they know?' query, because Izzy was almost certain that they did, and he didn't give a shit. He'd had people asking him the same question for the rest of the season—and even after they'd finished filming and they'd finally gone home.

Two bedrooms had become one as they'd merged the final piece of their lives together, Rowes converting his old room into an art studio where he mostly doodled and splashed paint against blank canvasses.

"That was mean," said Rowes, pouting as Izzy opened the door and the last flashing camera was cut off. The interior of the place was bustling, with servers moving around with drinks and appetizers as people chatted. Some of them were already moving beyond to be seated.

"Mr. Keppel, it's good to see you again," said the executive producer as he approached, shaking Rowes' hand with an easy smile.

Izzy wanted to gouge the guy's eyes out. Rowes seemed to sense his thoughts, tightening his grip on Izzy's waist.

"I wouldn't miss the premiere for anything, especially not an awkward reunion," said Rowes, his smile slightly more guarded as he glanced at Izzy.

"Always good to catch the last one when you're on your way out of the door," said the executive producer, grabbing a glass of wine as a server offered him one. Obviously, he was still in a bit of denial about Rowes, probably thinking he would quit on his own before the next season started.

"This season *was* a good way to end the show," Izzy cut in, grasping a glass and handing it to Rowes. "Here, sweetheart."

"Thank you, love." Rowes beamed, accepting the glass. His quaking nerves had disappeared and he'd really come into his own lately, taking control of a situation before it got out of control.

Of course, there was still one situation where he opted not to take control, and Izzy cherished every moment of it.

"I'm not sure what you mean—the end," said the producer, motioning to the crowd out front. "This is the hottest show on television, and every network is clamoring for it. We will be ready to shoot the next season in a few months."

"I'm almost sorry to miss it," said Izzy, snagging a skewer of something as a server went by. It looked like pork or maybe chicken with peppers and pineapple sandwiched between. He handed it to Rowes without a word, who chomped down as if he were starving while he watched their interactions with wide eyes.

Izzy would have fed it to him himself, but he didn't want Rowes getting anywhere near subspace when there were around so many people. He was too pliable when he was deep and would agree to almost anything.

The producer looked at him in confusion, taking a sip of his wine before swirling it around in his glass. "I don't understand. The bankruptcy rumors were purely rumors—nothing to worry about there."

Izzy had missed out on that little tidbit. He'd have to talk with Ainslie again. She always had the best gossip and had offered him some damn good advice on Dominance, too.

"I won't be available to shoot next season. My contract is up." It felt so good to say, but watching the producer's face fall before he turned to rage was even better. When he pointed a finger toward Rowes, Izzy stopped him in his tracks.

"There's an upcoming series that have signed both of us," said Izzy, drawling as if he were talking about the weather, while cackling on the inside. "I'm really excited to start working on something new, but good luck with next season."

The producer crossed his arms, his face almost fully red. "We don't need you, anyway. Connley is a superior actor, and he seems to pair well with Ainslie. It's barely a rewrite and the fans will hardly notice."

This guy had to be delusional. Izzy wanted to giggle.

"That's strange." Izzy touched his chin, not able to resist sending a smile to Rowes. They'd planned for Ainslie to be present for this conversation, too, but her cold was a nasty one. He spotted Connley coming their way, though, his strides set with purpose.

"Ainslie and Connley are joining us on the project, as well," said Izzy. "It might be a little trickier to replace all four main characters."

Rowes squeezed his hand, giving him a look that said to tone it down. Izzy only shrugged. He would never forgive them for what they had done to Rowes, even if he had to hurt the fans a bit. He had a feeling they would stand behind him once they saw the new show. *Gunlover* had had its day. It was time to move on.

"But I think we'll take a stroll around and enjoy this last one." He gave the producer one last grin before turning away and dragging Rowes along with him. He hoped the dumbfounded look on the man's face would stick with him for a long time.

"You're a diva," said Rowes, rolling his eyes as they headed to their seats. Connley tagged along like a lost pup.

"A diva who has the controls for that vibrator in your ass," said Izzy, reaching into his pocket and clutching the remote.

Rowes winked. "A diva I love."

Want to see more from this author?
Here's a taster for you to enjoy!

Falsely, Madly, Deeply: Knot Real
M.C. Roth

Excerpt

Sunlight filtered through the small, slatted window, the floating particles a fairy dust of white specks. Each time he turned the page, they were buffeted about, the ones close by swirling and dancing before they calmed to drift slowly down again.

Vale grumbled as he flipped the page again, kicking his legs out. His head was resting in the curve of Zyke's back, and every time his best friend moved, he lost his spot on the page. He'd flipped back and forth a dozen times, trying to make sense of the paragraph that was full of technical jargon that the author had thrown in. It was fun to read this kind of fiction but took every bit of his focus.

Zyke shifted again and let out a soft sigh, this time moving enough to nearly make Vale's head slip to the ground. He'd been wriggling around for the last half-hour as he progressively got more antsy.

Vale sat up and set his book beside him, his finger still marking his spot. "What are you doing?"

The attic was stuffy and close, the dust tickling at his nose in a near-constant assault, but they found themselves here more often than not. The house below them was vibrating with sounds and people, but here they were in the relative silence…again. It was a secret place that most of the people in the house didn't know about, much to Vale's satisfaction.

"Zyke." Vale touched his friend's shoulder. Warm brown eyes met his, and Zyke reached for his earbud, plucking it out and setting it on the ground.

"What?" Zyke tapped something on his phone and the whispering sound of music cut out. Vale hadn't even realized it had been there until it stopped, as he was so lost in the continuing vibrations of the house. "You ready to go down now?" Zyke seemed to perk up, his expression full of hope.

"Um." Vale looked toward the small door that led to the back of his closet. Beyond that was his somewhat-soundproofed room and the rest of the house that was brimming with enough people to make his senses squirm. His housemates, at the moment, were the type of people who had more friends than he could count, and they all seemed to like to party. "You can go. I know some of your friends are here."

Zyke got along with nearly everyone and had made fast friends with the latest batch of students. It made it easier to explain having Zyke in the house nearly all the time when he wasn't working, sometimes to visit Vale and others to be the life of the party.

Opening his book again, Vale hunched over, reading the same line of the paragraph that he was going to have memorized soon. Zyke's gaze burned along the back of his neck and shoulders, prickling over his skin.

"My best friend is right here," said Zyke, rolling onto his back and tucking one arm beneath his head. "I'm fine staying here with you." The hem of his dark shirt rode up, showing off a dusting of hair on his stomach and a tease of his abs as he stretched out along the wooden floor. "Tell me what you're reading."

Vale grinned, tugging down Zyke's shirt so he was covered again. That bit of skin was not for him to see. "You'd like it. It's about serial killers."

Zyke blinked, arching one brow. "Not what I expected. You were giggling earlier." He shifted until he was sitting next to Vale, plucking the book from his hands. "I feel like I should be worried. You should be reading romance or something."

Vale scrunched up his nose. "I was a psychology major. I'm basically just reviewing my studies." *Not exactly true.* The author had taken a lot of liberties and had gone through a completely inaccurate depiction of schizophrenia during one of the scenes—so far off that he hadn't been able to stop laughing because of how ridiculous it sounded.

"Yeah." Zyke flipped through a few pages of the book, his eyes going wide. "Wow. I'm so glad I graduated as a biology major. I thought omegas liked romances."

Rolling his eyes, Vale snatched the book back. "And I thought omegas and alphas couldn't be friends." He pointedly looked between them. He'd heard that line dozens of times in his life when people found out he was friends with Zyke.

"That's not it," said Zyke, laying back with a grin. "Omegas and alphas can't be friends without fucking. That's what everyone downstairs is thinking we are doing right now." He humped his hips, laughing when Vale chucked the book at him.

"You wish." He stood, strolling over to the window and looking out. It was barely daylight anymore, the golden streams starting to die off as the sun shifted lower. "I have the nicest ass you've ever seen."

"Nope." Zyke shook his head. "Wendelin has the best ass I've ever seen. Six-five, abs like washboards and an ass like a stallion. You could cook bacon on him, he's so hot."

True. Vale had caught himself drooling a few times as Wendelin did laps around the local track in the early morning hours. When the air was still cool and fresh, Vale would head to the track, parking himself beneath the same tree while he read. Lately, he'd left his book at home, preferring the view.

"Oh, I found a sore spot." Zyke reached for him and pulled Vale onto his lap. He landed hard, and they both let out a loud grunt. "You want Wendelin all to yourself." He dug his fingers into Vale's sides. "Well, guess what? You have to share him. That is an ass that needs to be cherished by the world. It deserves its own social media account. I'd follow that any day."

"Me, too." He flushed, ducking his head and squirming as Zyke tickled him. The attic was getting warmer, especially since the windows were the kind that didn't open. Sweat prickled over his scalp as he tried to pull away. Zyke only chuckled and tugged him closer.

"You smell like Oreos," said Vale, smacking Zyke's chest until he finally let him go. Sometimes, being the smaller guy was the same as having older brothers who thought you were half punching bag and half psychiatrist. Luckily, Vale was the oldest of his siblings, so he hadn't had to deal with that much.

"It's cocoa," said Zyke, stretching out again. "Sorry… It's strong today. My rut's coming up soon."

"Probably the other reason they all think we're up here fucking," Vale grumbled softly, circling the small room once he was released. There weren't that many spiders, considering the small space and how isolated it was, and they could both stand up straight without having to stoop. When he'd first stumbled upon the space, he'd known it was the type of place he'd keep coming back to, even if Zyke barely fit through the door.

"That sucks." Vale paused at the window. The front lawn wasn't quite *littered*, but there were three beer cans that he could see. They were going to get in trouble with the city very soon if they weren't careful. That, and Reimer was passed out in the long patch of grass again. "Won't suck for much longer, though."

Turning, he waggled his finger, climbing into Zyke's lap with his back facing him. He grimaced as he was immediately assaulted by the scent of cocoa beans.

"Don't joke about that stuff," said Zyke, wrapping an arm around Vale's chest. "You're lucky your family is exempt."

"Sorry." He leaned his head against Zyke's shoulder, closing his eyes at the sound of his steady heartbeat. They'd been friends since they'd awkwardly stumbled into each other in grade three, and they'd rarely been apart since. After going to the same high school, they'd continued at the same university where they'd always kept in touch. "Are you scared?"

If Vale had been in his situation, he would have been terrified. Hell, he probably would have hidden in the attic when his mating contract came up for bid. Luckily, he'd been born in another country, and people had formed the consensus that he was a bit of a slut. He wasn't, for the record, but he didn't bother correcting them. He had no pressure to marry well — not like Zyke did.

"Terrified," said Zyke, his chest shaking as he suppressed a laugh. "What will a poor alpha like me do when my parents choose a mate for me? As long as it's not a fucking kangaroo, I'll be fine. I don't think I'll ever fall in love with them, regardless. Respect and tolerance goes a long way."

Vale grinned, turning so he could smoosh his face into Zyke's chest, despite how sweaty and warm he was. "Kangaroo shifters are awesome. You just haven't met the right one." He rubbed his belly where he had the same softness almost every omega seemed to have. "I'm sure they'll find a muskrat or something for you."

"That would be preferred," said Zyke. "I'm more worried that I won't get to see you anymore, so whoever it is, you'll have to pretend to be their friend. That way, we can hang out."

The floor thumped from the music below, someone shouting loud enough to be heard over it. Any louder, and the cops were sure to show up and start searching the place for drugs. They would find alcohol in spades, but Vale was very strict on the household policy on drugs.

"We should get down there." Zyke patted Vale's hip before helping him stand. His palm was sweaty and slick as he dragged Vale toward the exit, before releasing him and going to his hands and knees.

The moment he opened the small hidden door, the music got louder, pounding at Vale's ears and throbbing just behind his sternum. Zyke shot him a grin over his shoulder before he started to make his way through the hole, tilting his hips sideways when he got caught on the frame.

Vale crawled through after him, tugging the door shut behind him. The clothing that had been pushed aside, he quickly shuffled back in their spots, hiding the entrance behind jeans and a bathrobe he had in his room for some reason. He'd left his book behind, but he'd be back for it soon enough.

"Someone should turn the music down," said Vale, shouting as he pressed a finger to one ear. He'd always been sensitive, but he was tired, and a grouchiness that could only come from an impending heat was nipping at him.

"I'll take care of it," said Zyke, rubbing Vale's shoulder. "You okay? Did you want to stay in your room while I clear the rest of them out?"

Vale bristled, standing to his full height. He wasn't huge, but he was fucking mighty, and he could kick someone's shins until they backed down from a fight. "I'm not afraid of them."

About the Author

M.C. Roth lives in Canada and loves every season, even the dreaded Canadian winter. She graduated with honours from the Associate Diploma Program in Veterinary Technology at the University of Guelph before choosing a different career path.

Between caring for her young son, spending time with her husband, and feeding treats to her menagerie of animals, she still spends every spare second devoted to her passion for writing.

She loves growing peppers that are hot enough to make grown men cry, but she doesn't like spicy food herself. Her favourite thing, other than writing of course, is to find a quiet place in the wilderness and listen to the birds while dreaming about the gorgeous men in her head.

M.C. Roth loves to hear from readers. You can find her contact information, website details and author profile page at https://www.firstforromance.com/

PUBLISHING

Sign up for our newsletter and find out about all our
romance book releases, eBook sales and promotions,
sneak peeks and FREE romance books!